Ex Libris

I n *White Lady, Black Christ,* Charlson Ong draws on his intuitive understanding of the Filipino psyche and goes beyond the familiar and superficial tropes of Philippine politics to take on Philippine culture itself—the sources of our deepest longings, fears, and beliefs. His protagonists emerge from the murkiest shadows of our obsessions—a milkish revenant, a swarthy Jesus-incarnate—whose unlikely union portends both catastrophe and hope, while in the foreground stumbles our dysfunctional middle class. There's laughing gas aplenty in this novel, whose absurdity—an imaginative stretch from Ong's traditional realism—mimics the often more bizarre twists and turns of Philippine history and society. This book establishes Ong firmly as the most versatile and inventive Filipino novelist in English of his generation.

–JOSE Y. DALISAY, author of *Soledad's Sister*

TO MY PARENTS
Nenita and Conrado

1
DEATH STAR

WHITE IS THE presence of all colors. He was awakened by this thought as much as by the shaft of crimson light that burst across his mind's screen like the supernova he had recently seen on The National Geographic channel. It was a feature on giant exploding stars—"death stars"—thousands of times larger than our sun. He didn't know when it became "ours"; it seemed more like *we* belonged to *it*. Death stars were said to send shock waves across the galaxies and knocked other star systems off kilter.

A scientist said these explosions were the reason why we were probably alone—or one of a handful of inhabited planets—in the universe. Exploding giants regularly blew away planets that likely host civilizations far advanced of ours, like some cosmic grim reaper. One such burst in our galactic backyard would incinerate us in minutes. All those skyscrapers, satellite dishes, menacing SUVs, billionaire CEOs, super athletes, and that sweet young thing with her endearing lisp, who seemed to be whispering something into his ears the other night—*"It's my tongue, doctor. It's a bit short, I think, but it's very quick."*—gone in minutes!

It was just a matter of time. It could happen the very next moment, or tomorrow while he was sipping coffee, or doing surgery, or having a rubdown at the spa, or yet take another billion years. We were like microbes cultured on a Petri dish lying inside an abandoned laboratory, where lab rats and stray cats now roamed and fought over spoils. Sooner or later, some creature was bound to step on us. The idea didn't perturb him so much as it caused a pesky irritation in his privates that wouldn't go away despite some heavy scratching.

Still, he had called up the hospital next morning to cancel the triple coronary bypass surgery he was scheduled to perform on his seventy-five-year-old high school mentor, Fr. Briccio Canlas. Fr. Brix had put off the operation for a month. Another day or two wouldn't matter, Dr. Chesterfield—*Chester*, to everyone else but his father—Limhuatco decided. He couldn't risk his privates itching up, just in case the itch was symptomatic of some organic dysfunction, while harvesting an artery from the good priest's calf or while grafting the vessel to his aorta. He didn't care to have to motion his long-time surgical nurse, Loretta, to scratch him "down there" in the midst of trying to heal a "soldier of the Lord."

Color, he was recently reminded by another episode from The National Geographic channel, is a *sensation* produced when a light of different wavelengths falls on the human eye. When the wavelengths that cause our brains to register red, orange, yellow, green, blue, indigo, and violet are mixed in equal proportions, we see white light. A red object—like the heart—illuminated by white light, absorbs all of its components and reflects only the wavelength we see as red. A white object absorbs none of the components and reflects the entire spectrum.

Strangely, this thought saddened him more than the possibility of an exploding star roasting planet earth and ending all life and activity, including cardiovascular surgery.

He lived in a world of white. The antiseptic corridors of the Saint Benedict's General Hospital were scrubbed clean daily. The medical staff was required to wear their white coats at all times inside the premises. Only in surgery was white replaced by green. Even then, the medical equipment and the surgical hardware all became shiny and gleaming, reflecting every movement, every tic.

So why should the sight of a shape—a woman, his mind insisted—in a white gown disturb him? It was at most a reflection of the spectrum that was somehow refracted by some medium in the night. Perhaps all those radio signals and cellular phone chatter had bounced off an ultraviolet or infrared light source, transformed into white light, careened towards his eyes and triggered an electrical storm in his oxygen depleted brain. After all, since he had been jogging for thirty minutes for only the sixth time in eight years, that it might have caused him to see a glowing female in the night just as one dying of thirst conjured an oasis in the desert.

Yes, it was a mirage, he concluded. But why did it recur?

"Why is it always a woman, dad? Why is it always some forlorn, bedraggled wench luring unsuspecting cabbies or horny bastards in the dark? It's an archetypal scare story that you've internalized and now it has emerged into consciousness because of your situation," his daughter Carmen said to him over the phone.

He had deferred calling her up, certain that her recent foray into cultural anthropology after three years in Vet Med School would elicit such dismissive views about his experience, but she was always the one who could settle him, cure him of his most unfounded fears and wildest worries, and remind him that all is as it should be in a universe of strings, quarks, bosons, atoms, genes, neurons, cells, tissues and instincts. But now, she moved in a world of shifting "paradigms" and "negotiated" knowledge; a world where neither Darwin nor Einstein was unassailable, where the "so-called" scientific was one of many methods and where spirits might communicate through human mediums attending academic conferences.

At first, he had sneered at all that "negotiation" and shiftiness of knowledge. "You sound more and more like that Internal Revenue agent with his *power of discretion* haggling with my accountant over my tax liabilities than scientists," he had emailed Carmen, who refused to take any more of his calls or answer his messages until he sent her flowers. It felt as if he was wooing back a lover and the thought upset him deeply. He decided to keep his distance and called her up sparingly until Carmen stormed into his clinic, demanding to know what was "wrong" with him and whether he had finally abandoned his family for another.

He had been estranged from his wife, Jackie, for five months but was living alone. Since then, he had kept up regular contact with Carmen for the sake of his equilibrium, and with Jackie for the sake of *hers*, or so he thought. But Carmen the prospective vet who would have told him of optical illusions that often occurred among "simian males" of his age was a lot more consoling and fun than this pundit who recorded the ejaculations of spirit mediums of Jose Rizal and the *Santo Niño* Christ child, but thought of her own father's as yet unexplained encounters as symptoms of cultural psychosis.

"What situation?" he had wanted to ask Carmen. "And who said she was bedraggled?"

But all he could say was: "I guess if it were the last thing you should see, you'd prefer it to be a pretty lass or a mother figure than some grumpy old guy."

"See, if it's on a dark street, it's female. If it's a near death, light-beckoning-from-the-end-of-the-tunnel thing, it's Ian McKellen as Gandalf in The Lord of the Rings."

"Could be worse, you know? I could've bumped into Darth Vader."

Chester suddenly remembered the six-year-old Carmen gripping his hand all those years ago as Luke Skywalker battled his evil father in *Return of the Jedi* at the Quad theater in Makati. It was her first movie. He had seen her wide-eyed and transfixed and saw her future as a fighter pilot or field marshal and the vision had troubled him briefly. Now she was thirty-four, with her mother's beauty and her father's brains—or so, Chester always believed—still single, chasing spirit mediums for her doctorate, and all father and daughter could often talk about were movies—the one constant in their lives; the one safe, uncomplicated bind.

"It was dark. How could it have been Darth Vader?"

"Come on, it's not the same for everyone. All right, maybe we each see what we want to in the dark."

"But it was that way for *you*."

It struck Chester that Carmen was taking *his* encounter personally. This also reminded him of his vision long ago of his daughter as a fighter pilot and he quickly vanquished it.

"Okay, come off it, enough about me. How are you? That Swiss guy calling still?"

"Swedish, Dad. His friend's the Swiss. And he's gay."

"That's what they all say before they become bi or tri or multiple...."

"Dad, he's researching the Black Nazarene. We're working together."

"Black Nazarene? In Quiapo? Ran out of Santo Niño mediums?"

"They're related phenomena, Dad. Most, if not all, mediums channel all three—the Child Christ, the Nazarene, and God the Father—sometimes successively within one session. They proceed from being childlike to being intensely grave."

"*That* bad?"

"Okay, call it multiple personality disorder if you will, but lots of people go to them for help and they've been known to do wondrous things."

"Like provide Ph.D. tracts for former vet med students?"

"I like what I do, Dad. I enjoy where I am."

"Okay, better than fighter pilot, I guess."

"What?"

"Nothing, delete that. How's your mother?"

A deep silence came over the phone line and Chester panicked for a while. "Carmen, you still there? Everything alright?"

"You know what? No, Mom's not all right, dad. I think she's just as miserable as you. I think you guys should stop this nonsense and get back together. What are you trying to do, Dad? You trying to live the bachelor life you never had because you got hitched too early and had me? You regret now having been a father too soon? You want to make out with girls my age? No, younger, I presume, much, much younger. You want to pluck…"

"Stop it, girl, it is not about you! Why must everything be about *you*? This is between your mom and I."

"And nothing to do with me."

"I'm sorry, Carmen. We have to work this out, if we can. Can't rush things. We've been together a long time, perhaps… too long."

"Oh, *Dad*."

Carmen had said the word with such exasperated finality before the line went dead that Chester went numb for a moment. In his mind's screen, he saw his daughter as Princess Leia coming at him with her lightsaber and he might have sought cover behind the cushioned sofa had not the explosion rocked his condominium unit on the 50th floor of Corinthian

Towers in Pasig overlooking the south of metro Manila and the Marikina mountains.

For an insane while, Chester Limhuatco thought some death star had indeed struck. He held his breath and counted to ten but the fireball didn't come. He opened his eyes and saw his home swathed in a brownish red glow. Early sunlight poured through the huge window panes as he had slept without closing the blinds. It was five in the morning. He had left a message on Carmen's mobile the previous night and the first thing she did when she got up in the morning was call him up about his "white lady".

No, it won't end with a bang but a whimper, the thought stabbed him from behind and he wanted to go back to sleep but he heard people screaming and, perhaps, gunshots. He rushed to the veranda and saw what seemed like a gigantic reptile lying dead on the ground below, with people swarming all over it. The creature appeared to be exhaling thick clouds of smoke. Perhaps some extra-terrestrial had indeed crash landed, he thought excitedly. There had been several supposed UFO sightings in the area in the past.

Then Chester remembered how the long lines of people winding through the street below for the past three days had looked to him at times like that dinosaur-sized anaconda in the movie with Jennifer Lopez. The crowd was lining up to get into the Legazpi Sports Complex at the bottom of the street, which was to host a special presentation of a noontime TV show called *Milyong Pangarap* (A Million Dreams) that gave away nearly a million pesos worth of prizes weekly. It was a variety program with songs, dances, and games. The big show promised a jackpot of ten million pesos and was to be held on Sunday.

By Thursday evening, people had started to camp out at the sports complex gate, hoping to be first in line for free tickets to the event. The gym only could hold five thousand people but many more were expected. By Saturday morning, the lines had stretched to ten kilometers causing alarm in the neighborhood. People from far away provinces were flocking to the place as if a shrine to a Marian apparition, a miraculous site. They brought food and makeshift tents. No one dared to leave his or her place. Chester was unsure where or how they went to the toilet. By nightfall that Saturday, the air out in his veranda didn't smell right to him.

Dr. Limhuatco hadn't known what the long lines outside his residence were for until Loretta asked him whether he had seen them. Apparently, the network had been featuring the lengthening lines of people outside the complex in its news programs in order to drum up even more excitement about the forthcoming "extravaganza." Chester realized then why choppers had been hovering over Corinthian Towers early in the morning since Thursday.

"You think it's safe, what they're doing?" Loretta had asked him.

Chester who didn't care too much for crowds—he was stopped from going to EDSA during the 1986 uprising despite having campaigned for Cory Aquino among fellow doctors not by the thought of runaway tanks but of stray microbes—stared at the nurse and shrugged. "Who?"

"The people? The network? The organizers?"

"I hope most of them have had their shots," was all he had said, before cutting open the General on his table.

Now he cleared his eyes and realized what had happened. The crowd had stampeded. The street was a cul-de-sac that narrowed downward into the gate of the complex and increasing pressure from tens of thousands of people at the back had forced people in front to ram the barricades and topple the makeshift structure being prepared for the show.

That had caused what sounded like an explosion. Perhaps the guards had panicked and fired their weapons. Perhaps some mischief in the crowd and sparked a riot.

He could see people running about wailing. The crowd behind had scampered back up the street but could not disperse for its sheer size; there was nowhere for all of them to go. It was like watching a whale that had wandered into a river channel trying desperately to find a way out. It thrashed and bobbed, whipped its limbs and moaned, expelled water through its blowhole but remained stuck. Up front the imaginary severed tail, he saw bodies sprawled on the ground. Some were pinned against barbed wire barricades, some piled in heaps. Chester was sure many of them were dead.

He called up the hospital to send ambulances and put on his running suit, grabbing his medical bag, and rushed to the elevator.

Outside, the air reeked of fresh fear and blood. He saw a child on his haunches, crying. He saw shoes, slippers, bags, and a dismembered cat. Then he saw the dead and dying but knew he was of no use to them. He didn't know what to do, where to begin. It had been a decade since he had worked in the ER. He wished Loretta or some veteran nurse were around to set him straight, remind him of things to do, turn on the right switch in him so he could get going.

He bent over a woman, who held onto her forearm screaming. He knew she had dislocated her shoulder. "Let me help you," he said, "I'm a doctor." But she wouldn't stop screaming and he couldn't get her to be still. He hadn't refitted a shoulder ball to its socket in ages and feared he might do her more harm than good. In any case, the pain might knock her out and he wasn't sure what he would do with her then.

He left the woman and tried to deal with the wailing child. He saw she was covered in fresh bruises. There was a deep gash beneath her breast. He touched the wound and thought she must have a broken rib but the child screamed and he fled. He decided he had never been good at mending wounds and fixing bones, or calming panic-stricken people and rushed over to tend the seemingly lifeless bodies instead. He felt for pulses and breaths, listened to heartbeats with his stethoscope. He might still find a life hanging by a thread, administer CPR, but he would have to choose carefully. Every second counted. It would have to be a body, a life more worth saving than the rest. It shouldn't be too old, too broken down, with a close enough expiry date. It might best be a middle-aged person or young mother—there were mostly women fallen, many of them elderly—with children to raise, someone with possibly two, three more decades to go; someone with long years left to live, with enough things left to do, enough joy left to fulfill, enough lovers left to pleasure and be pleasured by... A storm rushed through his mind as he scanned the mayhem for the right body, the rightful beneficiary of his expert intervention.

Then he saw *her*: the lady of his nights, the one he had seen four, five, perhaps six times since he started jogging in the evenings around the neighborhood two months ago. At first, the sight of her had baffled him. She seemed to be approaching—a woman in the distance wearing something white and diaphanous, like a nightgown—but he couldn't reach her no matter how long he jogged. He quickened his pace, but the distance between them remained the same. Then he was running, struggling to reach her but now it seemed she was moving away unbelievably quickly. In the dark, she seemed to be flying like those warriors in Chinese martial arts movies. She rounded a corner but when he got there, she was gone.

The second time, he was able to catch a glimpse of her face. It was two weeks after the first encounter. He jogged along the sign that marked the high point of the hill road when he felt someone staring at him. He turned and saw her, yet he couldn't figure out just how far away she was. She seemed both near and far at the same time. And it was, in fact, a nightgown she was wearing: something soft and sheer and he thought he could see her breasts in the moonlight.

Suddenly, she turned around and jumped over the side of the road. He shouted for her to stop and rushed over. It was an almost twenty feet drop. He flashed his penlight, his heart racing like a crazed stallion but there was no white gown in the clearing below, only shrubs. He peered desperately into the dark but could see no sign of her, of anyone. He rushed home and thought of calling the police but wasn't sure what to say. He couldn't sleep that night and spent the whole time trying to remember her face. Then he took out his pad and sketched her.

For the next few days, there were no reports of any dead body found in the area but he kept from jogging for a few evenings, fearful of another strange encounter. Still, he yearned to see her again. It seemed as if he was *hooked* on her. He had never been addicted to anything: not nicotine, not alcohol (though he had his occasional drinks, usually after a long surgery), not women (he hadn't been with anyone else since marrying Jackie nearly thirty years ago; even before his internship until their separation these past eight months, and even then he had only had sex twice with two different women and neither occasion was memorable), not golf, or poker, or porn, or fast cars or any of the myriad toys that six figure surgeons like him—whose actual incomes are unknowable to revenue agents since few subscribe to private health insurance in the Philippines while government insurance remains utterly corrupted and many big ticket clients issue checks "paid to cash"—might be prone to. He began to think if he was lacking something, maybe some gene for obsessing.

The last time he saw her in the dark, she seemed to be saying goodbye. It was as if she was telling him that she would disappear from his life like the others, like everything and everyone else he had flirted with but passed up because he didn't have the gumption or drive to pursue. She was beneath the acacia tree where she seemed to be sinking into. He rushed over to save and pull her out, but as he reached the tree, there was only brown bark and damp air and a sadness so oppressive he had to call up Carmen who could not be reached at the time. And so he sent her a text message about the white lady, *his* white lady, knowing his daughter would dismiss, if not mock, him.

Now the woman lay beneath him, seemingly lifeless, perhaps asphyxiated. Her face was paler than it had been in the dark, but he had no doubt it was his lady and she was alive. He felt a pulse, placed his hands over her chest and began pumping rhythmically. He saw her eyelids flutter and gave her mouth-to-mouth. He felt for a moment that he would suck the soul out of her, and into himself. He panicked as she seemed to fade, but he kept at it until she stirred. She was back from the dead, back from the darkness. A flesh and blood being, a pretty woman, fair and clear skinned—a beautiful woman, he realized.

He felt an overwhelming need to embrace her, to be with her, to keep her with him. It wasn't a simple desire. He didn't want to have sex with her. He just wanted to be in her presence. He tried to imagine her as he had seen her in the dark: in her white gown, looking at him, *through* him. He felt himself hard and was embarrassed. Just then, ambulances arrived.

He waved down an ambulance from Saint Benedict's. "I'm Dr. Limhuatco," he called out to the paramedics who recognized him and he led them to the woman.

"Here, this one," he said.

"But she's breathing," the paramedic said as he felt her pulse and breath.

The younger man looked to the surgeon a bit puzzled and agitated. The doctor felt some embarrassment and looked towards the other bodies. "Okay, see if you can revive any of those over there," he said.

The paramedics picked up their portable defibrillator and gear to move quickly towards the other injured. One of them looked back to the doctor, who stayed hunched over the woman. The medic didn't know why the surgeon was spending precious seconds with someone who was out of immediate danger while many were waiting to be resuscitated.

"All right, I'll be with you in a while, just do what you can," he shouted to them.

Chester knew she mustn't be his priority at the moment. Her chances of survival now were likely higher than many others who lay sprawled and unconscious. He had already done what he could, what he *should*, for her. For the first time in twenty-five years, he acted against his own best medical sense. Rather than rush over to lead the medics, Chester found himself picking the woman off the ground and running towards the ambulance. She felt surprisingly light. As Chester was about to place her inside the ambulance something nipped the small of his back and he instead asked for an IV bottle instead from the nurse inside the ambulance and carried the woman to his condominium building.

He carried her past the dumbfounded guard at the entrance. "It's okay," he said to Nestor, who quickly rushed over to help the doctor with the elevator door.

Chester brought her inside his home and laid her down on the bed, thinking to undress her if only to make her comfortable and free up air passages but ended up deciding against it. She was wearing a fashionable white-knitted frock over a pink blouse and flesh colored slacks and he was all the more convinced the woman was misplaced among the crowd. He took off her faux jewel-studded sandals. Her serenity was like a balm on his frayed nerves. He knew he must bring her to the hospital to be checked. She could be hemorrhaging. She could have an aneurysm or worse. He listened once more to her heartbeat and found it regular. He placed the ammonia to her nose and she stirred once more. His heart leapt. Still, she remained asleep and he could not be sure what was going on inside her.

What if she never woke? What if she died on him? What would he tell the police? The hospital? Yet he could not let her go. Something told him that if he took her to the hospital, she would be gone and he would never see her again. He would lose control. It was madness, he knew. There was no reason to think so, no reason to want her the way he did. No reason to keep her here in his home alive but unconscious, like a living doll. No reason to want to breathe consciousness into her, no reason to think that it was in his power to do so.

What would Carmen say? He felt briefly nauseous and knew that he should never tell his daughter about this. This was either his noblest or most basic act, his highest or lowest point.

He hooked up the IV and found, after some difficulty, a vein in her soft, supple arm. He still could not believe that he had found this fair, bright woman in a heap of mostly brown, beaten bodies. It was a crowd of the poor and downtrodden, to which this woman clearly did not belong.

Her body turned warmer now and his own doubts and uneasiness passed through him. He felt confident, convinced that he had done the right thing. However, the sound of mayhem continued to rise from the street to disturb the tranquility that the unconscious woman seemed to have brought with her. He decided to go back down to help whomever else he could.

More ambulances had arrived from other hospitals and local governments, and the injured were being loaded onto them. A medical tent had been set up. There could be nearly a hundred who had died there, he thought, as something steely ripped through his gut. He had never been surrounded by so much death. He imagined that all the patients who had died, or were yet to die, had suddenly been gathered in one place.

Consoling relatives and explaining how everything humanly possible had been done in the attempt to save lives had never been his forte. He often left the task to others, to his assistants, to interns, or to Loretta. He envisioned a crowd of bereaved relatives rushing towards him and felt like heading back to his condo building. Should the morgues be sending over their vehicles now, he wondered, or would all the corpses have to be taken to hospitals first? Would he have to pronounce people "dead" on site? Was there any other doctor on the scene?

"Doctor, we need you," Chester heard the paramedic from Saint Benedict, the one who had seen him carry the woman away earlier, call out to him and he rushed over. He saw that paramedic M. Fernandez was pumping on the woman's chest while the other paramedic, C. Serantes, held the defibrillator over the woman, waiting to shock her wayward heart to stillness so it could restart in proper rhythm. Fernandez gave way to Serantes, who placed the pads on the woman's chest and gave her 110 volts of electricity. Her body shot off the ground like a piece of flotsam left behind by a storm, yet she remained unconscious.

"Again!" Fernandez ordered, and Serantes obeyed but got no better result.

"Should we increase the voltage doctor?" Fernandez asked.

"Doctor?" he inquired again but Chester was stunned. The woman was clearly dead. She must have been seventy years old and her windpipe appeared crushed, her neck nearly torn. What were these two fools doing? Who trained them? He wanted to explode, to shout at them but he saw M. Fernandez's eyes on him as he remembered the look the paramedic gave him earlier when, he, Dr. Chester Limhuatco, Chief of Cardiovascular Surgery, one of the country's best known open heart surgeons, had opted to stay with a breathing young woman while others required urgent assistance, and then spirit her away.

"She's gone. Call it," Chester whispered. C. Serantes looked at the doctor, confounded. He seemed to be pleading with Chester, who thought the younger man would burst into tears.

"Enough," the doctor repeated, sternly.

"She resembles my late grandmother," C. Serantes mumbled.

Chester took the pen off the paramedic's shirt, peered at his own watch, and wrote *6:29 a.m.* on the dead woman's blouse. "Go look for others," he ordered the paramedics. "Check carefully, every second counts." He wondered why he was asking the two young men to do what he himself refused to do: pick survivors. Was it because he had already saved the *one* for him?

He slapped himself hard the way he sometimes did before a major surgery and went over to work with the paramedics. They went through bodies, rearranged remains, found a couple of injured people still breathing and brought them to the tent.

By seven, police had cordoned off the area and corpses were laid out in rows like in a war zone. Chester felt worn down. It was as if someone, something, had reached down and turned him inside out like laundry, like his pants pocket; emptied him out, but left him unwashed, flapping in the wind.

He remembered hearing former New York City Mayor Giuliani say on television that the final casualty numbers in the collapse of the World Trade Center Towers might be more than what Americans could bear the day after 9/11 that Chester thought his own heart might quit. There were no exploding planes and crashing buildings here, no bodies leaping a thousand feet to their demise, no clouds of debris, no intimations of an apocalypse; but these deaths were no less horrendous and unjust, maybe even more so, because unclaimed by malice, or hatred, or anger, or desire to martyrdom but resulted only from callousness, from crassness, from another circus for the poor who could dream only of sudden wealth, sudden redemption—like Dimas— and whose pain must pass once the next circus or crucifixion hits town.

Chester was disturbed by his own anger. He had not felt like this in a long while. He had always thought it best for someone in his profession to keep his emotions in check— sedated, as it were. Neither did he consider himself a social activist or do-gooder—despite the occasional pro bono work or provincial outreach—to be too pissed about other people's unconcern. In any case, the doctor decided his work down here was over. It was now a crime scene, a police problem. He hurried back up to his condo unit, where for no discernible reason he thought his future beckoned.

Inside his home, Chester was shocked to find his bed empty, save for his pencil sketch of the lady. The IV bottle hung forlorn from its hanger and he saw a dab of blood on the bed sheet. He saw the glass doors to the veranda open and was gripped by sudden cold. Had she jumped off? This was no twenty-foot drop but fifty stories. He rushed to the veranda and saw her staring down at the street. A profound sense of loss washed over him before he was alerted to his good fortune. The woman was awake, which meant he would not be charged with criminal negligence.

He had no words for her. He did not want to break the spell that seemed to have been cast over her by the sight she beheld. Then she turned to him slowly with a look that bespoke much grief but he refused to believe all it foretold.

"Who are you? Why am I here?" she asked him in Tagalog, with an accent he didn't find provincial.

"You were down there, with them, unconscious," he said. "I brought you up here to revive you. This is my place. I'm a doctor, a heart surgeon."

"Why?" she asked as she continued to stare down at the street below.

"I didn't know what else to do," he whispered.

"You should've left me there. Let me be."

"I know," he wanted to say but held his tongue.

"I'm Dr. Limhuatco. Chester Limhuatco," he said, holding out his hand. The woman glanced at him briefly, seemingly pissed but cowed, as if he were a traffic cop handing her a speeding ticket or a landlord giving her an eviction notice. Then she turned away as if in fear. He was bothered and bewildered but went back inside for his breakfast.

"Here," he said moments later, handing her a cup of coffee.

She took it in her unsteady hands and looked down to her feet, as if searching for firm ground.

"Come inside," he said, "have some breakfast. It will steady you."

She nibbled her bread but looked distracted.

"What's your name? Were you trying to get inside the stadium?"

She looked further away. "I don't know," she mumbled, "I can't remember. I can't remember a thing." She was falling apart and he longed to gather her pieces in his arms and restore her but he knew he must keep his distance and not force her off her precipice.

"Take it easy. You've been through a traumatic experience. Rest. It will come back to you. Don't panic."

"I can't remember. I don't even know my name," she was trembling, hyperventilating. He placed a hand on her chest and another on her back as he felt himself become hard again, mightily struggling to ignore this reflex. As of the moment, she was his patient, he reminded himself. "Easy," he whispered. "Relax."

"You're in good hands," he longed to say, but controlled another reflex.

"I don't know who I am." She was in tears.

"But I do," he wanted to say, but kept his peace.

She did not have a purse or an identity card on her. She had absolutely no memory of her past and didn't know why she was outside the stadium. She only remembered being trapped in a crash of bodies, the screaming and shouting, a terrible pain in her gut and breathlessness. Then she seemed to have drifted above the mayhem and saw herself on the ground amidst other fallen bodies. She remembered a light, a feeling of deep serenity, then, waking up inside a strange room, alone, with a charcoal portrait of a woman with some resemblance to her beside the bed.

"It could take a few hours, perhaps a couple of days but I'm sure it will come back to you," Chester said but she did not seem to believe him. "You could go on radio, television…"

"No," she said with sudden alarm and gripped his hand. He felt some fear enter him. "Don't do that." She sounded certain of her words but still looked confused.

"All right," he said.

"What will I do now?"

"You can stay here a while, until you figure things out. You can stay as long as you need to."

"I can't. I shouldn't," she whispered.

"Why? Are you in some danger? Are you in trouble?"

She shook her head. "I don't know. I don't know anything."

"Do you want to go to the hospital? We can give you a thorough physical. Perhaps a neurologist or a psychiatrist can help. You may have suffered a concussion."

"No." She gripped his hand once again, in mortal fear, and he enclosed her hand with his other hand.

"All right, relax. Just stay here for a while. We'll figure things out," he said.

"I'll take care of you," he wanted to say, "always." Only he feared spooking her even more.

He gave her a mild tranquilizer and convinced her after much prodding to let him massage her shoulders and back. He had learned a bit from his physical therapist at the spa and always believed he had a natural talent for massage. It had to do with the tactility of one's fingers and he was a surgeon, after all. He was half convinced of the reality of the *chi* of traditional Chinese medicine that supposedly flowed through the body's meridian points from the rest of the cosmos. He had heard of it since childhood, had been to China and seen surgeons operating without anesthesia but acupuncture. He didn't care for any of that mystical "astral body" crap, however, that Loretta sometimes talked about. It was all biochemistry and neural transmission.

Chester didn't dare ask his houseguest—he didn't think it proper anymore to consider her a patient—to undress. He touched her through the fabric of her blouse and imagined passing his own *chi* through her meridian points, allowing their "life forces to blend," and was embarrassed by his own mystical fantasy. Still, he felt her relax, her stiffness giving in to his kneading. He was both relieved, yet mildly alarmed that such contact had not given him another erection.

"I think you should sleep," he suggested, "it will help. Who knows? When you awake, this may all turn out to be a bad dream." He found himself rather saddened by his own words.

"Yes, I'm very tired," she whispered and stood up, disoriented. He led her back to the bed and she was suddenly embarrassed.

"It's okay," he said. "I'll be off to the hospital. We can talk when I get home. There's food in the kitchen. You can fix yourself something if you get hungry."

2

HORIZONS

AT THE HOSPITAL, Chester checked in on some of the thirty-three injured that were brought to St. Benedict's. Some seventy-five people had reportedly died and nearly a hundred others injured. So far, none of those taken here had died. One had a fractured skull and was being operated on. Loretta tried to pry Chester for details about the stampede. She liked the game show's host, Wowie Perez, but denied she was a fan. She said Wowie had called up to ask about the injured and was coming to the hospital.

Chester did not know Wowie and had no opinion of him. He was uncomfortable with celebrities in hospitals since they caused too much fuss and lured nurses away from the ER. From what he had seen at the crime scene, Chester thought it best for Wowie and his staff to make themselves scarce. "Don't let them in," the Chief surgeon was inclined to say but only shrugged his shoulders.

Chester asked Loretta to inquire among the survivors and relatives whether anyone was looking for a woman in her mid-twenties, wearing a white frock, fair and medium built *and smelling of jasmine.*

"Why?" Loretta asked.

"Someone's looking," he said and went on to the cardiac catheterization lab where he was supposed to sit in and watch while the hotshot fresh grad from Johns Hopkins, Dr. Steve Raquiza, nephew of erstwhile Hospital Director, Dr. Joven Raquiza, inserted a hair-thin, video-guided, balloon-tipped tube into the patient S. Rodrigo's artery. Inflation of the balloon cleared the clogged blood vessel of its plaque, restoring the artery to normal service of the heart without the need to cut open the patient's chest. The lab was trying out a newfangled stent—to be inserted into the vessel— from Germany that would supposedly last longer and cause no scarring. Non-invasive technology had become so advanced more and more patients and doctors were opting for angioplasty rather than open heart surgery. "Cutthroats" like himself—Chester preferred "old butcher" than Steve Racquiza's joke—were being swept to the sidelines as standby surgeons, just in case something went terribly wrong with the hi-tech gadgetry and that trusty "chainsaw" had to break open those rib cages once more for him to "grab the bull by the horn."

Chester loved to use *that* imagery in class. He was fascinated with Hemingway as a teen-ager and often thought of cardiac surgery in bullfighting terms. It was all "blood and guts" for him. He remembered his old mentor, Dr. Carlos Ortiz, reaching into the patient's chest and squeezing the heart, massaging, urging it back to life before the seventy year-old surgeon suffered his own heart attack. Chester, not yet twenty-eight, had to step in and take the patient's heart in his own hands, wrestle with it, pump it, and coax it back to activity in the nick of time. That memory never failed to brighten his mood as he sat through interminable administrative meetings or angioplasties. He felt potent once more, with some power over life and death, like a warrior at the messy, muddy, mildewed trenches of medicine battling the progression of death and disease.

Now it was all computer simulation and video games, MRIs and radioactive dyes. The tykes didn't even have to practice on cadavers these days. They just plugged into the latest digital 3D, 5G gizmo. Robots and A.I. were taking over and he was often bored. There was little art left in the practice, in *his* practice, and he wondered how long he would stay on. Perhaps he would go on a safari or big game fishing or climb some mountain in Mindanao or in Africa like Hemingway. Why not Everest? Perhaps he would take up the brush again. He had done some passable watercolors as a youth.

"Doctor," Loretta caught him as Chester sneaked out of the catheterization lab. Nothing ever went wrong with the million dollar equipment and even if it did he was almost sure some back-up robot would set things right.

An old woman stood beside Loretta.

"She's looking," Loretta said.

"What?"

"The woman you described. This lady says she's looking for someone like that."

"Oh?"

"Her name's Emily. She's my daughter. Have you found her? Is she okay?" the woman asked him frantically.

He scanned her for signs of the younger woman and found little to go by. Like his houseguest this older lady seemed well-kept, though, unlike the rest of the victims. Still, he suddenly felt protective of the woman at home and suspicious of the one before him.

"Who? What is this about?"

Loretta scowled. "You said…"

"I never said she was with me. I said… I saw her. Well, I saw someone who didn't seem to belong with the crowd, lying on the street and…"

The old woman began to plead with him, even as Loretta wore the look she often had on after a patient expired on the table: a little pained, a bit confused, anxious. She would be expecting him to tell her to "inform" the relatives.

"Tell them I'll be out in a while," he would say, but seldom showed himself to the family. Loretta always thought she understood this reticence of the doctor. At first, she found him too sensitive. She thought he was overcome by guilt. Later, she would suspect he was just too even-keeled, too bereft of emotion to even pretend sadness. Still, she was often the first to meet the relatives, considering it to be part of her job to protect him this way, but now she felt betrayed by the doctor for the first time. She knew he was lying.

"Your daughter, you say?"

"Yes. My one and only."

"You have a photo?"

The woman desperately searched her purse, but in vain. She took out a mobile phone and stared intently at it. "No, it's not in this one," she said.

"It's okay," Chester said. "I…. We will contact you should anything come up. Leave a number with the nurse."

Loretta's scowl turned into a grimace. She felt that the doctor had crossed the line this time. "I'm afraid you'll have to deal with the police, ma'am," she said.

"Maria Olivia Mahiwo, that's my name. She's Emily, my daughter. She's very young; she's a singer. We live in Mandaluyong. On Monday evenings, she sings at the Horizons Bar in that restaurant strip along Ortigas Avenue. It's not too far from the Legazpi Stadium."

"I know," Chester said, his heart was racing. The woman he had saved did seem like she could be a lounge singer. "So what makes you think she'll be among the victims of the stampede?"

"*Kutob*," Maria said. "I've been having a bad feeling in my gut since she started dating the Chinese mestizo about two months ago. He doesn't look right and he's too old for her. He's a friend of the bar owner, I'm told. I'm sure he's married, perhaps not just once, though he claims otherwise. The rake. She's changed, doctor. Acts strange these days. I raised her since…" the woman seemed stumped, uncertain. Then she recovered: "She's always been a good girl. He's done something to my *hija*. Got her hooked on something, I fear. She didn't come home last night so I called up the bar this morning. The guard said she left early last night. Didn't do her third set. She seemed to be in a dark mood, he said. Then I saw the news on TV about the stampede and I just sensed she might have gotten herself caught up in it somehow. She likes Wowie, watches the show sometimes. This is the closest hospital to the stadium so I rushed over to check."

Mahiwo spoke in a mix of English and Tagalog, but her accent didn't sound quite Manilan to Chester. There was a harder edge to it; something convent-bred but not quite. Mahiwo. He thought she might be from the Ilocos or mountain provinces.

Emily Mahiwo. Chester was a bit disappointed with the name. Singers always jazzed up their names, he thought like Anne Brazil, Diana Ross or Sting. Still, the woman in his home could be an Emily. He could indeed be savior to both her and her mother, though the woman before him looked more like a grandmother to the younger woman and he saw little resemblance.

He felt that empowering, elusive pride since the last time he held a patient's heart in his hands, though. That was nearly six years ago and he had massaged the boy's enlarged heart that had seemed to surrender to its own weight during surgery—only fourteen years old and born with a leaking valve. (And who knows? He might have imbued the organ with his *chi*!) He had revived the juvenile heart and replaced the valve with a synthetic implant that had given the boy a new lease on life, and his parents, life's greatest joy. But soon they would be able to replace valves without need for surgery as well. He wouldn't even be able to think himself some high-priced "plumber" anymore, or just another backseat driver.

He wanted her to be Emily but he needed to be certain. He did not want to provide anyone false hope or endanger the innocent. He had taken an oath that said: First: do no harm. And he must be true to his calling.

"We'll be in touch, Mrs. Mahiwo," he said again as Loretta stared at him and counted all the ways he had sugar coated his answers to patients and their relatives through the years.

"Why don't you just tell them straight, give them your best prognosis," Loretta had wanted to say to him many times but demurred. His reticence endeared him to her, though she'd always denied this to herself. This time, however, she knew he was withholding a truth that could finally haunt anyone who basked in its shadow. She decided she would not be a party to his elisions this time and refuse to play on his team.

"You should go to the police if she doesn't show up by tomorrow," Loretta said, but the woman held on to Chester's hand. "Please, doctor," she begged. "Please help me."

Chester was unsteadied by the woman's plea, her faith in a stranger. He withdrew his hand from hers gently. "Of course. I'll do everything in my power," he said, with little to no conviction. "Loretta, ask info to call up the other hospitals, they may have something," he said, but the nurse had already turned away and moved on.

"My phone number and address." The woman handed him the note she had scribbled quickly on a stationary. "Please," she said again and this time he felt the discomfort in his gut—like having drunk too much alcohol on an empty stomach—that often followed the death of a patient. This was why he seldom chose to meet the relatives, he feared expelling bad air and a coldness on his brow.

"Wait," he called and took out his mobile to take a photo of her. "Just in case."

She seemed stunned for a bit then nearly smiled. "It's Miss," she said.

"I beg your pardon?"

"It's miss," she repeated. "Miss Mahiwo."

Then she turned and left.

When he got home, the woman was gone. He panicked a while but was settled by a shot of whiskey. It was all for the best, he decided. He had done his bit. None of this was his business. At least now he wouldn't have to lie to an old woman, if ever. The memory of the younger one would not leave him, though. If she was indeed Emily Mahiwo then it was his duty to tell her so and bring her home.

He decided to drive around the area and look for the woman one last time. He cruised along the stampede site that was now cleared and restored to vehicular traffic, coasted through his usual jogging path and drove several blocks from his condo building without seeing anyone in white. Then instead of heading back, he turned another corner and headed for the restaurant and bar strip where Horizons was. He knew of it as a jazz place but had never gone there. He parked and saw the bar's neon sign a few meters away. He was anxious to check the place out yet wary of what he might discover. He scanned the area that teemed with neon but not patrons.

Then he saw her, standing on a promontory some five meters away from the strip but she was looking away to the distance. "Oh, no," he thought to himself. "She's going to do it this time, she'll jump." And he scurried towards her. "Emily!"

She turned to him, surprised. "What are you doing here?"

"What are *you* doing here?"

She looked lost. "I wanted to get some air. I started walking. I don't know. I just found myself here. I'm sorry. I've been enough trouble. I can't stay at your place. Thanks for everything."

"No. It's no bother. You can't…. Where will you go? Stay a few days. Until you… remember something. Please."

"What did you call me?"

"Emily."

"Why?"

"There was an old woman at the hospital this afternoon looking for her daughter. Fits your description. She says her daughter's name is Emily Mahiwo."

The woman tried to let the name sink in. "And this woman's name?"

"Olivia Mahiwo… here."

He showed her the photo on his mobile. The woman stared at it then walked away, appearing distressed. "I don't know. God, I don't know a thing." She covered her face with her hands, sobbing.

He wanted to hold her but caught himself. "It's okay. Give it time."

She wiped her tears as she sat down on the stone bench.

"Do you know that place?" he asked her, pointing to Horizons Bar.

She looked hard. "Should I?"

"The woman says Emily sings there. Do you sing?"

She shrugged and held her forehead. She looked towards Horizons again then cringed. She turned away, distraught. "I don't like it."

"Listen, I'll go check it out. Ask around. Who knows? I might learn something."

"I don't think I'll come with you."

"Okay, but do me a favor. Come stay inside the car. Don't stand out here. It's dark."

He brought her to his dark green Volvo and proceeded to Horizons by himself. Inside, a bossa nova tune was playing in the background, but no one was on stage. He could see a drum set and an electric guitar. There were around eight people scattered about the nightspot that could perhaps sit thirty. He picked a seat close to the bar and ordered a beer.

"Is Emily Mahiwo singing tonight?" he asked the waiter.

"No, sir. She's here Mondays and Thursdays."

"This Thursday?"

"Yes, sir, but I'm not sure if she'll be in. You better call up first," the waiter answered in Filipino.

"Why? Is she sick?"

"I can't say, sir, but she wasn't feeling very well last time, so she might be absent."

"But she *is* okay?"

"Sir?"

"I mean, she's not missing, or... I mean, she's still singing here, right?"

The waiter looked wary. "It's best you call up, to be sure... if she's the one you really want to hear, although we have other good singers on other days."

"Excuse me. You're looking for Emily?"

"Yes, I heard...." The face reminded Chester of someone, somewhere.... "Jefferson?"

"Chesterfield. Chester Limhuatco! Son of a... You old dog! How long...? I haven't seen you since high school! You're a doctor or something, aren't you? Our class genius! No, you're an astronaut, right? Something I read in the papers... I saw your mug. No, I think you're that rapist..."

"I'm a surgeon. Cardiovascular. At Saint Benedict's."

"I always knew you'd become some big shot something even if that flat head Johnson Yap made valedictorian. He's the astronaut, right?"

"I don't know. I think he works at NASA. We were batch mates at U.P. He was in physics. Went on to CalTech, I think."

"No shit. Maybe he can help us build a space sex motel, huh? Fuck your brains out in zero gravity. I'll find the girls, you be the doc, what do you think?"

"Don't think so. Got enough troubles down here with the tax hounds. How about you? How many billions you got?"

"Billions? Shit, I got nothing but this dump. Don't have the brains of you guys."

"You own this place?"

"Well, partly. I run it."

"You're into jazz?"

"Jazz, my ass. My partner's the music guy. I do the ladies."

"You have G.R.O.'s here?"

"Nah, not allowed here. This happens to be a classy joint, you know? It's too near a church and a school, and all that shit. I do co-own another place in Timog, however, where.... Wait a minute, is *that* what you're looking for? Well, well, we *have* come a long way, haven't we, doc?

"No, no, I just thought..."

"No problem, doc. Fate has brought us back together. Leave it up to the Pope..."

The Pope. Chester was reminded suddenly of their high school days when they punned each other's Chinese surnames. Peter Ong was *pag-ong* (turtle) because he was stout and slow. Sleepy Victor Ngo was *alima-ngo* (crab) because he was spindly and lean and seemingly hard-shelled though he ran like the wind. Billy Cua was *kwago* (owl) for his large eyes and wide forehead. And Jefferson Po was sometimes "Pope" because of the time he dozed off while Fr. Brix was lecturing on the "infallibility of the Pope". Jefferson snored and the good priest said, "And to you as well, Mr. Pope." Jefferson could also be *ponkan* (mandarin oranges) for his penchant to gift teachers with fruits that apparently signaled other transactions, *postiso* (for his early dentures), and *pokpok* (for the "working girls" he reportedly dated and sometimes pimped).

Chester could not remember anyone having a code name for himself. Perhaps his long surname—derived from his grandfather's full Chinese name, Lim Siong Huat—was too unwieldy for punning or perhaps he was just the semi nerd no one bothered to mock. This thought slightly unsettled him. He remembered how much he had disliked Jefferson Po—the batch bully, the squid-faced, tough-skinned football fullback, who always had his bunch of losers hanging around him. Chester couldn't recall Jefferson ever picking on him but he was always wary of the guy, always watchful.

"I just thought Emily Mahiwo...."

"You know her?" Jefferson suddenly perked up, turning serious that Chester felt his heart kick.

"I've heard of her... from friends."

"Oh," Jefferson whispered after a while. "I thought you'd seen her."

"Why? Has something happened to her?"

"Waiter said she seemed to be in a bad mood last time and left early. No one's heard from her since. I just hope she's okay."

"Is there reason to worry?"

Jefferson seemed distracted for a while. "What? Oh, no... you know women, can't ever tell what's bugging them. I just don't want people coming here to hear her sing and being pissed if she doesn't show. Bad for business," Jefferson said.

"How about you, man? Happily hitched? Kids?"

"One."

"One wife? That's all? Big time doctor?"

"One girl…."

"Well, I sure hope so."

"No, I mean, I just have one kid. She's 34, wanted to be a vet but… not anymore."

"A dog doc? You're a big time surgeon and she wants to treat dogs?"

"Not anymore. She's into other stuff now."

"Not monkeys, I hope. I met *pagong* last month. Remember him? Peter Ong? Says his son is digging for bones in Palawan. Shit. He spent a fortune on the kid. Sent him to England for studies and he comes home to dig for bones in the jungle. Kids these days…"

"He's a paleontologist? Archaeologist?"

"I don't know. Something or other."

"And you? What do your kids do?"

"Eat. Screw. Live off the old man."

"Come on."

"I don't know. Took after me, I guess. Good for nothing. One's with her mom in Canada, we're separated. The boy's… in Tokyo, last I heard."

"Business."

"Clothes. Designer stuff."

"Big bucks."

"Well I haven't seen a cent. Anyway, I got my own life."

"So you run bars and nightspots?"

"Well, sort of. It's just this one and Stefano's in Timog, where I first saw Emily. It helps to have your own place where you can meet people, you know, for business."

"So you have other businesses?"

"A little here and there. I know people."

"Shabu?"

Chester immediately regretted saying that. He wasn't sure whether it had sounded like a joke but Jefferson's eyes only seemed to light up in the dimness and held his breath momentarily. Chester felt funny down in his gut and remembered the time he saw Jefferson Po throw an elbow across the face of the center forward from Don Bosco High and broke the guy's jaw forty years ago.

"What? Don't tell me you're looking for that shit, doc. I'm sure you can get your hands on much meaner stuff in the hospital."

Jefferson's laughter disturbed Chester, before it comforted him.

"Just checking," he said.

"You're going to get me in trouble, man."

"Sorry."

"It's okay. You know these cops, always looking for something or other to pin on you."

"They bother you?"

"There will always be the shitheads but I got enough people upstairs to call on just in case. Why? You need someone to call? Some trouble?"

"No, nothing serious."

"Come on, tell the Pope."

"There's this girl...."

"Well, didn't I know it...."

"It's not like that."

"You want to send her boyfriend a final warning?"

"She's a stranger."

"What?"

"More or less. I mean... we just met."

"The best of times. Cheers to you."

"She can't remember who she is."

"What? What kind of shit is that? You're into amnesiacs? Are they hot?"

"I found her... outside my home."

"A stray? Better go slow on that.... You don't know where it's been, or what's been inside it."

"She was among the crowd... got hurt in the stampede this morning. I live at the Corinthian condos near Legazpi Sports Complex."

"Oh, that mad riot with the million-pesos show? People died there, I heard."

"Seventy-five."

"Serves them right. Good for nothing slobs, think they can get rich sitting on their asses and running after these show business freaks."

Jefferson's reaction bothered Chester somewhat. He briefly recalled Jefferson tackling another Don Bosco forward and kicking the fallen guy on the gut.

"You think it's safe to take her in from the street just like that?"

"Just until she gets her wits back."

"You sure she's not scamming you? It's hard to remember you're from some rat's nest while slumming inside a luxury condo unit. "

Jefferson could be right, Chester thought. The woman might have sensed his desire for her and decided to cash in. "I don't think it's like that," he said.

"You're the doctor, but if you need someone at Pasig police or at the NBI to look into it..."

"Yes. Perhaps, if she remains clueless in the next few days..."

"Sure, give me a call. I'll bring you to headquarters or to the NBI myself."

"Thanks. I appreciate it. By the way, you have a photo of Emily?"

Jefferson seemed stunned for an instant then he looked about.

"Ah … I don't think so. No posters yet. She should be here on Thursday, though."

"How does she look?"

"Oh …" his former classmate cooed and rolled his eyes.

Bastard's in love, Chester thought and quickly swallowed the acridness in his tongue that almost reminded him of his ancient dislike for Jefferson Po.

Jefferson closed his eyes, shaking his head slowly as he pinched his lips and kissed his own thumb to raise it before Chester. "The best," he said.

Chester felt the distaste rising up his throat again and had to push it back down, hard. The thought of this creature before him planting his snout anywhere on the white lady made him nauseous. It must be a different woman, he insisted to himself.

"It's not just the looks, man, great-looking food can sometimes taste bland. But this one … I tell you …" He shook his head slowly once more.

"I get it," Chester said, forcing a smile.

"Chester, my man, big-shot doctor, you should be laying Angel Locsin or Anne Curtis or their lost twins rather than some stray off the street who can't even remember her fucking name. Get rid of it, man. I'll show you what you need."

"Next time," Chester said and took a photo of Jefferson with his mobile phone.

Jefferson roused from stupor and sprang at Chester like a wounded cat. "What are you doing?" he growled as he grabbed the phone from the doctor.

Chester felt like a trapped rodent as he recalled all the forwards this erstwhile fullback had maimed. The next thing he knew, he was pinned against the bar. "Just a photo for my file," he tried to explain.

"You don't ask permission before taking a piece of someone's soul?" Jefferson asked and Chester was surprised the guy even knew that old Native American belief.

"Sorry. It was just a picture."

Jefferson deleted the photo and handed the phone back, eventually relaxing. "Sorry, too, man. I just have this thing about photos. I'm paranoid that way."

"It's cool."

"Come on, drink up. On the house. What are you having? You go for single malt whiskey?"

"No thanks, I can't stay long. I have surgery tomorrow."

"Hey, man. I said I'm sorry."

"No, I really have to check in early, might cut into the wrong vessel tomorrow. It's some German guy with an aneurysm. "

"You should circumcise him while you're at it. *Achtung*!"

"I'll try to come by on Thursday."

"Please do. By the way, is it true you guys transplant pig hearts into people?"

"It's been known to happen."

"You think I can have one when this outhouse pump gives in? I've been short of breath lately."

Perfect match. Donor aplenty. No chance of rejection.

"You look trim enough. Had a physical lately?"

"Nah.... What you don't know won't matter."

"That's the kind of thinking that kills you before your time. Have an executive annually. Look me up at St. Benedict. I'll only charge you what my daughter would've charged those dog owners."

I know there's a vessel right under your left temple that's about to burst. I know it will do so five minutes after I leave this place. You will be nauseous and faint, your tongue will turn to

*stone, your speech will slur, your eyesight will blur. When they get
you to the hospital, you will have been long gone, your brain dead;
your soul in hell ....*

"You docs are always trying to fleece us poor blokes. The
bill will kill me before any aneurysm does."

"Sign up for the charity ward. I'll vouch for you. See you
Thursday."

Once outside, Chester raced to his Volvo, afraid that the
woman would disappear once again. He found her there,
sleeping. He drove home then. He didn't have the heart to
wake her, so he tried to carry her up to his condo unit from
the parking lot. She stirred and leapt off him in revulsion. Still,
she just stood there like a lost child. Sighing, Chester took her
hand and led her to the elevator.

3
WHITE NIGHTS

SHE WAS A bit disturbed by their last phone conservation. He seemed impatient and agitated, but she had made no effort to calm or humor him, because she was pissed off with her father and his alleged white lady sightings. Roger was just back from a weekend in Boracay with his German friend Klaus, who flew off immediately to a conference in Tokyo. Carmen suspected that the two had had a lovers' spat and this further soured her mood, though she seldom admitted her feelings for Roger to herself. She had always known he was gay but could not quell the murmurs of her heart whenever he was near her, whistling some folk Swedish tune or admiring her China doll looks.

The first time they met at New York University where Carmen, then 20, was visiting her cousin, Belen, she had imagined being swept off to Asgard by this Viking, who betrayed none of the swish or swagger she had then associated with his gender. He was working on his graduate thesis in Anthropology and became interested in the Black Nazarene. When he learned that the girls were from the Philippines, Roger Geisler introduced himself and followed the cousins all over upper Manhattan, asking them about the 400-year-old, black-toned, cross-bearing, genuflecting Christ housed in Quiapo Church, in the heart of downtown Manila, the *Nuestro Padre Jesus Nazareno*.

However, Belen was doing Creative Writing and Carmen was a junior Vet Med student. Neither had even been to Quiapo, save for the one time when Carmen was around nine and she had gone with the house help on a whim, without telling her parents. She rode on her first passenger jeepney all the way there, only to be scared out of her wits in the pedestrian underpass when an old beggar darted out of nowhere, whom she thought was a leper like the one in her illustrated Bible. The cousins were raised in the suburbs and always thought of old Manila as a lair of petty thieves and beggars. It was the "armpit of Manila" that Belen could remember of Quiapo per some poet.

To keep Roger interested, Carmen recycled stories about miracles performed by the Nazarene which were told to her as a child by her *yaya* Pining. She told him about the millions of faithful who flocked to the environs of Quiapo Church every year on January 9, when the statue is paraded around the district atop a flower bedecked carriage to commemorate—the traslación— its transfer from the Luneta to Quiapo Church hundreds of years ago, in a bid to touch the miraculous icon, wipe it with kerchiefs that would henceforth be deemed miraculous, or pull on the thick ropes that moved his carriage forward.

She had seen the event a few times on television. It was fascinating and frightening at the same time. It was a stormy sea of humanity pushing blindly, ebbing and flowing, swirling and eddying, barefoot people, mostly men, piled atop one another struggling to reach the maroon-robed, cross-bearing black figure that seemed to toss and turn atop the waves of bodies while yellow and maroon-shirt men cordoned off the Nazarene from his most fanatical devotees. Devotees would throw handkerchiefs to the men protecting the icon who would then wipe the kerchiefs on the Nazarene and toss them back to the crowd, like in a rock concert. The devotion had been going on for as far back as anyone could remember. Every year, there were scores of injuries even as ambulances waited in strategic places. There were two deaths during the last festivities. The authorities tried their utter best to maintain order. A few celebrities, including a radio and television broadcaster who became Vice President, came barefoot every year to pull on the ropes of the Nazarene's carriage. It was in fulfillment of some vow he made as a young man.

"It takes 22 hours to complete the 6.5 km route," Carmen said.

She also told Roger about a barber who pleaded for his ten-year-old son stricken by leukemia. The boy was cured and every year hence, the barber and his son would camp outside the church on the eve of the Nazarene's parade, climb up the pillar of the church gate so they could touch the hem of the Nazarene's robe as the statue left church grounds. One year, the barber fell and broke his leg, but the Nazarene came to him in a dream and healed him. Soon, the son became a healer.

There were also women who walked on their knees inside the church till their kneecaps bled as penance for favors granted. She spoke, too, of those who prayed for a fee. "Prayer, after all, is the currency of faith."

Roger's eyes brightened upon hearing this, and Carmen imagined herself tiptoeing on the edge of a precipice. *Yes, take me,* she said with her eyes, *touch my hem, my brow, once, twice and I will grant your deepest yearning.*

Then *he* arrived, the friend, Earl, she still remembered. He was black, but unlike the Nazarene, Earl was a *mulatto*. He was lean but toned like a dancer and he was handsome. Carmen almost lost her balance when she saw Roger and Earl kiss. She seemed to have been thrown off her *carozza* just as she was about to touch the Nazarene, hustled back down the waves of humanity, and pushed to the ground.

Before she could be trampled by the horde, Carmen Limhuatco stood up, brushed off the dust and extended her hand. "Hi Earl, it's great to meet you," she greeted, but worried if she would ever come any closer to surviving a miracle.

That was fourteen years ago, and she too had since turned to Anthropology, leaving the relative precision of Veterinary Medicine for the more unwieldy types of healing involved in her present study, while Roger's lover Earl had given way to Arnie, who gave way to Steve, who then gave way to Klaus.

Meanwhile, Roger's fascination with the Black Nazarene had deepened. He had gone to Mexico to investigate similar devotions and claimed to have found the village where the unknown mulatto artist carved the Nazarene before it was brought to Manila in 1606 by a friar of the Recollect Order. The Mayas and Aztecs worshipped black deities that scholars surmise were transformed into "Cristos Negros" after the Conquista. They were all over Latin America.

"Roberto Duran famously joined the Cristo Negro procession in Portobello before his comeback fight in '82 after the "No Mas!" fiasco," Roger once said to Carmen, not a boxing fan, who had no idea what he was saying until years later when Filipino boxing idol Manny Pacquiao himself communed with the Señor Nazareno in Quiapo before flying off to Las Vegas for a big fight.

Las Islas Filipinas was a colony of the Spanish crown that ruled via Nueva España, later Mexico, from the 15th to the 19th century. The galleons, built in the port town of Cavite, south of Manila, ferried European wares, friars, imperial messages, Mexican goods and silver—much valued among the Chinese traders in Manila—from Acapulco to Manila and returned months later with ceramic, silk and tea from China and beeswax, hardwood, and abaca hemp from the islands. Roger agreed with another researcher that the color of the icon was due to the mesquite wood used by the sculptor.

"It was a cult in Mexico," Roger said. "The story goes that a priest started each day by kissing the feet of the crucified Christ in his church. A parishioner with a bad reputation asked permission to marry the priest's sister but he refused. The man, aware of the priest's devotion, placed poison on the feet of the Christ. The next day, the priest, as always, kissed the feet of the crucifix but nothing happened. The figure had absorbed all the poison into its system and turned black."

"Great story. Very telenovela," she quipped with a wink.

"I think that story marks the time when the Catholic Church accepted the indigenous devotion and absorbed it. A new faith was born out of the crossbreeding of the olden and colonial religions."

Carmen was awed.

The statue being paraded now isn't even the original, Roger said. "That was destroyed along with the church that housed it inside Intramuros during the bombing of Manila in 1945. On January 9, 1787, the Augustinian Recollects donated a copy of the icon to the Quiapo Church. That event is what has been commemorated on the date."

"So does that mean that what has come down to posterity might actually have been sculpted locally by local artists?"

"Who knows?" Roger shrugged. "Maybe by Chinese artisans."

Roger first came to Manila in 2004 to experience the traslación firsthand. Carmen felt obliged to join him but backed out at the last minute. The thought of being trapped amid all those bodies was enough to give her migraine. Chester disapproved of it as well. Roger went on alone. He lost his camera and earned a bruise over his right eye but was so enamored by the experience he seemed on hallucinogens the next few days.

He spoke of how spirit was the "movement of matter, immeasurable." He had paid some men to get him close enough to the Nazarene. Just as he was about to mount the carriage, someone grabbed him and he was thrown to the ground, suffering a mild contusion. Still, Roger would return to join the festivities on several more occasions, like once on Good Friday, when the statue was similarly paraded. He even went to the province of Pampanga, north of Manila, to witness the live crucifixion of penitents performed annually. He was convinced that only by experiencing a crucifixion, even vicariously, could he begin to understand devotion to the Nazareno.

At first, Carmen was amused by Roger's fascination with Filipino folk Catholicism. She egged him on as his research provided them a chance to work together. However, when Roger spoke of being crucified in Pampanga one year, Carmen was agog.

"Are you insane? Is this a joke?"

"No, I think it is a very profound solemn rite, which has unfortunately been degraded by touristic voyeurism. But if they see a white man on the cross, it could shock them into realizing the original gravitas of the act."

"You crazy Swede! I doubt if your travel insurance covers crucifixion."

"I feel my research has reached a point where I must take on the heart of the subject."

"Do you hear yourself? You want to do a Castañeda? Man, he only had to pig out on mescaline. You want to be nailed to a cross?"

"This is important."

"Shut up and stop insulting me and my people. Who do you think you are?"

"You're missing the point."

"You think you can just waltz in here with your white ass and green money and turn the thing into a circus? Those friggin' friars already did a number on us and we're still hooked on their bullshit, but you hanging beside some peasant who only wants his wife cured of cancer or to get his land back from usurers isn't going to create a United Nations of penitents. Quit your nonsense or I'll nail you up there myself."

"This isn't some weird practice that is particular to the Philippines. They have it in Mexico and other places in Latin America. It's also not even specific to Catholics. Other cultures practice corporal punishment as well like Hindus or Native Americans. Mortification creates an altered state of consciousness. This is something primal, before God was Love; it's trial by ordeal, worship by blood sacrifice. Unpalatable to the modern mind."

"If you do this, don't ever show your face to me again. However this thing started, it's *ours* now, *our* devotion. We own it, or at least those guys risking their lives do. You can't buy it," she said.

Roger didn't push through with his plan, as far as Carmen knew. The organizers in Pampanga told him there were too many volunteers that year while another group in Laguna offered to crucify him for $2,000. He left the country in a hurry and was out of touch with Carmen for several months. Then he emailed her that he would do research in Thailand instead. He did say he was to go with Klaus to Boracay and to interview a member of the *Cofradia* (Confraternity of our most Holy Jesus of Nazareth) that supported the Nazarene. The statue had suffered injuries through the last four hundred years and only members of the brotherhood, founded in 1620, were supposed to know whether the statue paraded each year was the original or a replica.

Some members of the confraternity were unknown to the public according to certain sources and initiation into the brotherhood was arcane. Still, Carmen feared that Roger might have been taken in by some fraud out to fleece him.

"You sure about this guy? How did you meet?" She had asked him when Roger told her about his new informant.

"It was perhaps destined. I was in a bar in Amsterdam listening to the band and there was this Asian guy on keyboard. He was very good, played everything from Beatles to ABBA and Steely Dan. I tried talking to him during the break but he didn't want to. Then he saw my amulet that I got from Quiapo and became curious. I told him about my research and he seemed thunderstruck. He began to weep. He said he was Filipino, Basilio Ambahan, and that he was from a line of Cofradia members. He was supposed to take over his father's place in the inner council when he turned 22 but Basilio refused. He didn't share his father's devotion, didn't believe in any of it. He was a musician and he wanted to see the world. "It is your destiny," his father, Conrado, wrote Basilio, before the older man passed away. "He will always be in your shadow." Basilio worked as a cook on a merchant ship but he was restless and jumped ship in Naples. He wandered through Europe until he found work with a band in Amsterdam, who protected him. "He is calling me home," Basilio said and promised to help me with my research once he came back to the country."

"Are you sure you're being objective about this?" Carmen asked.

"Who knows? What does it matter, really?"

"You're a researcher!"

"And I'm following my instincts."

"Sounds strange to me."

"Strange? From you?"

That was the last thing they said to each other before Roger left for Boracay. He called her when he got back and said he was meeting Basilio. He sounded annoyed and she didn't care to pursue the matter. He had been in the country several times before and knew enough Tagalog to get by, but now he hadn't been in touch with her for three weeks and she was worried. He always kept in touch whenever he was in the Philippines and it wasn't like him to leave the country without telling her. His mobile phone service repeatedly indicated that he was out of reach.

That evening, Carmen remembered how Roger described the "white" summer nights in Stockholm during August when there are nearly twenty fours of sunlight. "The sun would set around midnight and we would be walking down the street, which seem alit with a cold, incandescent, sulfuric flame. "I think that's why we produced Ingmar Bergman along with so much porn, white nights make you either morose or horny," Roger concluded.

That night, Carmen dreamt she was walking along a dark street lined with tree stumps. She seemed to be looking for someone, but was unsure who it was. Then she saw a white light in the distance beckoning to her. As she approached she was filled with a sadness so deep, she awoke with tears in her eyes. The next day, she went to Quiapo to see if she could find out what happened to Roger.

She was right in thinking that Fr. Jaguar Jimenez was too young and cool for a parish priest, as he confided to her that he was a temporary deputy to Fr. Dimalanta, who was on sick leave and whose future remained uncertain after surgery on his prostate.

"I prefer a small provincial town, perhaps near a beach, with just one cockpit and one brothel, much easier to come up with penances," Fr. Jimenez said, with a glint in his eyes that surprised Carmen. "But we must serve where we are called to."

"You mean the guys who frequent cockpits and cat houses go to confession?"

"No, but their wives do, and sometimes ask to do the penance for their husbands."

"That's allowed?"

"No, but it consoles the women. Also, how else am I supposed to know about cockpits and brothels?"

"What? You're pulling my leg, aren't you? You're a bad priest," she said, suddenly at ease with the young pastor, to whom, she would later admit, she was instantly attracted.

"What other sort is there?" He asked, and she might have flirted with him through her eyes and lips.

"Let's see, a Swede. Yes, there was a white guy, who came by a few weeks ago. He spoke pretty good Tagalog and had a deep tan. He asked about the Cofradia, said he was researching the Nazarene. I told him all I knew, which isn't much. I've been a priest here for less than a year. He seemed to know a lot."

"He's been researching the Nazarene for many years, for his thesis in cultural Anthropology. He was supposed to meet a man named Basilio Ambahan, whom he met abroad. Basilio claims to be a descendant of a Cofradia member."

"Ambahan?" The priest squinted and shook his head in a manner Carmen found charming. He wore his hair short but spiked every which way like that of a pop singer. There was some apparent method to the madness of the coiffure but Carmen couldn't figure it out at once. She was surprised he was allowed such hairstyle. "Makes me more approachable to the kids," he said, apparently reading her mind.

"The name doesn't sound familiar but sometimes they use pseudonyms. Certain traditions may put off outsiders but people tend to make more of the Cofradia than what they are, especially after that Da Vinci Code hype. Now, everyone's looking for secret brotherhoods, black rites and conspiracies."

"You've read it?"

"No. Saw the movie. I'm a Tom Hanks fan."

"So am I."

"Really?"

"I have a DVD of *Saving Private Ryan* at home. We can

see it on my plasma TV with red wine and chips ...." she was tempted to say to Fr. Jimenez. Instead, she said, "Conrado, that's supposed to be his father's name."

The priest frowned. "Conrado?" He squinted once more and Carmen would have pinched his boyish cheeks had he not said: "I heard there was a Cofradia member who died last year.... Yes, I think he was named Conrado."

"You sure? How did he die?"

"There's some uncertainty but ...."

"Please, I have to know, Father. It could help, my friend's missing; he might be in trouble."

"Well, there's a rumor that he committed suicide."

"Suicide?"

"It's just a rumor."

"So it's probably true."

"I see you have much faith in your fellow human beings."

"Only in their nose for a good story."

"And what is *your* story, Miss... Limhuatco?"

"Carmen."

"Are you perhaps looking for one? Are you a journalist?"

"Anthropologist. Well, working to be one, at least."

"Oh? Just like your friend. So you'd like to figure out where faith comes from? Why do people allow themselves to be scourged? Nailed to a cross? Is there a gene for devotion? Is it due to some wiring in the brain?"

"I think nurture plays as big, if not a bigger, role than nature. Faith is culture, mostly."

"Really? So you don't believe."

"I'm agnostic."

"And what does that mean? You're a fence sitter, *balimbing*?"

"It's not a matter of taking sides, Father, it's not politics. I just don't think I am capable of knowing God even if he, or she, or whatever, does exist."

"Conceit disguised as humility, always fascinating."

"I'm sorry if I don't share your certainties."

"No, don't be sorry, please. It's not every day I get a devil's advocate.... I miss the seminary sometimes, and its pleasures."

"I'm not... please, I just want to find Roger, or at least know that he's safe."

"What's the sound of one hand clapping?" the priest asked Carmen after looking deep into her eyes.

She was shocked. This was Roger's favorite Zen koan. There was no answer to it, of course. It was just a code between her and Roger whenever they were bored silly by some empty lecture or unwanted company. One of them would pose the riddle and the other would slap her, or his, own face before they leave the lecture hall.

Carmen slapped herself. Father Jimenez smiled and handed her the slip of paper he took out from his desk drawer. It was sealed by candle wax. "He said you might come looking for him but that it was best to make sure it was you," the priest said.

She unsealed the message with the priest's paper knife and it read: "I am safe. I can tell you no more at this point but I was a happy baby in Nigeria where the fairy rests in the south. All that glitters is not gold."

"What's this? What does he mean?"

Fr. Jimenez shrugged. "I'm just the mailman."

"Nigeria? I know he was there for a month two years ago but... a baby? Doesn't make sense. What's going on?"

She turned to the priest and nearly climbed on top of his desk. "Listen, you, I don't care if you're the assistant parish priest or the Archbishop's black boot! You better come clean with me!"

"Back off!" Fr. Jimenez warned, almost raising his crucifix against the woman but holding up a firm finger instead.

Carmen took deep breaths and paced the floor. "I'm sorry," she whispered, "but how did he give you the note? Where did he write it? Was he alone?"

"He was receiving communion."

"Communion? I didn't know he was Catholic."

"Probably not. He didn't know how.... He just took the host in his hand; then he pulled me down and whispered into my ear. He said a Chinese looking woman named Carmen might come to look for him and that I should give her the note if she slaps herself after I pose the riddle. It was a five a.m. mass so there weren't many people around. Then he left in a hurry. I didn't see who he was with."

"This is crazy.... Why doesn't he call or text me?"

"Maybe he's not allowed to do so. Maybe whoever he's with has confiscated his phone."

"Why? This isn't right." Carmen felt pin pricks all over her. "Is there anything you're not telling me, Father, please...."

"I've told you all I know."

"Is this something to do with the Cofradia?"

"Look, the Cofradia is just a group of devotees, respectable citizens, I might add, who help raise funds for the statue's upkeep and plan religious activities. The confraternity was founded in 1621, one of the richest at that time, and was officially authorized by the Pope in 1650. Locals couldn't join the priesthood back then, so joining the Cofradia was the next best thing. Fathers often bequeath their memberships to sons so some present-day members hail from a long line, but it's by no means an exclusive club. The guys in yellow, maroon and white long sleeve shirts atop the carriage who protect the Nazarene while on parade are the so-called Hijos de Nazareno—the sons of the Nazarene. They protect the statue with their lives, especially from over zealous devotees. Some of them are descendants as well of Cofradia members, while others are volunteers. There are some 600 members drawn from six church-based groups. You have to apply for the task like for any job, do 60 hours of parish service; attend formation and recollection meetings. Last year, one hijo died of cardiac arrest while serving the Nazareno, the first in 400 years. So you see, this is no trifling matter," the priest said.

"I'm sure it's not," Carmen replied.

"They're like the Pope's Swiss Guard, if you will," Fr. Jimenez went on, inspired it seemed. "Perhaps this Ambahan is one of them. I'm not too clear about the matter of descendants but elders usually pass on their devotions to their young."

"He's in trouble. I just know it."

There was a moment's silence when Fr. Jimenez thought he was in the presence of a grace once nearly his, but long denied. He would have reached out and touched the presence before him but someone spoke.

"He's armed then?"

"What?"

"You said they're like the Swiss Guard? So they're armed?"

"What? Who...? Oh, no, no... I didn't mean it that way."

"They're not armed?"

"I... I guess not."

"How do you know? How can they protect the Nazarene if unarmed? What if some nut, some terrorist, got on the float and threatened to destroy the statue, or hold it hostage?"

"Why would anyone do that?"

"Why not?"

"It's just a...." The priest checked himself. "Look, I... assume they're armed... only with their deep faith and commitment."

"That's... absurd."

"Why don't you pray for him? It might clear your mind."

Carmen turned to the priest and saw a large black cat

instead. She panicked. Was she confusing the person with his name? Or was it that whoever had named him had a similar vision? She quickly shook off the vision and only the dark, slightly bearded man with deep black eyes was before her, reminding her of someone, something sad and encumbered.

She gasped, as sudden chills went through her. She was staring at *Him*, at the Nazarene, but lighter skinned.

Fr. Jimenez realized that the woman was now staring at him—as though he were a ghost—and felt himself cold, then warm, then hard. He was embarrassed though certain she could not have noticed any unusual movement beneath his soutane.

"What is it? Are you alright?" He heard himself ask.

Carmen took three deep breaths.

"Would you like some water?"

She shook her head and tried to shift her focus away from the priest. She scanned the banners festooned across the office, the standards of various religious organizations.

"I have to go," she said. "Thanks for everything. I'm sorry."

"Beware the devil's advocate with angel scars," his old mentor at the seminary, Fr. Martinez, used to say. Though he could not see them, the young priest knew the woman before him bore wounds. Jaguar Jimenez found himself pursuing her as his prey (*He didn't know why he suddenly thought of her as such, she wasn't the first. Was it his name? Had he become his name?*) hurried across the vestibule before stopping at the Nazarene under the baldochino.

Carmen seemed transfixed. Roger had explained to her how there were now two statues made from the single original. To protect the Nazarene from further wear and tear, in 1984, Church officials commissioned a maker of religious icons named Gener Malagui to make a replica. Malagui made a sturdier body using narra wood, for the original head that now stood under the baldochino designed by the National Artist, Juan Nakpil. For the original torso down to the genuflecting legs, Malagui created a replica of the head. This other image was kept inside a glass case in a corner enclave on the ground floor of the church, which was the one paraded.

"Why not make a *panata*?" Jaguar asked and Carmen turned to him with what seemed like fear in her eyes.

"What are *you* willing to do for your friend?" The priest had wanted to ask the woman but caught himself.

Then she was gone and it was all he could do to keep from following her beyond church grounds.

Carmen wandered aimlessly around the square fronting the church. It was her first time here since her early teens. The place looked cleaner, better organized than she remembered. City Hall had restricted vehicular traffic in the area and arrayed the fortune-tellers and sellers of prayer books, icons, amulets, talismans, and candles in their respective corners. She approached the middle-aged women selling candles of many shapes, sizes and colors. Church officials had limited the lighting of candles inside the church so many devotees light candles at the square that had become an extension of the church. The different shapes she knew represented bodily organs and devotees who were ailing or prayed for ailing loved ones bought up these candles. A vendor told her the peach candles would help her pass exams, the pink ones would bring her lover to her door, orange candles bring success, violet ones for wealth, yellow candles to help the soul, brown ones provide travel and black candles would work on the "conscience" of the malicious.

That disturbed her somewhat. She had never seen black candles. "If you are treated unjustly or humiliated before others by someone, light this black candle and your offender will feel guilty and lose sleep," the vendor explained, which convinced Carmen to buy it for the first time.

Carmen saw waxen hearts, livers, and even sex organs. A Sto. Niño with an erect penis granted fertility, another vendor explained. She also saw bottles of brownish liquid that were supposed to "cause menstruation." She knew they aborted fetuses and was amused by the fact they were being sold right outside church grounds. The Catholic hierarchy was adamant against artificial contraception and the Philippines remained the only country aside from the Vatican without divorce.

"Are you looking for something stronger?" A bearded man in a red shirt with a skull and bones design suddenly came up to her. "Cytotec, 80 pesos a pill," he whispered. "This works better than any of this crap, no foul taste, no vomiting." He looked her up and down. "How many months?"

Carmen was befuddled. "Pardon me?"

He pointed at her belly.

"Oh no…. I'm not pregnant."

He grinned. "Okay, it works on ulcers too."

She had wanted to inquire further if only to find out the man's source for the drug but someone, or something, bumped into her from behind. She felt a sharp pain on her left side and swung around to see a figure in green racing away from her. Carmen felt instinctively for her mobile in her right trouser pocket. It was gone. Her pocket had been ripped open. Her keys fell to the ground.

"Stop!" She shouted. "Thief!"

The crowd stirred. She began to give chase but she felt faint. Soon, blackness had overcome her.

<h1 style="text-align:center">4
IN QUIAPO</h1>

SHE AWOKE TO a scent from her girlhood: a mix of camphor and mothballs. Strange beings hovered about her, for a moment Carmen thought she had been abducted by extraterrestrials. It was a fear she once shared with her father. Then she saw a familiar face, her dad Chester looking down with a relieved smile and her fears flew from her like ghosts of dead ETs.

"It's okay, honey. You're safe now."

"Dad?"

"Yes, dear, it's me. We're with friends."

"What happened? Where am I? I was in the plaza..."

"You're in a medical clinic, in Quiapo. This is Dr. Anna Duran, a batch mate of mine back in med school. This is her place."

"I found your dad's card in your purse," the female doctor said. "Some bystanders saw you faint and brought you here."

"Someone in green, I remember. He hit me and stole my phone."

"Green?" Dr. Duran asked.

"It is sometimes the last color one sees before blacking out…"

Carmen heard an eerily familiar voice. The man in a dark buttoned-up shirt with white collar came into her line of sight. She remembered him. "Fr. Jaguar."

"Someone said that you'd been inside the Church talking to Fr. Jimenez so I sent for him," Dr. Duran explained.

The priest looked down briefly, embarrassed it seemed, as the others eyed him curiously. He shrugged.

"How do you know these things?" the doctor queried the priest.

"We don't just sit around singing hymns at the seminary, you know? It happens to be a place of learning as well."

"Really? Is that where you learned that conception occurs upon hard on and birth control pills abort fetuses?"

"And you give them away like candy to kids. You think you're being their fairy godmother? It's the road to perdition, woman."

"And having ten kids you can't feed is heavenly bliss, I presume?"

"You know I'm not Dimalanta…. Fr. Dimalanta, that is. I'm not some old conservative who can't stand the sight of rubbers but you're indiscriminate. You're telling them it's okay to be promiscuous."

"And you'd rather they're knocked up at fifteen with no job, no husband, and nothing between their ears."

"And that makes it okay to kill an innocent fetus?"

"The girl was suicidal and the fetus was damaged."

"But alive."

"I saved the mother, it was my call. You sent her to me."

"*Mea culpa.*"

"Right. Next time send her to those nuns who'll mess her up even more."

"Can you guys do this later? My daughter was assaulted."

"Don't exaggerate, Limhuatco," Anna Duran said rather curtly to the man she last saw nearly thirty years ago as an intern. "You were always prone to hyperbole."

"Hyper what? Someone injected her with anesthesia."

"Mild one."

"And I suppose this sort of thing happens all the time in these parts?"

"Could've been worse…" Fr. Jimenez said.

"What? Shouldn't we call the cops?"

"No, no cops!" the female doctor interjected, a bit alarmed.

Chester scanned the premises; something nipped him. "Why? Is he right?" he asked, pointing to Jaguar. "Is this an abortion clinic?"

"Of course not! I'm an obstetrician-gynecologist! Don't listen to that half-baked friar. Half of my patients come from his confessional."

"The good half," Fr. Jimenez cut in.

"Is he a thief? Is this his modus operandi?"

Modus operandi. The word made Anna smile a little. It was Latin, she recalled. "He didn't take the whole thing. Is there anything missing?" the doctor asked, handing Carmen her purse.

Carmen rummaged her purse and shook her head. "It's all here, money, cards…"

"So what's he up to? He just goes for cell phones?" Chester asked, feeling cold sweat on his brow.

Just then, the doorbell rang. Anna's teen-aged aide, Lara, brought them a pink colored mobile phone after a while. "A boy handed this to me and just fled," Lara said.

"That's mine," Carmen said, taking the phone, and stared at the screen. "He left a number. Should I call…?"

"Wait," her father said, grabbing the phone from her. "Shouldn't we inform someone about this?"

"Who?" Dr. Duran wanted to know.

Chester shrugged. "I don't know...."

"A cop?" Anna insisted.

"Well, someone in authority, at least."

"How about the mayor?" Anna sneered.

"Look, she's my daughter and I'm not letting some freelancing street anesthesiologist near her again!"

"Still, the same gutless choir boy," the doctor chirped.

"I don't give a shit how you remember me, Duran, but no one's exposing my daughter to anymore danger."

"You need any authority higher than him?" Anna asked, pointing to Fr. Jimenez. "What do you say, Father?"

"What do you want to do, Carmen?" the priest asked.

"She's just been traumatized so she can't think clearly," Chester protested.

"Shit, Limhuatco! You're a cardiac surgeon, for Christ's sake! Grow some balls!"

"There's no need for that," the priest cut in.

"I'll text him. Find out what he wants," Carmen said.

"He's watching us," Chester said, "he knows you guys. He's a local."

"Ambahan," the priest whispered.

"Basilio Ambahan? So he does exist. He's Roger's contact. And you *do* know him after all?" She clarified, looking hard at the priest.

"He came to me a while ago, with some strange story. He'd been gone a long time. I wasn't sure what to make of it," Fr. Jaguar Jimenez said, rather sheepishly. "He said he'd decided to come home after meeting Roger Geisler in Amsterdam, to help with the man's research on the Black Nazarene. He's Conrado's son."

"The Cofradia member whom you said died last year?"

"Yes. Basilio suspects that his father was killed by Tata

Peping, a quack who dresses up like the Nazareno and heads a cult."

"Don't you all?" Dr. Duran taunted. "With your Latin and your incense?"

"I'm not here to debate with you, Anna. I'm just relaying to the girl what I've been told. This Peping used to be a cop and a penitent crucified in Pampanga every year on Good Friday. His father was an American from Clark Airbase, who abandoned him at birth. And Peping had vowed to be crucified yearly until he met his dad."

"So he's met his dad?" Chester asked.

Jaguar made a popping sound with his lips. "His father reportedly sent word that he was not interested and urged junior to get on with his life, and that seemed to have changed Peping."

"So he wants to avenge himself on another white man and this Swede somehow fits the bill?" Chester asked no one in particular.

Jaguar stared at the surgeon. "He's black."

"What?" Chester seemed lost in his own thoughts.

"Peping is black. I mean... African-American-Filipino. That's the proper term now, right?"

"The Nazareno," Carmen said, still groggy as the others looked towards her. She then sat up. "He must have deemed himself as some kind of avatar, an incarnation... the living Black Christ."

A stunned silence passed among them but Chester started pacing: "No, no stop this, you don't know what you're saying."

"You'll have to make contact with this Basilio if you hope to find that Roger," Anna chimed in.

"Inform the Swedish embassy. Let them deal with it. This is no longer our business," Chester said, shaking his head.

"I'll meet with Basilio," Carmen said, now on her feet and searching for her shoes. "Roger mentioned him some time ago."

"Stop it!" Chester barked. "This isn't a game and you're not Princess Leia. Grow up!"

Another stunned silence came over the room. Carmen shook off the embarrassment: "*You* grow up, dad! I'm a big girl now and I'm responsible for my friend."

"Who has willfully put himself in danger. I warned him! I warned you! You wouldn't listen. You're responsible for…" Chester backed off as Carmen faced up to him.

"For what?" She seemed to be daring him to say but he looked away.

"For me…" Chester might have said in another time and place, "for your own father."

"I'll bring you to him," a voice broke the impasse. It was Jaguar. Chester wanted to rip off the priest's head. "He told me where he might be found, but only you, Carmen. Only you can come."

"I'm beginning to think there's more to you, priest," Chester said menacingly, followed by an awkward silence.

"Okay. I'll come," Carmen said.

"What? Do what you want. I'm out of here," Chester nearly shouted and harried off.

Jaguar gave Carmen a batik shawl to cover her head as they entered the Muslim neighborhood by the local Mosque. She saw stacks of CDs and DVDs on sale in various stalls and caught a glimpse of a favorite- Bergman's *The Virgin Spring*. She thought for a moment of buying herself a presumably pirated copy, to save herself the trouble of downloading on line, but Jaguar tugged at her sleeve.

They reached a halal coffee shop where a man in white skullcap stared at them and nodded. Jaguar led Carmen up the stairs by the rear and knocked on the door. They were allowed in after a while.

The air-conditioned room was spare but clean, with only a bed and worktable. The man wore a black beret, dark glasses and a week old beard that reminded her of a Che Guevarra portrait. Jaguar gestured to Carmen.

"You're Basilio Ambahan?"

"Who's asking?"

"Carmen Limhuatco. I'm Roger's friend. You know where he is?"

"Maybe."

"Why'd you knock me out?"

"Let's say it's my calling card."

"Why do you have anesthesia?"

"You ask too many questions."

"Alright where is he?"

"Why do you want to know?"

"He's my friend. I'm responsible."

"How well do you know him?"

"Enough. I know his research. I know you met him in Amsterdam. I know about your father, the Cofradia."

Basilio stared at Jaguar.

"We grew up together in these parts," Jaguar said to Carmen. "We're old Quiapo folk. His father was my godfather."

"And you think your father was murdered by this Tata Peping?"

"He was found floating in the river with his blood full of alcohol. My father never drank. He was allergic to liquor."

"What if he'd finally given in?"

"To what?"

Carmen shrugged. "Depression, maybe? Your mother died. You were away, their only child."

"I wrote him to say I was coming home."

"And you're sure he wanted to see you again?"

"Why not? What do you know about me? About us? My father was a devout Catholic. He would never commit suicide."

"Not intentionally."

"Did you come to malign my family?"

"Okay, stop this," Jaguar broke in. "Listen, Carmen, I brought you here in good faith. We all want to find Roger and figure out what this Peping may be up to. You can't be shooting your mouth off like this."

"I'm shooting my mouth off? *He* injected me with anesthesia without consent!"

A tensed silence came over them.

"Alright, I'm sorry for putting you out," Basilio admitted. "I had to be sure you were really serious about finding Roger."

"Do you know where he is?"

"I met him once, briefly, since returning to Manila, in Chinatown. He told me about Peping. Roger seemed taken in by this guy. I told him to be careful. My father had written to me about this ex-cop, a Tondo guy, some Lenten penitent who wanted to join the Cofradia and the Hijos but was rebuffed. So he organized his own *Kapatiran ng Tunay na Anak ng Poong Itim na Nazareno*—or the Brotherhood of the Blessed Black Nazarene in English. The BBN was supposed to be nobler and purer in spirit than the old group. He talked of cleansing. Father distrusted him, thought he was crazy and up to no good. When I came home a month ago, I found out how my father died and I knew at once it was Peping. I remembered him. He was a Tondo boy, ward of the lesbian trader one-eyed Gloria and her partner. Some years before I left the country, I saw him in Quiapo Church once, costumed like the Nazareno. He walked towards the parish priest during Holy Communion like he was going to beat him up. Fr. Dimalanta looked so terrified that it was a bit comical," Basilio related, nearly smiling.

He went on. "Before that we used to knock him around when we played basketball with the Tondo boys. He was supposed to be their big import but he was a dolt. We called him Dennis Rod*mani*. I saw him and told him I was taking over my father's place. He invited me to join his Kapatiran instead, but said I had to be initiated like everyone else."

"Initiated? Like in a fraternity?"

Basilio shrugged.

"What sort of cleansing?" Carmen persisted.

Basilio shrugged again and lit a joint.

Carmen panicked. "What's that? What are you doing?"

"It relaxes me," Basilio said. "I got used to it in Amsterdam, though this local stuff is still better."

Carmen turned to Jaguar whose turn it was to shrug.

Basilio offered the joint to his present company but both demurred. "Don't worry about the anesthesia. I was a paramedic in Holland. We used it for euthanasia," he said to Carmen.

"Well, that's a relief," she quipped but suddenly turned serious. "You have to find out what Peping is up to."

"He killed my father. He won't think twice about doing me in."

"You're the only one who can find out where Roger is, what really happened to your father and what this guy's planning."

"She's right," Jaguar agreed. "You're our only link."

"Fine, but you have to help me."

"Sure, we'll do what we can," Carmen said.

"You have to swear."

The woman and the priest looked to each other and nodded.

"You have to help me kill him."

Jaguar gasped. "Hey, I'm a priest."

"And he's the devil. Your sworn enemy."

"I can't..."

"Of course, he will," Carmen answered for Jaguar. "I'll see to it. Now we have to plan this out. You have to join the BBN."

"Initiation's on Friday, three in the afternoon."

"Where?"

"I don't know. Someone will meet me by the side entrance of the Church."

"We'll keep watch from a distance," Jaguar said.

"I'll be contacted after lunch."

"We won't be far," Carmen told him. There was a part of her that regretted her boldness, while another part was fascinated by the stranger whose gaze she had yet to meet head on.

5
TATA PEPING

ALL HE WANTED from the man Conrado was respect. After all they were comrades in arms. Ambahan was from a family that had served the Nazareno for five generations. The first Ambahan to join the brotherhood was a civil servant named Lazaro, who became a member in 1885. He had inherited some money. Back then, only the well heeled could enroll in the Cofradia. The Ambahans had joined the Revolution against Spain and lost their money but remained active in the brotherhood until, Basilio, the latest among the line and Conrado's only son, refused to be part of the Cofradia and the Hijos and fled abroad.

Now, he knew he would have to deal with Basilio who had vengeance in his heart.

"It was an accident," he wanted to say to Basilio at the first instance. "Unfortunate but necessary. Your father was a man of principle but he could not see past his history. Sadly, he had a weakness. He was of the past and you are of the future. I know why you left. You had no choice. You could not carry the weight of the dead. But you and I together can do what must be done. You have traveled the world, seen the plight of our people, and know the fate that must be fulfilled in our homeland." All this he would say to Basilio, when the time came.

According to the National Statistics Office, Jose Catapang Crenshaw was born in Angeles City on April 2, 1970. His mother, Andrea Ruiz Catapang, was a resident of Tondo, Manila but went to Angeles to work as a bar hostess at seventeen. She was the youngest of five sisters. She left home more out of wanderlust than from a dire need.

There she met Lawrence Earnest Crenshaw, an American civilian employee of Clark Air Force Base. He was an accountant. At eighteen, she was pregnant with Crenshaw's child and dreamt of snow and apple trees even as Crenshaw left for home with nary a word. Still, when the child was born, black and curly-haired, she had Crenshaw written down as the father on the certificate of birth. She made inquiries with base personnel about Crenshaw's whereabouts but received no reply. She obtained the help of a lawyer to no avail. A year later, she brought the child to her parents' home in Tondo.

"You went all the way to Angeles to get knocked up by a baluga?" her mother hissed.

"Ulikba," her father quipped.

"Crenshaw," Andrea introduced. "His name is Jose Crenshaw."

"You can call him whatever you like, but it won't make him worth one centavo more," her mother said.

"I like him," Andrea's elder sister Rhodora, who worked in the post office, chimed in.

"You can have him then," her mother callously replied.

Rhodora took the boy home to Gagalangin, a few blocks from her parents' place, where she lived in an apartment block owned by her lesbian partner, one-eyed Gloria, who trucked vegetables from farms in Laguna to Divisoria. Gloria wore a black patch over her left eye that was blinded in a fight in a gambling den. Gloria Respicio made her fortune trucking vegetables and advancing credit to farmers, the main reason Rhodora's parents tolerated the relationship. Her father, Luis, once asked Gloria for a loan he never repaid. But as much as she made in business, Gloria lost huge sums in gambling tables. She nearly died from the fight that half blinded her at twenty-eight. An irate gambler who accused Gloria of cheating in mahjong had stabbed her in the face, chest and stomach. When Gloria awoke from a week-long coma, she became a devotee of the child Christ—the Sto. Niño.

When Rhodora brought baby Jose home, the couple doted on their ward as if he was their very own Sto. Nino, despite the jeers of neighbors, who preferred their Holy Infant Jesus porcelain-hued with golden hair. Still, every year, on the feast day of the Sto. Niño, every third Saturday of January, the black boy would be at the head of a throng of children parading with the statue of the child Christ from the Church through the streets of Tondo. Gloria was the Church's main patron and headed the Cofradia of the Sto. Niño.

Meanwhile, Andrea returned to the Pink Eden in Angeles City, where she met many more Americans, and none of them remembered Lawrence Crenshaw. Every afternoon, before work, she would hang out by the gate of Clark Airbase, hoping to espy her child's father.

As a child, Jose disliked his name, Crenshaw. He thought it clashed with his blackness and made him even more the target of nasty jokes. He had heard it said that he turned out as he did for being the child of tomboys. His classmates often wondered about his foreign sounding name, though. Even as a boy, he knew things would have been worse, if not for the fact that half the neighborhood owed his "Papa" Gloria money and that the Catholic school only allowed him in after his "Mama" Rhodora paid for a new classroom.

At five, he knew his aunt Andrea was his "other" mother, who lived in Angeles and visited occasionally and that his "other" papa was a black man in America, who would send for him one day. He never said any of this to neighborhood kids and classmates—unsure whether being "overcooked" by the incubator after birth or having a mother who hankered for black chicken while pregnant—was better or worse than being a black man's spawn.

At twelve, he was a foot taller than his classmates and made center of the class basketball team but he couldn't play for his life and was all the more despised by his mates for failing in the only thing he was supposed to excel at. His grades were middling, though he managed to pass, sometimes with help from Gloria's loans to his teachers.

At thirteen, he ran away to his other mother in Angeles, taking the bus, but she bawled him out and brought him back to Tondo. She was now with a white American, Uncle Tim, who was sixty and did not take to black kids.

At seventeen, he was accepted to the University of Sto. Tomas, where he thought he might learn to become an architect. He was always good with a pencil and sketchpad, but Gloria's health was failing as she was diabetic and her debts were mounting. Their home was mortgaged and he worked part time for his tuition. Again, he was urged to try out for the varsity basketball team and earn an athletic scholarship because he was a shade over six feet tall but he still couldn't play. He even considered the seminary, fascinated by some of the things he learned in Theology class but his aunt dissuaded him. "They'll just make you a missionary basketball player," she chided him. "You'll play for God, but no money, no girls."

Jose worked as a police sketch artist to pay his way through school as a career in architecture became more distant by the day. His height and heft made him a shoo-in for the police force.

It was either that or a bouncer for strip bars. So at twenty-two, Jose Crenshaw took the test for police recruits, spent a semester at the Police Academy, where his previous college units were credited, and became Police Officer 1 Crenshaw assigned to the Western Manila Police District (WPD), the district's first black beat cop.

It was 1992. Those who liked the rookie called him Michael Jordan when in good cheer; Dennis Rodman, when in a bad mood, while his enemies, in uniform or otherwise, still said ulikba behind his back. Jose patrolled Avenida Rizal and Quiapo, places where he grew up and knew by heart. His size intimidated petty thieves and fences but he kept away from cat houses and gambling dens protected by other cops. He would be called on to kick down a felon's door, or wallop a thug or even sketch the likeness of a suspect. He still couldn't play basketball, to the dismay of his colleagues at the WPD who had thought they would at last win a national police championship.

When Jose turned twenty-five, his Papa Gloria finally succumbed to disease and a Chinese rice trader—Gloria's creditor—repossessed the apartment block where he lived. Rhodora moved back to her parents' place but Jose knew better than to join her. His grandparents disliked him so he rented bed space from his superior officer, Superintendent Alvaro Lumauig, who lived a block from the police station. Alvaro was a good friend of Gloria and Rhodora and took Jose under his wing.

When Lumauig was made head of the anti-kidnapping strike force at the height of kidnap-for-ransom cases that victimized mostly the local Chinese, Jose became a member of the five-person team working directly under Lumauig. Jose learned all about surveillance tactics and equipment. Before then, he had no idea that mobile phones could be tracked and messages could be intercepted so he became wary of using his own phone for months. Still, he was astounded by the speed with which the team could often identify the kidnap gangs involved whenever an incident was reported, going by what he thought was sketchy information: the make of a getaway car, the accent of a perpetrator, the place of abduction.

It didn't take him long to figure out that there were perhaps three major gangs operating in Manila who employed police stooges and involved dismissed cops. He realized it would take perhaps a month to neutralize or chase away the gangs from the city if only the police would strike before the criminals did. The cops often seemed to be playing a waiting game, though, sometimes even taking bets on who the next victim would be or where the next abduction would occur, until some order came down from higher ups. Only then would they raid an abandoned warehouse stacked with surveillance equipment and would even discover some cash. Jose felt uneasy about how the strike force functioned but he understood why he had been tapped for the team. He had been on the force less than three years. He had no family, therefore, he wouldn't be missed. So he kept his peace and did as he was told until that time when the twelve-year old boy was snatched from outside the school in San Juan. He was in civilian clothes, but he had borrowed the service car for an errand, and the police radio was on when the report came in.

"I'm in the vicinity," he radioed PO2 Ricarte, another task force member.

"You're off duty, aren't you?"

"So what? I can cut them off. What are they driving?"

"I don't think that's a good idea," Ricarte said. "Follow protocol. It's dangerous to engage the suspects by yourself. The victim's safety is paramount."

"Is it the Ugarte gang? Blue Toyota Corolla, car-napped last week. I see it."

"Don't go in."

He had never defied authority, save perhaps for the time when he ran off to Angeles at thirteen to see his mother. No one told him to go see his mother; he just decided to go on his own without telling anyone.

"He has the fool's wind in him, the *ipu-ipo*, the dust devil," Jose had heard his mother say to his aunt when she brought him back to Tondo, "like his father. You never know when it blows."

"You're the fool," Rhodora shot back. "He's your son, you have to come see him more often."

"*Ipu-ipo*," he wondered what it was until many years later in Pampanga, after the lahar from the Mt. Pinatubo eruption had turned much of the province desolate. A gust had raised a cloud of dust and gravel that swirled around him and lashed his skin.

"Dust devil," his father had called it, he who was from the land of giant tornadoes, his mother Andrea said, and Jose understood.

Now he could feel it rising from inside him, from the pit of his gut, after catching sight of the blue Toyota race across the road, he could taste the dust in his tongue as he tailgated the Toyota. The Toyota signaled for him to pass but he refused and continued to pursue the car that now took evasive action. Jose decided to turn on the siren and the pursuit quickened. Suddenly, the Toyota turned into an alley and stopped. Two men got out of the car and shot at Jose, but he fled towards a narrower lane. Jose scampered towards the Toyota and found the boy crouched in the back seat but thankfully unharmed. PO1 Crenshaw realized he was not armed and quickly pulled the boy towards himself, shielding the boy with his own body should the kidnappers return. After a while, he led the boy back to the police car and brought him home to Greenhills.

The Lim family was ecstatic yet confused. The mother said the family chauffeur had just called to report the abduction while the father had just raced home after receiving his wife's message. Mr. Wellington Lim was dumbfounded. He took his son aside and they spoke in Chinese. Then he went over to Jose and handed him a business card that read, WELLINGTON LIM, CEO COMTREX ENTERPRISES: Makers of industrial grade plastics.

"Is there something we can do for you, PO1 Crenshaw?" he asked.

Jose shrugged.

"Listen, this is all very strange. I'm not sure what happened but I am just grateful my son is safe. We owe you and you come to me if you ever need any help but I think it's best if you leave now," he said.

Jose Crenshaw brought the car back to headquarters and walked home.

Nothing was said of the events of the day. A week later, Supt. Lumauig asked him to look for other lodgings. "I can't be seen to be coddling you."

"What did I do wrong? I rescued the boy, didn't I?"

"You were lucky. What if things had gone terribly wrong? We follow protocol Joe, I told you that from day one. You're part of a team. You don't rush into a situation like that on your own. You have things to learn, kid."

Jose bunked with another bachelor cop and was assigned to desk duty and after a month he wondered if he'd see another beat. He was in the freezer and he knew that more than flouting protocol he'd messed up someone's big payday.

"I don't think this is the life for me," Jose finally said to Lumauig. "I'll hand in my resignation letter."

"And do what?" Lumauig asked, shaking his head. "You're a good kid, Joe, you got a lot of heart, but you have to use your brains more. See, the big picture."

"I know what's going on," Jose whispered.

Supt. Lumauig eyed the younger man briefly. "You think so? You think you're better off not being cop? You think you'll be safer? We still take care of our own, kid."

Jose raised his eyes to Lumauig, who thought he had glimpsed a hint of madness in the younger man's gaze, causing him to swallow hard. Jose felt a storm stirring once more in the pit of his gut. It was all he could do to hold it in.

"Listen," Lumauig said. "Take a week off or, better yet, take two. It'll be the Holy Week anyway. Think things through, then we'll talk when you get back. Everyone deserves a second chance."

Jose then sought out Wellington Lim at Comptrex Enterprises in Pasig. "My superiors are pissed with me, I'm thinking of quitting."

Wellington stroked his chin, thought deeply, frowned, stood up and paced the floor. "Wait." He left his office briefly before returning with a white envelope that he handed to Jose. "I already have a security officer. I thank you again for rescuing my son, but I think we should call it quits for both our sakes. Don't come here again."

Jose saw that Wellington Lim had written out a check to him for 500,000 pesos. He wasn't sure what to do. Something in him wanted to hand the check back but Wellington said, "Keep it. You have six months to cash it in."

For the Holy Week, Jose visited his mother in Angeles. She was alone again as Timothy Lowry had relocated to Thailand. His mother said there was still no word from his real father. He shrugged. If truth be known, it had never really mattered to him.

"I just want to talk to him, hear his voice before its too late," Andrea said.

Jose noticed that his mother had shrunk into half the woman she had once been. She had aggressive ovarian cancer and it had spread. There was nothing more to be done by doctors or faith healers. Jose thought he should feel shock, pain, sadness but he didn't know where these emotions were kept inside of him. He tried to conjure compassion even for a stranger, and fumbled. Yet Andrea understood, tapping his hand. "Promise me, son. When I'm gone, seek him out. Don't give up. Let him know who you are. You are Jose Crenshaw."

Jose went to the adjoining town to look for Anselmo Dela Cruz, a carpenter who had been crucified every year on Good Friday for the past ten years ever since his son was cured of leukemia.

"Does it hurt?" Jose asked Mang Selmo, who was preparing for his annual ordeal.

"How much do you love your mother?" Mang Selmo asked Jose. He had no answer. "Are you willing to give up your own life for hers? Half your life?" Jose still had no answer.

"God doesn't bargain, brother. It's all or nothing. You must be willing to lay it all on the line every time."

Jose went home, knowing that his time had not come yet. He returned on Good Friday to watch Anselmo and four other men and one woman crucified then tended to their wounds. Andrea died that June. Her son was with her until the end. He never returned to the WPD, never handed in his resignation. He cashed in Wellington Lim's check and buried his mother. With the rest of the money, he bought himself a modest home in Angeles and a carpentry shop. Jose hired Anselmo to train him in carpentry and serve as his foreman for projects.

When Holy Week came, Jose walked to where river and farm turned into a desert of grayish volcanic ash and glass stretching to the far horizon. He asked for a sign and felt the earth tremble beneath him. A wind borne by many wolves howled and a gray cloud swirled about him. He was whipped by gravel and lashed by sand, pilloried against rocks and dragged through winds. When it was over Jose was covered in blood and ash. He found Anselmo gazing at him in wonderment.

"How long were you in the wilderness?" Anselmo asked.

Jose only shrugged.

"You were gone for three days and nights. What did you see?"

"A child, the boy I rescued, borne by an eagle, and three angels with wings afire. Then a black man appeared. I remember thinking he was my father. "Father," I said to him. "It is I, your son, Jose Crenshaw." "Why do you seek me?" He asked. "Because I am your son. You must know I am your son." "Fool," the man said, "you seek your own darkness."

The first time he was crucified, Jose felt his heart being stabbed as the nails were pounded unto his palms. He was certain his heart was torn and bleeding even as the sun baked his skin. "Father! Father, why have you forsaken me?" He wailed, looking at the skies but hearing the mockery from below: *Itim na Nazareno*, the black Christ.

On the next season, a TV crew arrived and interviewed Jose as he was about to be nailed to his cross. The questions he was asked were: Was he doing this in order to find his father? Did he have any message for his old man? Did he want to go to America? What was all of it for?

In truth, finding his father was the farthest thing from Jose's mind. He knew now, more than ever, that he was of dust and would return to dust. The dust of him was an angry cloud that would be a storm; that would flay the unjust and mark the unclean.

"It is my father who has found me," he said to the interviewer in English, "I am his will. I am the hour."

His words made the evening news and upset the Cardinal, on his exercise bike, who had heard of wilder, stranger claims. Somehow the words of this black man with a scraggly beard nipped him in the gut.

"Judas," the seventy-year-old priest whispered to no one. He was just reminded of the actor who played Judas in the movie version of Jesus Christ Superstar he saw years ago.

6
BASILIO

WHEN HE WENT aboard the Musashi maru, Basilio Ambahan had no idea where he was headed. He only knew he must leave Quiapo, the place of his birth, the home of his forebears. It was a place that had claimed and demanded too much from his clan. His great-grandfather was exiled to Guam by the Spanish, his grandfather was imprisoned by the Americans, his uncle was killed by the Japanese while his father was maligned by malicious enemies. His mother Dolores had died early of leukemia, though he always suspected that it was shame and a broken heart that did her in.

Now he was expected to accept the mantle and protect a black idol that was supposed to have blessed his family, his people with immeasurable favor. It was the noblest task anyone could desire. His boyhood friends would walk through burning coal bare feet and suffer every dignity for such an honor. Basilio could never fully believe any of it: the alleged miracles, the seasonal transformation of sinners and sudden renunciation of evil by vile men. The syndicates pushed their dope all year round and the cops took their cut, the hired killers worked their trade and the pimps peddled their ware.

On January 9, they would all trudge bare feet across steaming concrete, pressed against each other, cheek by jowl, towels over their napes, pushing, shoving—a heaving, groaning animal crawling inch by inch across the urban mire, driven by the black cipher at its heart.

Why did they have to risk life and limb on this day of the year to pull at ropes that moved the carriage carrying an idol that they could visit safely at its perch any other day of the year? It made little sense to Basilio. He always thought of it as a sort of madness but dared not say so to his folks. Perhaps, it was a necessary kind of madness, like the gentler strain of a virus that immunized against some killer disease and the faithful, or faithless, were somehow vaccinated annually.

He had done it only once, at eighteen, to fill in for his father who was too ill that year and it only made Basilio feverish for days after.

"It's a form of trial by ordeal for males in animist cultures," a social science teacher had said to their class once as they discussed the traslación. "Every civilization has a version of it, an initiation into manhood and a way of preserving social cohesion. In Japanese villages, men in loincloth form teams to fight for a totem in honor of the local deity, the kami, on feast days. The Yakuza usually participate."

Perhaps it was the thought of seeing a Japanese village festival that made him board the Musashi-maru that Basilio knew only as a Japanese ship. In fact, it was Greek registered.

It was 2001, he was twenty-four years old, when another Philippine President had been chased out of office and was now in jail like a common criminal. Basilio hadn't been to EDSA when the nuns and priests and the folk from Makati and U.P. and other big name schools massed together again to call on the generals to get rid of Erap. He hadn't gone either when his father and cousins and neighbors had trooped to the Marian shrine to call for Erap's restoration and marched on Malacañang. *That* had led to riot in the streets of Manila where his boyhood buddy Manito Santos ended up in jail for a week. Unlike his father and uncles, Basilio was no fan of Erap. He never thought of the guy as one of their own, despite his movie roles as hoodlum from Quiapo and a Nazareno devotee. Actually, he thought Erap was a bad actor but never said so out loud. He preferred George Estregan, Erap's younger sibling. Erap was likely as dirty as any of the people lambasting him. Basilio had also never voted in any election.

Still, when Basilio saw the deposed President's mug shot on TV, when he visited Manito at home after his release—battered and bruised, refusing to speak like a child nursing some irredeemable hurt—Basilio felt emptied out, like someone had stolen his heart and his spirit, and buried it in some desolate, faraway land. He couldn't bear getting on to that carriage again to protect an idol, whose beating heart was the sea of humanity surging towards it.

His father, Conrado, had insisted that Basilio learn to manage the family business, a Liquefied Petroleum Gas retail outlet, if he was done with school. Rusty LPG tanks didn't seem to need much management, in his opinion.

He signed on as drummer and vocalist for a show band, G Men, led by his mate Dinks Suarez, whom Basilio met at university where he spent four semesters as an Accounting Major before dropping out. They played mostly "oldies" since most of the tourists were retirees. Basilio always thought of oldies as *Let it Be* or *Light My Fire* and other Beatles' and The Doors's hits that his father and uncle, Jonah—an occasional band guitarist—often belted out in karaoke. Now he had to learn Tom Jones and Jack Jones: *What I Did for Love* and the theme from *The Love Boat* (most requested) and even older tunes like *Moon River* and *As Time Goes By*.

Now and then, he would do Filipino songs like *Ngayon at Kailanman* just to feel grounded, as well as to stem the sense of drift as he looked out to sea. The old timers, often Filipino-Americans, would sit him down and buy him a beer or whiskey to tell him about nostalgic times, stories about Diomedes Maturan and Rose Tattoo, about the time the Beatles were chased out of Manila by Imelda, about Rico J and Bayside and the Flame…

All of it sounded alien to him. Nothing reminded him of home and that was good. It was a four-month gig that would take them to Australia and back as tourists came on and off the ship, while it cruised the south Pacific.

One night, a middle-aged widow invited him to her cabin because it was her wedding anniversary and she wanted to be with her late husband once again. The husband had been a musician who worked on cruise ships, and she often imagined what it was like for him in his months away. She was lonely, especially when their only daughter went away to college. They spent the night together and she gave Basilio a tweed jacket that had belonged to her husband. It was only later that he would find the two hundred dollars inside a secret pocket.

When morning came, he felt sadder than when he saw Manito beat up. Basilio knew he could not spend another day at sea. They were docked at Yokohama for thirty-six hours. He didn't have much luggage to begin with so he packed a tote bag and went on shore leave with no plans of returning. He spent the afternoon roaming the streets, had dinner in a Chinese restaurant, sat atop a hill and watched the Musashi-maru sail away near daybreak. He felt nothing. He wondered if anyone, perhaps Suarez, had gone looking for him, whether his absence had been reported to the authorities. He had no visa to stay in Japan. He was now an illegal, an interloper, a vagabond.

The next day, he found a place that seemed familiar, safe: a Catholic church. St. Catherine's didn't feel as old as Quiapo church. Although not that small, it felt like a school chapel to Basilio rather than a parish church. There was something too easy-going and lenient about the place. He was almost reminded of the first time he entered a carnival "funhouse." It was hard to imagine this church being home to anything, *anyone*, as awesome as the Nazareno. Perhaps God had these vacation churches, he thought where the Almighty could relax and put up his feet for a bit, deal with trifles, after listening to all those life-and-death entreaties and performing the tons of miracles for the devotees in places like Quiapo and Sta. Cruz.

Fr. Ignatius de Souza was originally from Goa. Basilio had never met a *bumbay* Catholic priest before. He listened intently to Basilio, aware that he was being told half truths, or perhaps truths larger than could be hidden inside his mid-sized church should anyone come looking. The Filipino seemed sane, if a bit troubled. Basilio said he had "jumped ship" after feeling a deep sadness and "sensing a call."

"I don't know if it was from God, but I had to make sure," Basilio said. He told the priest as well that the first Filipino saint, Lorenzo Ruiz, was martyred in Nagasaki over a century ago.

That bothered Fr. De Souza. He hadn't known there was a Filipino Catholic saint before. There were now a few Indian ones and wondered why there wasn't more?

"Do you plan to go to Nagasaki?" he wanted to ask the man. "You want to be sainted as well?"

But the priest only sighed. "You look tired. Fatigue can do strange things to people. You can sleep in the parish hall guest room."

After three days the priest called upon Basilio. "Everything you told me will be treated as sacred confession but I'm afraid you cannot stay here indefinitely. I cannot harbor an illegal."

What Fr. De Souza had to stop himself from saying though was, "Go away now. I will not be party to your madness or martyrdom, you fool!"

At church, Basilio met a number of Filipinos. The priest told him whom to trust. He went to live with Akiko—James Rosales, by birth—a Filipino transvestite working as a *hosto* in a bar. Fr. De Souza did not approve of Akiko's work but he trusted Akiko's heart and loyalty when it came to a *kababayan*. Basilio had known many transvestites in their neighborhood. At the yearly Sto. Nino celebrations that are largely festive rather than devotional as the traslación, transvestites joined the parade. The parish priest later exiled them to the rear, as they were attracting too much attention.

Basilio didn't mind gays but he always wanted to know whom he was dealing with. He preferred crossdressers to others, although he knew enough to understand that there were all sorts. Still, Basilio had never been close to any gay person. Akiko was from Baguio with an army officer for a father, who was never reconciled to having a homosexual son. While he was never violent with Akiko, the tension between them was always palpable. The disappointment over his son and a flagging career drove Capt. Rosales to alcohol. Akiko knew only his exile from home could save his father.

Japan was always in his radar. As a boy, James loved anime and imagined living in a world of round eyes, button noses, and flaming colors. He loved to design clothes and to dress up, but did so only in private, with his sisters, or among friends. He knew it would kill his father to see his only son—after two daughters—emulating a woman in public. So when James heard of bars in Japan where crossdressers served as hostesses, he applied through a friend who knew someone who had worked there.

At the Sakuragi, his boss, Shugi, took a liking to James and gave him the moniker Akiko, after her own daughter who had died in a car accident. Akiko was popular, though he knew only a spattering of Nihonggo. His regulars included salary men, merchant marine, even a lesbian. His first affair was with a dentist, who offered to pay for his sex change and never stopped pestering him about it when Akiko had never wanted one. Finally, he realized that Hiroshi was not in love with him but rather with some woman whom he thought he should be.

Basilio found occasional work as guitarist, cook's aide, English tutor, disc jockey and janitor. He shared the rent with Akiko whenever he could but Akiko didn't mind otherwise. Having another Filipino to talk to every day was heaven sent. Akiko told him of his own mother's pain, walking on her knees in church to plead for James's "cure."

"I'm not sick, mother," he confronted her once. "If you don't stop hurting yourself, you'll never see me again."

Mrs. Rosales stopped walking on her knees but continued the novenas.

"We ask too much of God, don't we? Not only does the machinery have to work but must perform to someone's specifications," Basilio said, the beer working on him.

"I've never wanted to be anyone else but me," Akiko said and belted out the first phrases of *The Lady is a Tramp* in Filipino, an adaptation by the National Artist, Rolando Tinio. "And you? What deep, dark secret do you harbor beneath that cool, calm exterior?"

"Why should I have any?"

"You're here, underground in Japan. Do you really need the money? You're an only son, with healthy parents. No wife and kid?"

"I want to see the world. I come from folk who die where they were born."

"You say that now. In the end, we all want to die where we were spawned… like salmon. That's what the Japanese say, the ones who pay for my drinks at least."

"I'd feel the same way if I were a salmon in these parts."

"Still no sashimi for you?"

"I'm getting the hang of it."

"You really want to go to Nagasaki?"

"Why not? But I might try Tokyo first. It's just a short train ride away."

"And straight to jail…."

Basilio shrugged. "You can get caught anywhere if you're careless."

"More bilogs in Tokyo. Desperate people will sell out their own kin not to say some stranger."

Filipinos with expired visas were dubbed bilog or "round" by other Pinoys—that is "o" for "overstaying."

"I have protection," Basilio said, showing her his *estampita* of the Nazareno.

Akiko smiled. "My father has one, too. He never goes to battle without it. Didn't protect him from spawning me, though."

"Oh, you're not too bad. It's just… technicalities… you know, sometimes life just throws us these… technicalities."

Akiko laughed. "Spoken like a true CPA."

"Cannot Pass Accounting," Basilio quipped, making Akiko laugh even more.

Perhaps she should have just finished her bottle and called it a night as she usually did whenever she felt too cozy around him, too bare during nearly three months together. This time, she reached out and squeezed his hand.

He pulled back as if jolted, cheeks reddening in embarrassment.

"Good night," she whispered and left him to his beer.

He was gone in the morning, leaving her a note that he would be out of town for a few days to help with a minor construction job. She knew he wouldn't be back.

It wasn't the first time he had been propositioned by a gay man. When he was a teenager, he had heard of some mates who were fellated by gays as a sort of initiation rite in their part of town but the come-ons were always in half jest and too crude. This incident with Akiko, however, was serious and Basilio felt a tinge of guilt. He wondered if it was something he had said or done? Or something he had missed? Had he been leading her on? Was it the time she massaged his stiff nape that he had been complaining about for weeks? Or when he fixed the tap while she was soaking in the tub? Why wouldn't she take more than one thousand yen from him a week?

Technicalities. What a stupid thing to say. What could he have meant by that? What could he have thought? It was just something to say. Neutral. Emotionless.

Technical: one of those words in English that came handy. Meaningless.

After a week bunking with Hiroshi, a half-Filipino band bassist, Basilio decided to clear things up with Akiko; part ways if they must but as friends. After all, he had taken him, a stranger, without fear or favor.

As he came near the street where he had stayed with Akiko for months, Basilio saw police cars and media vans. When he came closer, he saw that it was their apartment block that had been cordoned off.

"What's going on?" he asked an onlooker in halting Nihonggo.

"I hear someone died, or was killed. A foreigner, a Filipino," the man said and balked a bit when he looked at the person he was talking to.

Cold sweat started streaming down his temples. He felt acridness rise from his gut to his tongue. He thought that he was having a heart attack and fled the scene. Basilio made his way to St. Catherine's where Fr. Souza was waiting.

"It looks like a suicide," the priest said, "but you can never be sure. Someone might have made it look like one."

"Why?"

The priest shook his head. "I guess it's a danger in his line of work but the police know someone's been staying with him for months so you shouldn't go back there."

"I still have some stuff...."

"Forget it." Fr. Souza said and produced a Philippine passport. "This used to belong to a compatriot of yours. You might pass for him or you change the photo later. There's a cargo ship docked for the day. A Filipino will be waiting for you at Okayama, the sushi joint by the wharf. You know it?"

Basilio nodded.

"Ponce. He owes me," the priest said. Basilio peered at the passport photo of someone named Arsenio Manalastas and tried to see a semblance of his own visage.

"Move it," the priest barked. "They will be scouring all the Filipino haunts soon!"

Basilio rushed towards the door but something stopped him. He turned to the priest. "It wasn't me."

Fr. Souza stared at Basilio and shrugged, waving the other man away. "You're one for martyrdom," he might have hissed inwardly in a less generous moment, but he rose to the occasion and kept his peace.

The Andorra shipped cargo from Shanghai to Milan. Her German captain drank too much and left most things to his Filipino first mate, Santiago Ponce.

"Welcome aboard," Ponce said, shaking Basilio's hand. "Any friend of Fr. Souza is a friend of mine. Tell me what you can and are willing to do and nothing I don't need to know. I'll pay you something if and when I can. Don't blab too much, and steer clear of the captain. If he asks, say you're my cousin. If anyone gets too nosy, tell him you killed someone, in confidence. It shuts them up every time."

Basilio guessed from the accent that Ponce was from Mindanao. "I can cook, do some plumbing, repair some gadgets and… play drums and lead guitar," Basilio said.

Ponce's eyes seemed to light up. "Really?" He smirked. "I don't think you should fancy a fan club for now. Come, I'll show you to your bunk."

Basilio looked out towards the expanse of dark water and wondered where his country was in the vastness. "And peace be with you," he whispered finally and nodded, like the last time he attended Mass, to all he had left behind.

7
JAGUAR

HE NEVER FIGURED out how he got his name. Was it from the movie starring Philip Salvador, his mother's favorite? She had done some bit roles in the movies and was convinced that her slight lisp did her in. Jennelyn Jimenez met Django Dy, a movie stuntman, when she was eighteen. They never married but had Jaguar before Django was hit by live ammo in a botched stunt and died.

She sold insurance, real estate, health care and funeral plans, in between her odd movie jobs and never married or had any more kids, though Jaguar could remember any number of "uncles," who flitted in and out of their lives while he was growing up. She wished only for her boy to become a priest.

"You were so sickly as a child, I feared you wouldn't make it to your first birthday. You needed a blood transfusion. I offered you to Our Lady of Manaoag," she first told Jaguar when he was three. He thought his mother had tried giving him up to some rich woman living inside a big house, like on TV, until she took him to Manaoag when he was seven and he saw the statue of the Virgin Mother, looking down at him with her deep blue eyes that seemed to know his every secret—his wish, for instance, that he had been born into the family of their neighbors, the Ambahans instead.

He never said any of this to his "everyday" mother, Jennilyn, but he knew somehow that she and the woman with blue eyes had agreed on everything that was to matter in his life and he was glad.

Basilio was two years older and behaved like a big brother to him. They went to the same public school and Basilio brought Jaguar into his circle from the outset to protect him. He was always slight and shy, a sure target for bullies. The Ambahans, on the other hand, were a Nazareno family and untouchable in Quiapo. At grade six, Jaguar earned a scholarship to the Dominican School.

"You really plan to become a priest?" Basilio asked Jaguar over his first beer when he turned thirteen.

Jaguar shrugged. "My mom wants me to."

"It's not a decision for others to make, you know? My uncle says you need a calling for something like that."

"Calling? Who's supposed to call?"

"I don't know. Maybe God or the Holy Spirit or some other big shot."

"How will they call?"

"Beats me… you're the Catholic school boy. You know what it all means, though, don't you?"

"What?"

"You can't marry. You can't have sex… with girls… ever."

Jaguar shrugged again.

"You really don't care?"

Jaguar finished his bottle.

"Let's go to our place, no one's home. I'll show you your real birthday gift," Basilio said.

It was a movie called *Cherry Cheerleader*. It was his first porn flick and featured a bevy of buxom blondes, though it was the Asian girl Jaguar fell for. She was called Kitty in the movie. Basilio gave him the CD to take home. "I've got another copy," he said but Jaguar refused it.

"My mom might see it."

"So? You're not even a sacristan yet."

Jaguar wasn't really worried about his mom. She barely had time to fix her own mess much less go through Jaguar's. It was Jaguar who cleaned and kept their two-room rented apartment spic and span. From early on, he learned to cook and tend to himself when his mom was away. Jenny hardly watched any of the pirated CDs she bought, mostly featuring Philip Salvador, since buying a discounted player from the neighborhood pawnshop. There was nothing on the CD cover to give away its content.

It was Kitty whom Jaguar was wary of, actually. He feared he might not be able to stop watching her, though her only scene in the movie was a threesome with a black man and a white woman. He feared she too might lodge inside him like the woman with sea blue eyes and find out his secrets. They might fight over his thoughts and memories and take them all. What then would be left of him?

He knew it was a crazy thing to think so and said none of this to anyone, not even to his confessor in later years. He just chased Kitty away from memory and she seemed to oblige, until that day Carmen came to church looking for her missing friend and he thought he had seen her somewhere. It was impossible that Kitty and Carmen were one and the same. He had seen the movie nearly twenty years ago and even then it wasn't a new flick. Carmen was too young to be Kitty and too well-heeled to be in a porn movie.

And yet the thought nagged at him. He was unassailable with faces. He remembered faces, if not names. Jaguar was tempted to scour the video nooks of Quiapo to look for a copy of *Cherry Cheerleader* or its later incarnation but was sure he would be recognized even with dark glasses and fake moustache.

He thought of searching for Kitty on porn websites but feared he was courting moral disaster, not to say computer viruses whose provenance some whiz kid troubleshooter could certainly figure out. The last time he had the parish computer system cleaned and upgraded the technician warned not to indulge on "dirty" sites. Jaguar suspected the sacristan who sometimes asked permission to use the system for his homework, but then again, it was Fr. Dimalanta who spent most of his waking hours in front of the computer since walking became too painful. Who knew what "research" he required for his sermons?

So when Basilio suddenly showed up after a decade, the first thing Jaguar wanted to ask him was if he still had a copy of Cherry Cheerleader, but he stopped himself. After a bit of catching up, he told Basilio of the missing white man and the young woman just looking for him and how he tried to distract her.

Basilio lit up like a thousand watts. "He's the reason I'm back."

Basilio told Jaguar about his meeting with Roger Geisler in Amsterdam and of his dreams about his late father, Conrado. He said he hadn't gone home or contacted relatives fearing for their safety. Jaguar thought his friend was being paranoid but kept it to himself. He wondered what his travels had done to Basilio. They went out to the streets and spied Carmen checking out bottled herbs a block away.

"You think she might be pregnant by that Roger guy?" Jaguar asked Basilio.

"Who knows? I doubt he's into her that way."

"She's a tiger, that one. Had to ward her off with my crucifix."

Basilio gave Jaguar a look that reminded him of their boyhood when they could signal each other to drop a game of tong-its with neighborhood kids, or sneak inside a movie house just by eye contact.

"I need to get to her," Basilio said.

"Come, I'll introduce you."

"No. We have to make sure she's not with them."

"With whom?"

"They may be watching."

"Who?"

"I have an idea, listen," Basilio said, and Jaguar felt himself a thirteen-year-old again being given instructions by his elder. He knew he must resist this time, say 'no', say, "I'm the priest here. I'm the adult. I was the one who took on my burden while *you* ran away!"

It felt exciting to be thirteen again, though. "But she's Kitty," he whispered to no one, as he saw the hooded man wind through the sea of bodies towards the woman in blue.

8
ANG KAPATIRAN: Brotherhood

HE WAS BLINDFOLDED and led inside a van. It smelled of petrol and burned rubber and what he would later remember as day-old sex. They must have driven for well over an hour. Basilio surmised that they must be in Laguna or elsewhere in the southern Tagalog region, given the bits of conversation he heard on the way, or they might just as well have been going in circles. Still, the absence of heavy traffic and the vehicle's pace suggested that they had traversed expressways.

They drove into what seemed a rustic, unpaved back road as the vehicle swerved and buckled. Dogs and fowls and a pig, could be heard outside. As the vehicle stopped, he was led out and made to hold on to the shoulder of the one walking in front of him.

Suddenly, they were indoors, shut in from the breeze and the crickets and stray dogs. He imagined they were inside an enclosed space from the silence and the heavy air and the feel of the floor against his rubber soles. They went down some steps then he was left alone, as bodies seemed to retreat all around him. He wasn't sure how long it took before his blindfold was removed. They seemed to have been testing his patience, waiting for him to remove his own blindfold without instruction. But he had remained calm and trusting, and the gathering was assuaged.

They were inside a cave lit up by bamboo torches. There were stalactites and stalagmites, some oddly shaped, some reminding him of giant fangs and he briefly imagined himself inside the maw of some ancient behemoth. He thought he smelled sulfur. They were in Montalban or Tanay, Rizal, where the Katipunan once held council, Basilio quickly concluded. He had been in such caves a few times as a boy, with family or for school outings, listening to stories of olden heroes, asleep or chained to rocks, who would someday awaken and redeem the people from evil, both foreign and home grown.

Now, he saw Tata Peping behind a stone altar clad in a red robe over a white gown, a golden chalice before him. He appeared to be a priest celebrating mass, or like Jesus among his disciples. Basilio felt a coldness enter the crown of his head and slither down his spine like an invisible snake seeking the pit of his groin. He could be in far worse danger than he thought.

The other men, perhaps thirty, were all in white *camisa* with maroon sashes draped over them. Basilio recognized a couple of them: family friends and neighbors. Rizaldy Dimaguiba, an acquaintance since elementary school, whose grandfather was a cop. So was his father, Donato, who was made captain before being gunned down, reportedly by goons and rogue cops. Macario "Mac" Lim, another long-time Quiapo resident and beat cop forced into early retirement for refusing to condone the shenanigans of certain officers. What were they all doing here?

Then it dawned on him: Peping had gathered a group of mostly Manila police, or former police, around him. Those similarly dismissed or disillusioned as he was, ready to strike back, to reclaim their city from the wicked. It all made sense now: the corpses that had been showing up in garbage and construction sites marked with crucifix and numbers. They referred to Bible verses. *Do not think that I have come to establish peace on earth. I have not come to bring peace, but a sword… Ex 1:8-k4, 22…* Cops missing, rumored to have been "salvaged." The youngster who allegedly put up a website featuring clueless young girls having sex with his mates found tied to a post beaten and traumatized out of his wits. Pimps and drug pushers, and child pornographers, mauled and dumped outside precincts. This was a strike force that the ex-cop had formed to do his bidding.

I am the will. I am the hour. Peping's words echoed inside Basilio's head that he briefly imagined to be hollowed out as a cavern. How did he do it? Why did former officers now heed their once underling? The man was a healer, Basilio remembered. That was how he first espied the black man upon his return to Manila. He had seen Peping in the compound of Mac Lim, who now ran an auto repair shop, laying hands on the sick and suffering and curing all manner of affliction.

That is how it begins, anywhere in the world, Basilio thought. First, heal the sick. He had been to Lourdes and seen the crutches left behind in the grotto, to Fatima and Santiago de Compostela, walking among pilgrims, many of them Filipinos. It was always the cure that desperate people sought, the healing of the body, but more so, the soul.

The last time Peping was nailed to the cross, he went into shock and was in a coma for three days. When he awoke, as the story goes, he could heal and prophesy. He would sometimes walk around the environs of Quiapo Church in his robes greeting the curious and admonishing certain vendors. Kids would tug at his red frock and some would kiss his hand while he blessed others. The Parish Priest was annoyed and became increasingly alarmed.

While there had always been sackcloth-and-staff types and other costumed curiosities in the area, especially during Lent, this one's resemblance to the *Nazareno* was too close for comfort. Yet, there was no reason to keep him from the church where Peping would often pray in a back pew before leaving. Perhaps prayer would at least keep him temperate, if not sane.

One Sunday, he rose to his full height during Holy Communion and strode the entire length of the church towards Fr. Dimalanta, who was beginning to administer the sacrament to the faithful. Because of the large number of churchgoers, Fr. Jimenez, along with two other sacristans, and a lay brother were also authorized to provide wafers to the communicants. There were five of them in a line in front of the altar, but Peping walked straight towards Fr. Dimalanta in the middle like a guided missile or a warrior marching inexorably at the enemy.

For some reason, the other churchgoers gave way to the tall black man in red robe, as though a sea of humanity parted. There was a stirring in the crowd, a buzz, even as the choir sang Kordero ng Dios.

The older priest could see a dark red blur coming his way, wondering why the people were giving way, joining the other queues when they would normally prefer receiving Communion from him. Was it a politician or celebrity? Who knows, maybe the Mayor had finally come to hear Mass? *His* Mass. Elections were not too far off. The priest swallowed a smile then peered through his glasses and saw that it was *him*... that ...lunatic! That blasphemous *son of a*... He froze. Should he raise his chalice against this unholy presence? Or hurl it upon the demon before it came any closer?

Suddenly, someone else was in front of him. Fr. Jimenez had stepped in, blocking Peping's path, and offered him

Communion. Peping hesitated a bit, then offered his linked palms to receive the wafer, eyes locked on Jaguar.

Fr. Dimalanta could feel his heart racing like a wild horse and his temples throbbing. He breathed in deeply and endeavored to dispense the rest of his Communion wafers, but his hands shook and his knees buckled. The sacristans helped him to the vestibule.

At the corner aisle, Basilio Ambahan took it all in. It was nearly the best fight he had seen since Muhammad Ali fought Joe Frazier in Manila shortly before his own birthing. He had only seen the tapes but grew up with stories of how his father left his expectant mother at the hospital to rush to the Folk Arts Theater for the training sessions wherein the "Black Butterfly" taunted "Smokin' Joe" who huffed and puffed inside his red jumpsuit like an overgrown boy. Basilio smiled and thought he knew why they had to keep the Nazareno inside his glass enclosure whenever not on parade.

Later that evening, Peping would go pick up the white man at the police station, who had been found wandering about in his underwear, nearly incoherent but asking for a Jose Crenshaw. Someone said to inform the media or higher authorities, but the officer in charge knew better.

And now here he was, celebrating *his* own mass. Jose Crenshaw, former dud of a neighborhood ball player, former beat cop, former police task force member, former flagellant and former Lenten crucified. Now, he was Tata Peping: The Black Christ.

"Brothers, we are here gathered to welcome into our fold one who was born among us; one of old, noble blood. He has been to other shores and was called home by the Spirit to fulfill his destiny. He has listened to the call of his blood," Peping intoned. "Welcome, Brother Basilio."

"Welcome, Brother Basilio," the gathering echoed.

"We are not here to initiate. There is no need to initiate. We are one in spirit, the Spirit chooses. The Spirit that dwells among us, that has chosen our land as home and chosen us as his vessel. But as always, we must purify, we must cleanse, we must sacrifice."

"Sacrifice," the throng intoned.

The other man too was blindfolded, his hands tied behind his back. Led towards the altar by two brotherhood members, the apparent prisoner stumbled and was helped to his feet. He seemed lost and panicky. Basilio thought he knew the man from somewhere until the blindfold was removed. The man, in his fifties, looked blinded by the light and fell to his knees.

"Vergel Mamaril, are you ready to confess?" A younger man approached the prisoner and asked.

Basilio recognized him as his old friend, Manito Santos, whom he last saw all those years ago, beaten but unbowed, after the pro-Erap riots. He stopped his urge to call out to the man, who was now stockier but still wore the mien of aggrieved youth. Basilio also sensed that Manito was closer to Tata Peping than the others, perhaps a sort of "Apostle Peter" or "John."

"It was an accident," Mamaril stammered, in tears. Peping approached and whispered into Manito's ears. Manito helped Mamaril to his feet, led him to Basilio and motioned for Vergel to speak.

"He was my friend," the man said to Basilio, imploring. "Your father was my friend, Basilio. I would never hurt him deliberately. You must remember me…"

A light seemed to flash through Basilio's mental cavern. "Of course, Tito Vergel, you used to raise fighting cocks for Father."

"Yes, you remember, hijo! And I never cheated him. We always won."

"I remember that Texas father loved. He named him Rocky."

"Yes, yes…" Mamaril seemed effusive.

"Whatever happened…?"

Sadness suddenly came over Vergel. "He lost and… I didn't want him to fight that time. He didn't look right but your father…."

"What are you saying?" Something nipped Basilio. "You're telling me now that Father threw the fight, made bets against Rocky?"

Mamaril looked to the ground. "He had debts…."

"NO!"

"It was a sacrifice, wasn't it, Brother Vergel?" Manito cut in.

Vergel nodded sheepishly.

"So you understand… about sacrifice?"

"But that was a rooster," the man pleaded.

"Still…."

"Wait, what's going on?" Basilio asked. "What's one thing got to do with the other?"

"Why don't you tell Brother Basilio what happened?"

"I came to collect from your father that night, Basilio. He had ran up a tab at Mañalac's…."

Vergel looked to Tata Peping, seemingly wary of continuing.

"Salvador Mañalac's place…." Manito started to explain but Basilio cut in, rather peeved.

"I know… it's a mahjong den."

"A place for peaceable recreation," Tata Peping said.

"You own it?" Basilio asked.

Manito glowered and might have attacked Basilio, but Peping held him back.

"We do not own. Things are not for us to own in this world. We are stewards, who manage resources for a noble purpose," Peping said.

"So you offer protection."

"We all need protection, brother."

"From gangsters? Other cops?"

"From all manner of evil. You understand. You come from a line of protectors, guardians. You left because you sensed it was a false guardianship, it had been corrupted. You were being made to protect a false idol, to proffer lies. Now He has summoned you home. The true Godhood has beckoned. I saw you in a dream, brother. It is no accident you stand here among us. You are called. The Kapatiran is your true home."

The two men locked eyes briefly.

"What happened to my father?"

"Brother Vergel was sent that evening to urge your father to live up to his obligations," Peping explained eyeing Vergel.

"I showed him his signed chits," Vergel said to Basilio. "He owed the house seventy thousand pesos... plus interest. He'd been drinking lambanog...."

"Liar! My father...."

Peping silenced Basilio with a gesture and urged Vergel to continue.

"I swear, Basilio. I know you think your father never drank. He did. He only made sure you weren't around. He became different when he drank. He lost his temper, told me to pay his bill... went on and on about how I cheated him in the past, injured his fighting cocks. It was all in his mind, Basilio; none of it was true. Then he came at me with his bottle. I swear. I had to defend myself. I tried to fend him off with a stick, but he was like a crazed animal. So I shot at him with my handgun. The bullet grazed his temple. I only wanted him to stop but he came at me again, tripped and hit his head on some scrap metal. There was blood all over, so much blood. God.... I didn't know what to do. I couldn't save him, he was convulsing. And then he stopped. He wasn't breathing. I pumped on his chest but nothing happened. Nothing. He just quit breathing. There wasn't anyone else around so I dragged him out to the yard and threw him into the river. I'm sorry, Basilio. I'm sorry. I swear that's what happened, swear to God."

Basilio was stunned. He wasn't sure what he had heard. It was something about blood and convulsion and the river. A man was kneeling before him, pleading. Then Manito walked up to Basilio and proffered him a dagger.

"What's that for?"

"Him," Manito said, indicating Vergel. "A life for a life. Blood for blood."

"No… I don't want to…."

"I'm sorry," Vergel pleaded once more. "It was an accident. He was like a brother to me."

"This is brotherhood, Basilio. This is what you chose," Manito said.

"I can't. It was an accident."

"Perhaps, but brotherhood is bound by blood, nourished by blood. You make the first cut. You can make it easier for him by going for the jugular but each one of us then deals his own blow, his own choice. We all share in the act. We act as one. This is brotherhood. We are one."

"That's insane."

"It is time, Basilio," Manito said, thrusting the handle of the knife at his old friend.

"No! I won't."

"You or him, Basilio. Your choice."

"What? This is madness!"

"You or him? Blood must cleanse."

"Stop this, Manito! It's not happening. We've known each other since childhood, man. I don't know what's happened to you. You're pissed with how things are, so am I, but this isn't the way, *pare*, not this."

"Last chance," Manito said, holding the weapon to Basilio's face. "Do it."

"No," the other man said standing between Vergel and Manito. "You go through me."

Manito unsheathed the knife. Basilio backed off but made ready to defend himself.

"Stop." Tata Peping spoke finally. He approached Basilio, beaming and held the man's shoulders. He then gestured to the gathering that burst out in applause and approval.

"This is a man, is he not?" Peping asked the crowd. "This is a brother, is he not? One of true conviction: one who does not follow blindly but listens to his own conscience. One who is willing to defend another brother with his life! "

The crowd cheered once more.

Peping touched Vergel's head. "Rise," he said. Vergel struggled to his feet in tears. He had soiled himself.

"You are redeemed, Brother Vergel, you are reborn. Now, you are a shadow cast by the light of our Brother Basilio," Peping said, touching the man's nape. "*He* is your light!"

"Thank you… thank you Brother Basilio, I am in your debt," Vergel mumbled, shaking.

"No, don't say that," Basilio whispered.

"Now, remove your shirts," Tata Peping said.

Basilio was dumbfounded.

"Do it," Manito commanded.

Both men took off their shirts. Peping took the dagger from Manito and handed it to Basilio. "This is your instrument now, as you are an instrument of the Kapatiran, of righteousness and truth."

Basilio took the dagger and as per instruction, cut slightly just beneath his right nipple. Manito let some blood drip into a valise before staunching the wound with cotton and aloe. Basilio then cut Vergel in a similar manner. Blood from the two men were mixed in with lambanog and they were both made to drink from the valise. First, Basilio: then, Vergel.

Basilio hesitated but Manito stared steely at him. "It's safe."

"This is the blood of your new and everlasting covenant with the Spirit, brother," Peping said to Basilio. "Welcome home."

Just when Basilio thought the worst of it over, another prisoner was brought in. He too was blindfolded but seemed calm if not sedated. Basilio looked to Peping.

"Blood must cleanse, brother, this is the ancient and new covenant," Peping said.

"What are you going to do with him?"

"Not I, brother. *You.*" Peping said. "The instrument is now in your hand."

Basilio stared at the dagger he held. He realized suddenly that he was in the midst of what Roger had once described to him as a "black" Mass: an inversion of Catholic ritual. There were many forms, but all involved blood sacrifice that celebrants believed to be the origin of modern Church rites. He had heard of such practices in Europe.

"So you spare the one you deem innocent, now slay he who has defiled and slain the innocent."

"What has he done?"

"He raped and murdered a five year-old."

Basilio could taste the bile in his tongue. "He must have been under the influence of something."

"Does it matter?"

"We can't take the law into our hands, give him to the police!"

"Where do you think we got him?"

Peping now hovered over Basilio, who felt puny beside the large man, as if he could be crushed like a fly any moment.

"The brotherhood casts a wide net, Basilio. It is near and far, seen and unseen. It is earth and sky, flesh and spirit."

"I can't do this. I can't commit murder."

The giant smiled. "So be it. There is time." Peping extended his hand to ask for Basilio's dagger. Basilio quickly handed it over to Peping, who in turn proffered it to Vergel.

Vergel looked to Manito, who gave him a pair of rubber gloves to wear before he took the dagger from Peping.

"What's he doing?"

Before Basilio could utter another sound, Vergel had grabbed the prisoner by the hair and slit his throat.

"No!" Basilio felt his innards explode. He imagined worms creeping out of his gut and through his windpipe. He had to swallow his vomit back down as he turned away.

"He is now your shadow, Brother Basilio. Brother Vergel will do for you all that you are as yet unprepared to do," Tata Peping said.

Basilio felt cold sweat flooding out of his pores. "I'm in hell," he murmured to himself.

Peping took back the dagger from Vergel and tucked it inside his robe. "A bit of insurance for now, Brother Basilio. You will regain your instrument when you are ready. Now, you must complete your present task."

"What do you mean?"

"We know you are close to the younger priest in Quiapo, Jimenez, who secretly defies that old benighted one. He is not a bad priest, but he has yet to discover his true calling. You must help him."

"How?"

"You will know when the time is right. And bring her to us."

"Who?"

"The singer, Emily. Tell them, the white man is with us. She must come to us, if they want him alive."

Before Basilio could clear his head an acridness shot through his nostril and darkness overcame him.

9
HOUSE OF SADNESS

WAS IT A dream or a memory? Of late Chesterfield Limhuatco had difficulty telling them apart. Did it matter? It might be a memory of a dream. He was driving pass a tree-lined residential street. Balete, he remembered. He first heard of the street at ten from his buddy Jigs who said his brother was flagged by a woman wearing a white seamless blouse while he was racing for home to beat the curfew that was imposed from midnight to four a.m. when Martial Law was imposed in September of '72.

Jigs said his brother decided to give the woman a lift to save her from being accosted by the police or the military. She got into the backseat hurriedly and he asked where to drop her.

"Just drive, please," she whispered but when he glanced at his rear view mirror minutes later she was gone.

Jigs and his brother may have just been fooling around. But it doesn't explain why their family driver, Lorenzo, a former cab driver, would avoid the street whenever he could, or else rush through it. Lorenzo told Chester ghastlier tales he'd heard from other cabbies about picking up women in white along the street who, moments later, would turn out a bloody pulp on the backseat. There was that passenger too who allegedly asked the cabbie to wait while she went inside her home to retrieve her fare; he waited for ages but she never returned. When he finally inquired from the other people inside the house he was told the woman he described had long ago died in a car wreck. But the tale that stayed with Chester, he was no longer certain whether he heard it in full from some source or made up some of it, was of the cabbie who decided to enter the gate of the house where he'd drop the woman in white after waiting for an hour for the fare.

Past the courtyard he saw a run-down antiquarian house that was unoccupied. He was scared out of his wits and tried to flee but every time he reached the gate he would be overcome by a terrible sadness that forced him to remain in the premises to await the woman. He finally lost all fear he said and stayed on for what seemed an eternity, surviving on food that would appear on the dinner table. The neighborhood watchmen found him sprawled unconscious on the courtyard the morning after. He awoke at the hospital days later, vomited flowers, and became a healer. Why he always preferred that tale to the horror versions Chester was unsure.

"Don't be such a romantic," he recalled Agnes saying in jest after he told her the story once while they were resident physicians, "people die."

"Be careful," she said to him moments later as an afterthought. That might have been before his 'first death.' He'd been assigned to the ER graveyard shift. The senior physician was indisposed when they brought her in—after all it was a minor public hospital in a poorer part of the city where he had chosen to do his residency to better earn his chops or so he thought—and he had to take charge. Chester had been transfixed on medical dramas on TV growing up and had earlier imagined himself a trauma surgeon.

She was unconscious with nary a pulse, her nose broken. It wasn't the first time she'd been brought in like this, he was told. Last time she lost a fetus, the head nurse informed him. It's her husband, he was told, does it all time when he's drunk. A dirty cop but nothing anyone could do about him especially these days. 'Next time you may not make it back,' the nurse had told her last time. She nodded, she knew. But what could she do? Where could she go? He always wept and vowed to change. A pall of sadness more than purpose permeated the room. It was a play they've done before, too many times. Being repeated for his benefit, it seemed to Chester. He was the outsider, the audience of one. They were a family mourning a member and he was the stranger, it struck him. They did what was required: defibrillator; chest massage; pump. And then he held the syringe. Epinephrine? Lidocaine? He could no longer be certain. In any case something he could plunge right into her heart that might re-start it, bring her back. But they seemed to be pleading with him to put it down, to let her go. No more for her, no more for us. There was the subtle admonition too from the hospital director to be judicious with use of limited resources. He felt numbness creeping into him, put down what he'd always remember as his weapon and turn away.

"Call it," he whispered to the intern and walked into the night. A week later he would quit the hospital and get his father's friend to find him a place in St. Benedicts.

How long was it later when he drove through the street? What did he hope to see? He'd seen enough bloodied corpses for any ghost or walking dead to bother him. The first thing he'd probably do, Chester mused, if he were to meet one would be to check it out for authenticity. It was the abandoned house in the tale he was looking for, the house of sadness that would keep him hostage until flowers blossomed inside him.

A sadness it seemed that no death could infect him with not even of one who'd survived it so many times and whose passing he had finally to ascertain. Was it this quality that made him perfect for the job?

Had it ever truly cared for anyone? Were his own parents' deaths more like medical conundrums to him than personal losses? Would it pain him truly if his wife passed? Then there was his daughter Carmen. Yes, perhaps hers was the only pain, misfortune, and, God forbid, death that would matter to him. Chester quickly perished the thought and resolved to protect his daughter at all cost. Yes he would protect her even at the price of his own life or that of this stranger who might be named Emily.

10
EMILY

"EMILY."

It seemed right. She must be an *Emily*. She could live with the name until something else came up. *Mahiwo* didn't seem to fit the face that stared back at her in the mirror, though. She was fair, her eyes round and hazel, her cheekbones high, her nose tall. Who was she? Where was she? She seemed to have awoken from a long restful sleep. She felt invigorated, content, almost happy. Nothing seemed amiss, except that she could not remember her real name or her story. She could see bits and pieces in her mind's eye, hear names of people and places she could not fully imagine no matter how hard she tried.

There was this door in her mind's screen, the color of burnt wood, with the head of a tiger wrapped around a serpent, staring at her. She could feel its roughness. If she pushed with all her might, she might force it open; then everything could make sense, all the hidden pieces revealed, like in a magician's workshop. But every time she held the knob, she would freeze, then tremble. She would back off and return to the pleasant quiet of the room where she had awoken. It was an unfamiliar but safe place.

Who was the man? He said he had rescued her from some accident. Was he the cause of it? Had he stolen her from someone else? Somehow she felt at ease with him, sensed that he meant well. Now there was this woman claiming to be his daughter, eyeing her carefully as if perusing a pair of expensive shoes she was tempted to buy.

"I don't think you should stay here," the man's daughter said. The other woman kept quiet. "I'm Carmen... Limhuatco. You're Emily, right? That's what my dad said."

"I don't know. I'm not sure... maybe. I don't remember."

"Well, let's go by Emily for now. I'm not saying you're in any danger. I mean, not from him... he's not the sort but... still, people might get the wrong idea. I mean... unless you want to stay."

"No!" the other woman nearly shouted, shaking her head, although she didn't mean to. "I have nowhere else to go. I have no money on me, no I.D."

"Well, I could invite you home but I'm with my mom and that would be dicey."

The other woman nodded, though she wasn't sure why.

"I think I know where you can stay in the meantime. You might also want to undergo a physical, just to be safe. I don't think father wants to bring you to St. Benedict's. Here, I brought you some clothes."

She could hear the other woman speaking but her words made little sense. She liked the clothes, though, and felt a kinship with the stranger.

"Dad says you may be a singer. Are you?"

She shrugged.

"Well, there's a sure way to find out. You like karaoke?"

At her clinic, Dr. Anna Duran gave Emily a thorough physical and told her the good news: she was two weeks pregnant.

Emily was stunned then became nauseous. She felt little feet rushing up her windpipe and rushed to the toilet. Anna hurried after her but Emily locked herself inside the bathroom.

Anna gave Carmen a knowing look.

"C'mon," the younger woman whispered. "She's only been with him one night."

"And you believe his story? Found her among the fallen crowd... please."

Something nipped Carmen. "You don't seem to trust him a lot, do you?"

Anna shrugged.

"What's with you guys? Did you date? Back in the day?"

Anna smirked. "Date? Well... you might say we were an item."

"So... you...?" Carmen returned Anna's earlier look.

"No, not that far You didn't go that far back then, but we were intimate, short of... you know."

"Then?" Carmen pursued.

"Then... nothing."

"C'mon... tell me."

"Then he stopped calling, and then he was engaged to your... mother."

"Oh?" Carmen felt her throat tighten.

"I'm sorry," she murmured.

Anna shrugged again. "Not your fault."

They were quiet a while. "It's none of my business," the younger woman said to break the awkward silence, "but I think I can sort of guess what happened... they just didn't... couldn't do it... you know... then."

"Do what? Marry a *huanna*?"

"My grandparents were from China. They wouldn't have approved. They didn't approve of *my* choices but Dad... he fought for me."

"Good for you. I'm glad he's grown a pair, finally."

"I don't mean to defend him, I don't have to. We've had our spats but now, I sort of understand everything that was at stake…"

"What the fuck? He chickened out! We had plans! He was a wimp, always was, always will be."

"Hey."

"Sorry. He's your dad but…. We were both doctors. We would have survived. We didn't need money from your folks. We would have made it." Anna said, swallowing hard.

"Sometimes… it's not just about money. In olden times, exile from the tribe was a fate worse than death. They didn't have to kill you. You just wasted away on your own."

"Christ, what were we? Bushmen in sub-Saharan Africa? It was Manila, 1982! Everyone comes around eventually. "You think your folks will bear not seeing their grandchild after a few months?" I asked him and he knew they wouldn't but… please, sorry, stop… it's ancient history."

"Well, he was an only son… again, I'm not defending but it was sort of a big deal then."

"I know. Of course. Bloodline… and all that confounded bullshit."

"Not to pry but did you marry okay, anyway?"

"Got hitched soon after, just to spite him and it was the worst thing I could've done. Didn't last long…. I had a miscarriage, unfortunately. I use my maiden name now."

"If it's any consolation, I think he's always been sad about what happened. Now, I think I know what's really the matter between him and Mom."

"No, it's no consolation, girl. You never wish your own sadness upon the innocent, especially children. It's not your problem."

The bathroom door swung open and Emily emerged with a determined look on her face. "Jefferson," she declared. The two other women looked at each other, clueless. Emily refused to say anymore, and began to retreat into herself to sort out her memories.

"Jefferson Po," Chester spat out the name when Carmen told him what had transpired as he arrived at Anna Duran's clinic. "I knew it," he muttered under his breath, "scumbag, always was... must've drugged her."

"And who's Jefferson?"

"Fullback."

"What?"

"Old school mate of mine. He runs that joint near my place, Horizons. It's where Emily sings."

"So she *is* Emily Mahiwo."

"Well, she knows that scum, and he claims to know her."

"Don't like him much, do you?"

"Underhanded, sneaky...."

"Okay. I get the picture. So he's her boss? He just runs the place or owns it?"

"Says he's a minor partner of Wellington Lim, the plastics guy."

"Oh? Well-spoken of, that one—smuggling, money laundering...."

"His sort of trash."

"So, you think he's the father?"

Chester felt a phantom kick in the groin. "How the hell do I know? I don't know anything! This is a mess."

"My, my... we're going ballistic aren't we? This guy stole your girl or something?"

"Stole his balls or something." It was Anna Duran emerging from the examination room with a patient whom she led out the clinic before returning. "Of course he's pissed. His virginal white lady is knocked up by some fullback."

"And whose bright idea was it to bring her here?" Chester asked his daughter.

"You have a better option?" Carmen shot back.

"Sure, he does. He's full of bright ideas, aren't you, Chester?" Anna jeered, looking at the man with mock tenderness as Carmen cringed.

"My only concern is her safety. She doesn't remember a thing. She works for… crooks."

"And you know that for a fact?" Anna asked, approaching Chester with a compress in hand that she seemed to be wielding like a weapon, and Carmen thought her dad winced.

"We shouldn't let anyone know where she is, until she or we know more." Chester said, as he raised a brown leather bag to his chest, as if using it toward off Anna who was now upon him.

"And how do we propose to do that?" she asked, staring into his eyes like a punitive school teacher.

"I will talk to Jefferson again and…. See if I can find out anything… significant," Chester stuttered.

Anna grinned. "See what happens once we put our minds to it?"

"I found this in her frock," Chester said, handing the bag to Anna, who took it and inspected the contents. She turned it over to Carmen with a troubled look.

Carmen retrieved the handgun and stared at her father. "You kept this from her?" she asked.

"I …was worried."

"You have to show it to her. It could unlock her memories."

"And then what?"

"And then… show it to her! Emily!" Anna called out but the woman was already present, staring at them.

Emily took the handgun, stared at it a while and winced as if in pain. She held up the gun and aimed it at Chester.

"NO!" the women screamed.

Chester held up his hands. "No, stop, I'm not your enemy."

"I knew it," Anna said. "What did you do to her, you son of a.... Talk, now!"

"I did nothing! Shut up, this is no joke."

"Shoot him!" Anna said to Emily. "Put him out of our misery!"

"Stop this! Put the gun down," Carmen shouted.

Emily's hand shook. She pulled the trigger and looked away. The others sought cover but nothing happened. There was no gunfire.

"I removed the ammo," Chester said, after a while. Emily threw away the weapon and burst into tears. She went down on her haunches.

Anna brought Emily to the bedroom upstairs.

"So what were you up to?" Carmen asked her father, after settling down.

"You're right. The gun is crucial to her regaining her memory. Why did she have it? Was it to protect herself against Jefferson or did he give it to her? But why? I had to get her to use it again."

"She shot at you."

"She may have shot at someone else, another man, perhaps."

"You think she'll remember now?"

"Who knows? But then again, is it the best thing for her?"

"Memories are what make us, Dad."

"Even if they're terrible?"

"We can't choose our memories just as we can't choose our family. We can only ignore them so much. You think this Jefferson?"

"I don't know. I never liked the guy, I've seen him hurt people, but whether or not he is capable of rape, I can't say. We were kids together forty years ago."

"So you were close, too, with Dr. Duran?"

"Listen, I don't know what she's told you...."

"None of my business."

"She was my girlfriend, before your mom. I betrayed her. I hurt her. I can't fix the past but I can try to be a better person, right?"

Carmen shrugged. "You're not too bad, you're just... as she says, a bit... gutless."

Chester exploded. "She said *that*?"

"More or less."

"Why that lying...!"

Then Basilio arrived, looking ashen and deeply shaken. "It's worse than we thought, people, far worse."

"Should we call the cops now?" Chester asked.

"Who do you think we're dealing with?"

"What do they want?" Carmen asked. "For starters someone named Emily Mahiwo, a singer. Is she with you?"

"And Roger?"

"I think they have him."

"Is he okay?"

Basilio showed them a screenshot on his mobile of a half-naked white man with a weeks-old beard, gaunt and seemingly confused. He resembled a hostage kidnapped for ransom. Carmen gasped.

"It was just sent to my phone," Basilio said.

"We can't let Emily go to those mad men. What do they want with her? What's she got to do with any of this?" Chester asked.

"They know her, Dad. They've been monitoring her whereabouts."

"No way!"

"Where does she sing?" Basilio asked.

"At the Horizons, in Pasig near Legaspi Sports Complex," Carmen said.

"Where the stampede occurred?"

"Yes. You think these people had something to do with it?"

"I'm not sure but Peping went to see the crowd the day before. I hear he was mobbed, because people wanted his blessing for the raffle."

"That's it!" Carmen said, "They sabotaged the event."

"You're reaching," her father cut in.

"Peping went to check out the scene. Why do you think they're looking for her now, dad? She's with them, she's the operative… she did something…."

"That's insane."

"Is it?"

"No, she can't go to them!" Chester insisted.

"Yes, I can." It was Emily standing at the bottom of the stairs with Anna Duran holding a pair of forceps.

11
MARIA MAHIWO

SHE FIRST CAME to the CICM mission station in Kiangan as a six-year-old to join her father, who had come earlier to study under Fr. Jeffrey Cryuff. The fifty-year-old Belgian priest and medical doctor had vaccinated villagers in Lagawe against an outbreak of smallpox not long after the Big War. The elders were against it.

Their village was among those that had chased away white men who had come to deliver the "Good News" about a foreign God, who was slain by his enemies and rose from the dead to forgive his tormentors. It was either a bad joke or terrible lie. How can mortals murder their maker? These white people— Americans, Belgians—were up to no good, just like those who had come before them during the time of Amburayan who had cut off their heads. All they wanted was gold, as they had found in Lepanto, in Baguio. "The Ifugao have no gold," the elder shouted at a white one once. "Only red rice and tapuy and warriors!"

But Mahiwo, the *mumbaki*, had seen him in a dream: The white man with a bad eye and silver cross astride a two-headed eagle. Mahiwo himself had gone into the forest to hunt a wild boar, remove its entrails and read the signs. "We must allow him to heal our young," he said to the elders. "It is the only way, or our people will be no more."

So they let the white priest prick the skins of their young with his large needle and give them medicine. The sickness went away with the rains and the village slaughtered two carabaos to honor the priest before he left. He had not asked to sprinkle anyone with his spirit water or to call on his God.

"It is not what I came for," he said, "but you know where to find me, if you should ever need my help again."

The elders were elated that the people were cured. After the white man was gone, however, they told Mahiwo that he too must leave. "We need a new *mumbaki*," they said. "Your ancestral spirits have abandoned you, but your children can stay."

Mahiwo understood. He traveled to the mission house and asked the white priest to teach him about this God who rose from the dead, forgave enemies and healed with needles that pass medicine into the body.

"First, let me teach you the language of the white people," Fr. Jeff told Mahiwo in halting Ilokano. He taught the Ifugao how to read and write in English. "It was not his own language," he told Mahiwo but it was that of the people who now ruled the country. "It is best you know it."

Then the priest told him about the one true God mightier than any other who created heaven and earth and all that was in it in six days before resting on the seventh. He described the war between the loyal and treasonous angels and the one sent down to hell.

Mahiwo asked to be baptized.

"Do you believe in your heart?" Cruyff asked the other man, who had no answer. "It is not necessary then. You are my friend, I will teach you all I can, all you want to know and you can teach me about your people, your ways, your words, your gods."

Fr. Jeff wrote down everything Mahiwo told him of the Ifugao as well as of the other mountain peoples. He led the white man to other villages where they spoke to many people some of whom were baptized. Fr. Jeff took photographs and sketched on his white pad, but when they returned to Mahiwo's village the elders would not let them in.

"We do not know you," they said to Mahiwo. "Do not bring us your sickness."

Mahiwo felt an unseen spear plunge into him at what had been decided. He asked that his son, Kaban, live with his brother Bakon, and that his wife Agan and daughter Bagiw join him, but Agan refused to leave her natal home. She would rather raise Kaban alone so Mahiwo took his daughter Bagiw to Kiangan to live in the mission house. She will be baptized, he decided. She will grow up with the white ones and learn how to heal with needles and listen to the beating of hearts with strange devices. Should the sickness ever return to Lagawe, she would be ready to save her people.

Bagiw was sad to leave her home. The mission house scared her; she felt its anger. It was made of stone like the dapay in their village. She stayed with other girls and young women who had also come to learn from Fr. Jeff and two other white priests. They lived inside the mission house while the boys lived elsewhere. Some adults planted rice and vegetables for the mission in exchange for instruction for their children. Mahiwo chopped firewood and sometimes went into the forest to hunt boar, deer, monkey and wild birds for the mission. There, alone, he would occasionally read the entrails of the slain animals.

Bagiw was baptized Maria, mother of Jesus. She learned to read and write the languages of the lowlands and of the white people. She learned their prayers that Mahiwo thought powerful, but when they were alone, he would still tell Maria—whom he still called Bagiw away from the white ones—about the olden gods and ancestors so she would always remember.

"Why did you bring me here then?" Maria asked her father.

"Because the world has changed. We must know what the white ones know to keep us safe from the lowlanders."

Maria wondered what the lowlanders wanted from them. The priests gave her a "birthday," August 15, Feast of the Assumption, the day Mary rose to Heaven whole and unsullied. It was about that time Maria first came to the mission. They deemed it as a sign. She became curious as to how they read signs that were not entrails. Henceforth, they would bake a cake on that day, made from flour and eggs, put small candles atop, light them so that everyone could sing and cut up the cake to eat.

Not long after Maria's thirteenth birthday, Mahiwo entered the forest but never came out. Perhaps, he too had gone to heaven, whole and alive, to be with Mary and Jesus and their once living in Kabunian. A month later, some hunters came to the mission to return Mahiwo's knife they had found in a clearing. There were bones as well, they said, that they did not touch for fear of offending the dead, human or animal. Fr. Jeff handed Maria the knife to keep.

Days later, her brother Kaban came to ask for her. She had come of age, he said, and must now return home to join the akhamang and find a husband.

"I do not want a husband," she told Kaban, "I will be a doctor, as I promised father."

"Father is dead, so is our mother. I am head of our family now, listen to me."

"She is a Christian now. She cannot live in an *ulog*, or an akhamang," Cruyff told Bakan.

"She comes peacefully, or there will be trouble," Bakan warned.

Maria returned to Lagawe with Bakan. She recalled her former name, Bagiw, and her old tongue. She regained her childhood friends and wore her mother's clothes. She stayed in the akhamang with the other girls but was uneasy when the boys visited. She kept away from them.

"Bagud is a good man, brave and trustworthy," Bakan told her, "he will inherit his family's payo, he likes you but he cannot wait forever."

Bagiw had kept a Christian calendar and a missal with her. Every time Bagud visited, she would pray secretly. Three days before her fifteenth birthday, as the full moon shone brightly above and the village slept, Bagiw decided she would rather be Maria, so she crept out of the akhamang and traveled back to the mission house.

"You must go to Baguio. You will be protected there," Cruyff told Maria.

She rode in a truck then took her first bus ride to the big town. She had never seen so many stone houses of different color and sizes. A black stone road ran down a hill, then up a church that reached to the sky.

A priest older than Fr. Jeff welcomed her along with a local woman wearing a brown frock. The priest introduced her as Sister Anna. Many people were in mourning, Maria was told, because the leader in the lowlands, Magsaysay had died in a plane crash. She had only once seen an airplane fly over Kiangan.

She lived with Sister Anna and two other unmarried women in a wooden house not far from the church. She went to school with other girls and learned as well to sew and cook in the manner of the lowlanders. On the weekends, she helped out in the church, typing out Fr. Patrick Hazard's sermons on the machine he had taught her to use. She prepared his food and ironed his soutane but could not serve in the mass, as only boys did that, although she never understood why.

When she turned eighteen, she was told she had learned enough from the girls' school and need not come back. She could continue helping at the church or look for other work if she wanted more money.

"I want to be a doctor," she told Fr. Patrick.

The priest smiled, "I know," he said, "but that's a bit difficult right now. You'll have to go to Manila and there's little chance you'll get into a medical school."

Perhaps she can learn some things by helping out at the local hospital, they told her, so she could prepare to become a nurse, but the people there only made her wash clothes, sheets and diapers. She returned to work full time in the church instead, even if it earned her only free food, enough to pay rent for a small room and time to read to her heart's content at the public library.

When Martial Law was declared, Fr. Patrick was sent home to Belgium. His superiors said he had been away too long and needed a vacation but rumor had it that the military didn't like him. He had too many friends they found suspicious. His sermons bordered on the "subversive." Some of his students in St. Louis University where he taught Philosophy "went underground." At first, she had not understood what that meant and thought they had gone digging for gold.

Maria was saddened by Fr. Patrick's departure, as she had served him for fourteen years. His replacement, Fr. Gerard De Bruyne, was only in his thirties but seemed more fragile. Fr. Gerry looked pale and ashen to Maria, who made it her secret purpose to feed him back to health. She sourced black chickens from her favorite market vendor that she cooked with herbs, as her Chinese friend taught her, and he seemed to savor the entrée, although he ate anything she served up without much comment. He also seemed nervous most of the time. He tapped his fingers on tables, chairs and walls constantly, as if looking for some secret passage. He would wipe his brow and spectacles all the time and smoke his pipe that seemed like a chimney.

Maria would clean his pipe whenever he went to bed, which wasn't often. He was up and about at odd hours reading and writing. She would check out his study and find books like "Being and Nothingness" by someone named Sartre, which she tried reading once but couldn't wrap her head around. There were books on Buddhism and Hinduism as well. He had been to places like Nepal and Bhutan, and he showed Maria pictures he had taken there. He had statues of the Buddha and some deity with many limbs and arms. She was tempted to ask him once if he believed, like the other priests, in the one true God who created everything in six days and rested on the seventh but lost her nerve. He taught Anthropology and read everything Fr. Jeff had written about the highland peoples. He inquired often from Maria about the traditions of the Ifugao but she had been away too long and was no longer certain of her memories.

"I've been a Christian for many years," she would whisper and see his face strangely sadden like a child deprived of a beloved toy. She often wondered why he became a priest like many of the parishioners who understood little of the few sermons he gave.

The Constabulary officer, Major Vince Palou, who sometimes chanced upon Maria at the market or at Star Café would often ask what the priest ate, read or heard? Did he have the same friends as Fr. Patrick? Did he hear confession? Did he talk as well of liberation theology or preferential option for the poor or cultural justice?

"He talks of Nothingness," she said to the Major once to see his eyes grow dark and stony. Was she mocking him? She only stared back with all the might of the Lagawe payo behind her. She was unafraid. Even as a child, she had looked unflinching into the eyes of warriors returning with the heads of their slain enemies and saw their fear. They had called her Amdarangan as well, daughter of Kabunian, mother of tremors. That is why, she always suspected, Mahiwo had taken her away from their people for fear that her fearlessness would someday bring them ruin.

She saw the Major look away, the soldier who would own her spirit, turn her into his eyes and ears. The Major then stood up and walked away, troubled.

She saw herself as the young priest's protector, as the fire through which all his enemies must past. She prepared his food, wardrobe, schedule—screening out callers she deemed to be nuisances—typed up his sermons, cleaned his study and even wrote some of his correspondence. That was how she learned of his breakdown in India and the trouble he was having with superiors in Manila and in Europe.

"I'm hanging on by a thread," he said to her once. "I don't know how long I can last." She could see his pain and confusion.

"Why?" she wanted to ask, "What is so difficult with your life? You have servants and food, a bed to sleep in, a God greater than any other?" All she could muster was: "God will show you the way, trust in him." She said it, as if she was now his confessor and felt a tremor run through her.

"Why are we here?" he asked, and she saw for the first time how truly alone he was. "Have we done right by you?"

She had no answer for him and he realized the enormity of his query and how deep evening had turned and how her face was aglow and her breasts proud.

"I'm sorry to have kept you," he said. "It's late. Go home now."

In the morning, she heard the usual whispers: "*Mrs. Gerry… warmed the kettle ….*" Never truly nasty, more playful, perhaps even hopeful, she often mused. But he told her he would be away for sometime. He was visiting the missions, going into the mountain villages. A Filipino priest, Fr. Francis Domogan, would take over meanwhile. "Why?" she wanted to ask. "What is there that is not in front of you?" She kept her peace instead.

"I must know…before it's too late," he whispered. "What it is we have done."

"*I* am what you have done. I who stand here," she would have said, if only she did not know what he already knew in his heart.

Fr. Domogan was a Benguet native, an Ibaloi who did not like Bontocs or Ifugaos, so it was rumored, neither did he like rumors especially those involving priests and their female secretaries. He made this clear to Maria on his first day at St. Christopher's when he instructed for his office door to be kept wide open all the time, and for Maria's desk to be placed outside the room when it had always been adjacent to Fr. Gerry's.

This made Maria feel less as a colleague than a sentinel, but she consoled herself with the thought that things would return to normal once Fr. Gerry came back from his tour. The weeks rolled into months, even as correspondence from Manila and Brussels grew ever more urgent. Was Fr. Gerard De Bruyne officially missing? Was it time to inform the civil authorities? The military? The embassy?

Martial law was relaxed as elections were held for an interim Parliament, but the President continued to rule by decree and the military continued to do as it pleased. Few believed anything had changed. Major Palou was surprised and a bit discomfited to see Maria. A Manila native and part Iberian descent, he was raised to be wary of the supposed occult powers of mountain peoples who beat to death their fowl in slow tedious ritual. She spooked him when they spoke last.

"He's been gone eights months," she told him. "Something has happened."

"We can't interfere unless the Church or the embassy makes a request," Major Palou answered, his wariness warmed by her despair. For a moment, he imagined a life with her, this mountain maiden, this protector of priests but he knew his family would be agog. "What is this strange white man to you, anyway? This interloper?" he wanted to ask her but held his tongue.

"They won't do that. I think they're secretly glad he's gone. They'll wait a year perhaps. It doesn't have to be official," she said. "Whatever you can find out… anything, please."

He brought the infant to her place a week after Ninoy Aquino was gunned down at the airport in Manila. She saw the brownish wisps on the infant scalp, her tan, the high nose and dimples, the hazel eyes and felt tremors once more inside herself.

"Who is she?" Maria asked Vincent Palou.

"You know," he whispered.

"Where is he? Is he alive?"

The officer shrugged. "Someone brought her to the PC detachment in Mayoyao and told a spotty tale about a white drifter."

"But how can we be sure? Where's the mother? He would never abandon his own child."

"She had this on her."

Maria saw the silver crucifix and felt cold. It was the one thing of his that she never touched. "It doesn't prove anything. Someone might have found it somewhere, if indeed it was his."

Vincent Palou shrugged again. "I have to turn her over to Social Welfare, anyway. Do you want her or not?"

Maria named her Emily after a friend in city hall where she worked after leaving the parish, though she continued to do volunteer work, and took her to Fr. Domogan to be baptized.

The priest refused initially. "You have to inform the authorities first," he insisted.

"I found her, she belongs to me. This is God's will. I know people at city hall. She will be my child. I can have her baptized elsewhere."

Domogan called in a seminarian and the cook to stand as sponsors. At city hall, Maria registered her child as Emily Olivia Mahiwo, born in Baguio City, August 21, 1983. She thought it was a good day to be born.

12

JEFFERSON PO

WHEN HE FIRST saw the guy seemingly stumble inside Horizons, Jefferson at first feared he was running from crooks, or worse, the police. He looked Chinese and Jefferson hoped he was local as he was wary of expats, more so guys from China who were trouble. Then he recognized the wide forehead, the bubble nose, the reddish mark, the duck gait—it was Chester Limhuatco, from high school.

"Chicken," he remembered, as that was what they used to call him. He had already forgotten why, perhaps because of how Chester ambled or the way the guy 'clucked' when he talked, or his hair. He was one of the brighter boys, spelling champ, not so much teachers' pet, though the occasional altar boy. Jefferson couldn't recall having any beef with Chester, save for an intramural basketball game in Grade 6 when their class (in red) were trailing the opposing team (in blue) by a wide margin. The blues had sent in their bench, including Chester, just to mock the reds and Jefferson had kicked the guy's butt to send him sprawling. He wanted a dust up now that the game was lost but Chester just shrugged it off as did the rest of his teammates, and that was that. There was only a minute left so Jefferson took himself out of the game, pissed. It almost felt like he had kicked his own butt. Was it why he remembered the guy as "chicken?"

When Chester asked about Emily, Jefferson suddenly felt the kick on his butt again after all these years. "Chicken! I'll wring your neck this time!" He almost shouted, but the thought that someone else, someone he knew, was also looking for Emily, cooled his anger.

Jefferson suspected that Chester knew more than he was letting on, but decided not to spook him anymore than deleting the photo he had taken with his mobile. Jefferson was convinced Chester had come "fishing," after he had left and was confident his old schoolmate would be back in a day or so to say whatever he had really come to say. Perhaps, he was actually in touch with Emily but it had been four days and Jefferson was feeling the noose tighten. What if Emily had indeed been hurt in the stampede or been held captive by that mad Peping and his cohorts?

So when Chester finally returned, Jefferson felt awesome relief. "I'll never think of him as chicken again," he swore to himself.

"So who is she?" Chester asked.

"You have her?"

"Maybe."

"This is no joking matter, man."

"You want her, you tell me."

"This is government business, Chester, you don't want to get involved."

"What government?"

"This one, at least. It's police business."

"She in trouble?"

"She's undercover. NBI."

A light blinked inside Chester's head. "You shitting me?"

"No…. Well… so am I."

"What? You're a cop?"

"NBI."

"Don't bullshit me, man. We're not kids anymore. I'm not afraid of you."

"You were afraid of me?"

Chester stared at Jefferson and shrugged, feeling unhinged.

"I didn't plan it this way, man." Jefferson sighed. "Things just turned out the way they did."

"Tell me everything."

"I fronted for Wellington Lim in some of his import ventures."

"The plastics guy?"

"Yup, he was a batch mate of my elder brother, Christopher, remember?"

"So you were smuggling for him?"

Jefferson smirked and shifted his head the way he used to whenever he was caught angling his pocket mirror up some pretty teacher's mini skirt.

"Technically… you know how it is. I knew people who knew people in customs. My own ventures had bellied up because some mainland Chinese had scammed me. I was in deep shit and Wellington bailed me out, kept me afloat. In the beginning, it was just onions from Taiwan or motorbikes from China. Then there were chemicals…. He said it was for plastics, but the cops got on my case. They said it was for ammunition or… narcotics. Then before I knew it, I was in NBI headquarters. Avelino, remember him?"

"CAT corps commander… a batch ahead."

"Yeah. Ever the boy scout… anyway, he's now a lawyer."

"Right. I heard from his cousin once, Ateneo or San Beda. Top whatever at the bar exams…."

"Well, turns out he was pretty well placed at the Bureau, and he was my case officer. So he showed me this dossier that was all bullshit. "So you tell me what's what. In any case, it's you or Wellington," he told me, "and I hear *he's* got money to burn." What was a guy like me to do?"

"So you snitched?"

"Well, you know…. I gave them enough to save my own neck. Wouldn't be the first time we had to face the inquisition right? Remember Fr. Zallo? We called him Steve McGarrett, didn't we? Hawaii Five-O? All he did was glare at you and sound like he was snorting fire and you'd confess to every crime in third year high."

Jefferson chuckled. His reminiscences warmed Chester briefly, and he felt glad that Jefferson had chosen to include him now among their old Jesuit Prefect of Discipline's list of usual suspects. The truth is Chester was never among the "bad eggs." The worst he had done was forge a priest's signature once when he skipped confession after watching porn the night before.

"Anyway, they didn't have enough on Wellington, just wanted to keep tabs on him for bigger fish, and I was all they got. Then they arrested some Chinese mainlanders and those guys put out a contract on me! Where else could I go?"

"I thought the bureau only hired lawyers?"

"I took some courses. I'm not actually on the payroll, you understand?"

Chester shrugged. He had never trusted Jefferson.

"Confidential agent," Jefferson whispered, though they were far from hearing range of anyone.

"So this is a listening post?"

"People like to blab, you know, especially after a few drinks and with pretty women around."

Chester noticed only then a number of female food servers in the place, all in tight-fitting if tasteful black tops.

"Wellington comes here?"

"Never. But… one might get word to him."

"And Emily?"

"She majored in Criminology. Can you believe that, a pretty thing like her? She seemed fascinated with criminal minds. But I think she's really obsessed with finding her father."

"Father?"

"She suspects that he was a foreign missionary in the Cordilleras who turned rogue, and that he might have been involved in some ghastly killings in the 1970s and '80s."

"Really?"

"There's talk of a white Igorot back then who took heads."

Chester felt a phantom kick to the groin. "Took heads? As in…?"

Jefferson nodded and whipped an imaginary axe against Chester's neck. He ducked.

"It was during the building of the dam in Kalinga. Many of the locals were against the project, since it would inundate their villages, so they waged war, raided army outposts, took away enemy heads. Some survivors recalled seeing a white man among them who was naked but for his g-string and tattoos and bore an axe, although the locals were mostly in fatigues and carried firearms."

"So he was this Mahiwo?"

"She uses her mother's name."

"Maria? I've met her… seems a bit old to be Emily's mom."

"Who knows? I checked her out: educated by the missions, worked in the Baguio parish church for many years.

She was there when a Fr. De Bruyne, was parish priest. People remember him but there's no record of him ever leaving the country. His superiors say he abandoned his post and disappeared. No one's saying much. Anyway, Emily applied at the bureau and for some reason Avelino liked her. "Something curious about her," he said. "Our sort." He placed her under my charge, to train."

"Does her mom know?"

"No. She made us promise not to tell the old lady."

"Why?"

Jefferson shrugged.

"So why here?"

"We're casing this religious blowhard, Jose Crenshaw. Heard of him?"

"On TV… the Black Nazarene guy?"

"Yup… serious mental case, that one. The Cardinal's pretty pissed."

"So why is it an NBI concern?"

"He's an ex-cop who went AWOL. We think he heads this group of mostly cops and ex-cops—the Kapatiran or BBN— who seem to worship him as a Christ figure. They could be behind some killings of drug pushers and other criminals."

"Vigilantes?"

"More like Angels of the Apocalypse."

Chester was surprised Jefferson remembered anything from Religion class.

"They're planning something big?"

"We're not sure but his right hand man, Manito, has asked about equipment for fumigation?"

"Fumigation?"

"Yup, the metallic contraption used to spray stuff that kill dengue mosquitoes and sort. Ten thousand units, for starters."

"That much? Are they going into the business? Government contract?"

Jefferson shook his head. "That's what we're trying to find out. Also inquired about ammonia and sulfur, and phosphorus."

"So he comes here? Crenshaw?"

"He's been here four times. Always incognito: dark jacket, hood. Sits right over there," Jefferson pointed to a dim corner. "Manito arrives thirty minutes beforehand to case the joint, talk business. There are always five other guys. I make sure they don't carry firearms, but Crenshaw's off limits. Manito passes the detector over the boss himself. And the man meets only with Emily."

"So he likes her too?" Chester asked, just to drive an imaginary nail into Jefferson's forehead. He winced.

"Likes her singing. Tells her she's almost like a white girl who sounds like a black one."

"You think so?"

Jefferson shrugged: "What do I know?"

"Perhaps he fancies her as his Magdalene," Chester said just to drive another unseen nail into Jefferson's cringing forehead. He smirked.

"So these guys have other business with Wellington?"

"Sometimes there's stuff we can't sell through the stores or things they won't take—deodorants from China, or condoms from Vietnam—we pass them through Manito. They run a big network of hawkers in Quiapo and Tondo."

"Wellington needs to deal with these guys?"

"He hates them. It was my idea," Jefferson said. "I convinced him we needed to keep ties with these guys in case there *was* something we really had to sell through them. So he leaves it to me, doesn't want to know any of them. But I suspect he knows Crenshaw from somewhere, owes the guy some favor."

"NBI in on it?"

"As long as there's no drugs or explosives or bad shit like that."

"So Emily was here on the eve of the stampede?"

"We had an all-nighter. Some frat people were celebrating up to nearly four in the morning. I rarely keep the place open past two. I was planning to drive her home but she was gone. Waiters said she hurried off."

"With her weapon." Chester said.

Jefferson seemed struck. "So she had it with her when you…?"

"Yes. In her frock."

"Has it been fired? I mean…."

"Checked the clip, it's missing two bullets."

"Oh, man. She's never shot anyone. She's a good shot, though, at the range."

"What if she did? And she actually caused the stampede?"

"Oh… shit, but why?" Jefferson looked truly confused.

"She rushed off, you said? What if she knew that those cultists were up to something with that huge crowd?"

"I don't know," Jefferson seemed to be scanning the premises for clues.

"She's kept to herself lately. I couldn't pry anything out of her. I don't know if she's fallen for that Crenshaw or…."

"She's pregnant."

"What? How do you know?" Jefferson glared at Chester. "Stop shitting me. I've told you everything."

"I brought her to my friend's clinic."

Jefferson gripped Chester's forearm with both hands and for a moment Chester thought he would break it. "True?" he asked, almost pleading.

Chester nodded. "She's safe."

"You have to bring me to her, chicken," Jefferson said, and Chester knew they were back on familiar terms. "Stop messing around, we could all be in deep shit."

"Yours?" Chester asked. "The baby?"

Then they stared at each other as if simultaneously hitting on an answer in Math class. "No!" Jefferson growled, disdain written all over his face. "She couldn't have fallen that badly for that nut case… that creep." He looked like he was about to explode.

Chester's stomach rumbled triumphantly. "Let's go visit Maria Mahiwo. I have a feeling she has lots more to tell," he suggested, pushing his advantage and beaming confidence. He had never enjoyed more talking with Jefferson, who looked beat but relieved.

13
BORDEAUX

BORDEAUX TOWN HOMES in the heart of Mandaluyong City, Metro Manila was a letdown for Chester, who had long wanted to but never visited France. It looked rundown, at least thirty years old, and told little of why it was so named. Chester was briefly reminded of how many local Chinese families named their kids—after U.S. Presidents or trademarks; he himself might have been named after his father's favorite brand of cigarettes. Well better than *Camel*, he thought to himself and felt some consolation.

At the gate manned by two private security guards, Jefferson flashed them an I.D. that Chester hoped was genuine. Some hundred homes were spread out across a grid of six rows, around 60 sq. meters each with shared walls, single garages but no lawns.

Still, such residences didn't exactly go for peanuts and Chester wondered whether the Mahiwos owned or rented.

"They moved here ten years ago, and Maria bought it off her employers on installment," Jefferson answered Chester's mental query. "She clerked for a shipping firm before retiring last year."

Chester wondered how often Jefferson had been here, driving home Emily or visiting for Sunday dinner. Did he see Maria as a putative mother in-law and could he be hard on her now for information? He wondered why *he* was here? None of this was his business after all. Why not turn over Emily, or whatever her real name was, to Jefferson—NBI or not—and be done with it? Let Carmen find her own way to that Roger guy, if he was still in one piece. She always kept her own counsel anyway. What was he trying to prove? That he could get back at Jefferson Po? Kick him one in the butt this time around? Steal some girl from him? Or, more pathetically, conspire with him and be "buddies" finally? The term *middle age crisis* popped into his head.

"Let me off. I'll find my way home. You go do your job and I'll bring Emily to you later," Chester said.

"What?" Jefferson scowled. "What's with you, chicken?"

This time the pet name hit a chord. "Stop calling me that! We're not kids anymore!"

"Alright, cool it. I'm sorry, didn't know it bothered you that much."

"Just...."

"I said okay. We're here, man, hang in there. I need your brains on this one, Chester."

He wasn't sure if Jefferson wasn't bullshitting him again but hearing such an admission tempered Chester's dislike for the other guy and grew his confidence.

An altar with a portrait of the sacred heart of Jesus and another of the Virgin Mary was prominent. The rest of the furnishing was spare but tasteful, none of the knickknacks one often associated with middle class homes.

Horror vacuii. Filipinos were supposedly afraid of empty space and tended to fill it with clutter. Chester rather thought, from what he had seen from relatives and friends, that they feared slipping back to poverty and hoarding assuaged such fears.

From the looks of things, Maria had no such fears. She stared steely at Jefferson once the two men entered her home. "Where is she?" the woman demanded.

Jefferson looked to Chester. "So she *is* with you, doctor?"

Chester showed her the photo on his mobile. Maria looked at it and equanimity gave way to a warrior's mien. "Where is my daughter?"

"She's in a safe place. I found her at the site of the stampede. I had to be sure about you," Chester said.

"Bring me to her."

"First, we'd like to ask you some questions," Jefferson chimed in.

"What questions? How dare you? You've been trouble ever since she met you!" Maria lashed out at Jefferson. "I knew you were up to no good! What have you done to her?"

"Listen to the good doctor, Aling Maria, Emily is safe. We will bring you to her... or... anyway... just bear with us a bit."

"I'm not bearing one more moment with you, rascal! Predator! You know how young she is, you dirty old ...."

"She's past thirty ma'am, not quite a child," Jefferson said.

"She might as well be. She's so innocent."

The two men looked at each other.

"Who's her father?" Jefferson asked.

Maria glared at him. "What's it to you? That's none of your business."

"I'm afraid it is, ma'am," Jefferson said, flashing his I.D. that was beginning to get on Chester's nerves. "I'm with the NBI."

"What?" Maria asked, incredulous.

"And so is Emily. I'm a confidential agent and Emily has been working under me for the past six months."

"Liar!" Mahiwo shouted at Jefferson and looked to Chester, who shrugged.

"Enough of your lies," the woman said. "She sings at that place of yours… that's all. I never approved of it."

"She didn't want to worry you. Just tell us some things we need to know if you want her back safe," Jefferson said, calmly.

Maria sighed and sat down. "The past always catches up, doesn't it? I adopted her as a baby. A soldier brought her to me in Baguio, said she was the child of a foreign man."

"Fr. De Bruyne."

Maria was thunderstruck, hand on her chest.

"Are you okay?" Chester asked, moving towards her but the woman waved him off.

"He disappeared nearly forty years ago," Jefferson said.

"Never thought I'd hear that name again," Maria whispered.

"Did Emily know?" Jefferson asked.

Maria seemed lost. "I don't know. I don't think so but there were some people from abroad who made contact once, said they were family. I ignored them but Emily... I'm not sure. She was always curious."

"Have you ever heard of the white Igorot?"

"Lies!" Maria shouted, quickly enraged. "His superiors spread lies about him. They never forgave him for leaving, for showing what they were, hypocrites!"

"And is that how you see them, Ms. Mahiwo?" Chester asked.

Maria calmed down. "I have my own faith, doctor."

"Is this him?" Jefferson took out his mobile and showed Maria a photo of a long haired, bearded white man, in g-string and body paint, tattooed, wielding an axe in one hand and a severed head in the other.

Maria gasped.

"Look carefully, Aling Maria," Jefferson requested.

Maria began shaking her head but the rest of her body followed suit. She cupped her hands to her mouth and turned away.

"We have to be sure, Aling Maria. Look at the eyes," Jefferson said as he touched the screen, focused on the man's face and widened the angle. His eyes were blue, Chester saw. "Please...." Jefferson urged Maria, who refused to look but was now teary eyed. Po pocketed his phone and sat down, deep in thought.

Maria remained stoic, staring hard at the distance but her silence spoke volumes. "You can fake these things, these days, I know," she said after a while.

"This is genuine. It was taken years ago by a researcher who sent it to Emily recently. We scanned and digitized it," Jefferson said.

"Who took it?" Chester asked

Jefferson looked at Chester. "Come on, we've come this far... *haven't we*?"

"Another confidential agent?" Chester asked, smirking.

"A certain Roger Geisler."

Chester nearly dropped to his knees.

"What? You know him?" Jefferson asked.

"Carmen's in trouble. They could be after her too..."

Jefferson scowled.

"My daughter, Carmen. She knows this Geisler. She's been looking for him. He's an anthropologist, Swiss, or maybe Swedish."

"It seems he met this De Bruyne, or someone who might be De Bruyne, in the Cordilleras four years ago. When Emily went on line to inquire about the man, Geisler sent her the photo," Jefferson explained.

"So Emily's been in touch with Geisler as well?" Chester asked, agitated.

"Apparently."

"And she thinks De Bruyne's her father?"

Jefferson shrugged. "We have reason to think, De Bruyne's in touch with Jose Crenshaw, that they might've met or are in cahoots somehow. Its what got Emily interested in the case."

"But if that's De Bruyne, how old is he now?"

"Seventy-six," Maria said, staring into the distance. Chester and Jefferson looked at each other. She stood and walked away.

Then something nipped Chester in the small of his back.

"You've been using Emily as bait all this time haven't you? You lying…"

"Shut up! The both of you!"

The woman's voice stunned the two men. She was brandishing her knife that once belonged to her father.

"Take me to my daughter, or I will gut the both of you like pigs," Maria Mahiwo demanded. The two men sensed she had never been more earnest.

14
THE HOUR OF THE JUST

HE HAD FIRST heard of the lost De Bruyne from his mother Helga who was part Belgian. This cousin Gerard, whom Helga was fond of as a child, had joined the priesthood and gone to Asia and never returned. The CICM admitted later that he had gone missing. They had no idea where he was, or what had happened to him. Then there was talk that he had gone native in the highlands of the Philippine island of Luzon; had shed his priestly garb for a g-string and tattoos.

This possibility fascinated Roger as a boy. He had seen *Apocalypse Now*, read Conrad's *Heart of Darkness* and imagined his uncle Gerard as Kurtz. He read all he could find on the Igorots of the Philippines and decided he would be among them before he turned twenty. Then he met Andrea Salas, a Filipino nurse at the Stockholm General, where he had his appendectomy. She had slipped a pamphlet with a cover of a dark-hued Christ in a maroon robe and laden with a large cross into his hand when she heard he was Christian. Their clan was Lutheran but his academic parents were secular and hardly practiced. The portrait disturbed him at first. The agony on the Christ's face seemed to be accusing him of having committed some horrendous crime, of wanting him to share its burden. He continued looking on and the gaze softened, the burden seemingly lifted. He was looking into a vast sea... of suffering then solace. He was tearful. He had been forgiven; for what, he did not know.

Andrea told him of this large black-hued Christ in a Philippine town called Quiapo who performed great miracles. Once a year, millions of devotees, mostly male and unshod, struggled to be in his presence as he was borne on a carriage across town. Every year, on January 9, she told him, Quiapo was the center of the earth, the hub of all creation. Filipinos, she explained, were now wandering the earth as the last apostles of the Christ, bearers of the Good News as the millennium approached.

Roger was stunned. For centuries, white people, like his uncle Gerard had roamed the earth to preach the white God to colored peoples. Now, Gerard might have gone native, and the black Christ had now come to an unbelieving Europe. It was a closed loop. The empire was preaching back.

He befriended Andrea, dined at her home, where she prepared adobo and lumpia, and saw her altar with smaller versions of the Black Nazarene, the Sto. Nino and Mother Mary. As long as they were with her, Andrea said, she was at home anywhere in the world. She had worked in Hong Kong and Israel and Hamburg, lived among Buddhists, and Jews and Protestants, and always there were those who found the true Faith through her.

"They never know they're looking," she said. "No one ever knows. They see a black figure, the likeness of a white child, the serenity of motherhood and are pleasantly amused. "Why worship wood and plaster?" They ask. "Why not say a prayer?" I say. It does no harm. They smile politely yet they do so, in their hearts. I know because they come back again and again. They want to know more and more. I teach prayer after prayer and lay my hands over them and feel the spirit pass into them...."

Roger gasped.

"Would you like me to lay my hands over you?" She asked.

Roger demurred. "Maybe next time."

And she smiled, certain he would return.

Roger did not come back to Andrea's place. He had never known such religiosity and he was wary of it, but he researched the Black Nazarene and the Sto. Nino, the first Christian idol worshipped in the Philippines. The Portuguese explorer Magellan, who sailed under Spain, had gifted one to the wife of a native leader who agreed to baptism in 1521. Nearly fifty years later, a second Spanish exploration found the idol in an abandoned hut. The locals sought to ransom it from the Europeans as the white child was now their rain deity.

A black man, a white child and, perhaps, a mixed race woman; what an unlikely family, Roger thought. He studied Anthropology and Comparative Religion at university. In 1996, he joined a church-based group of volunteers who traveled to the Philippines when he was only twenty-one. They met with other church groups, went to the "Smokey mountain" dumpsite, and helped build homes for the poor. When the group returned home, Roger stayed on and went to Pampanga for the Holy Week.

There he saw the black man on the cross. He was fascinated, hearing the buzz among the crowd about *Itim na Nazareno*, as he recalled some Tagalog he had learned from Andrea. He broke through the cordon and came to a place beneath the black man. The black man looked down at the white one. For a moment, Roger saw the same eyes that stared out at him years ago from Andrea's pamphlet. Then the black man looked to the sky and shouted in agony. The sun blinded Roger and he was being ushered back behind the cordon.

Later, as the five crosses were taken down and first aid administered to the "crucified," Roger tried to make his way to the black man but was turned away. He stayed the night and went to the carpenter's shop next day but was told Peping would be incommunicado for an indefinite period. He jotted down the address and left.

In Quiapo, he saw the life size Black Nazarene for the first time and was awestruck. He spoke with the parish priest, Fr. Dimalanta, who was non-committal about the miracles attributed to the idol. In fact, the priest seemed skeptical about the matter and admitted that veneration of the Nazarene verged on idolatry. He suggested that was why he was sent here. Parishes like these, he said, were "battle grounds" for the Church. He told Roger how in decades past, influential people could request the parish priest to be sent the hand of the idol in order to cure some sickness.

"It's like a fetish," Roger said, and the priest leaned his head slightly to one side in agreement.

"We don't like people going overboard in these matters, but then again, it's better than for them to go over to the other side," Fr. Dimanlanta quipped and seemed tickled by his own thought.

Roger nodded but wondered if the priest was referring to non-believers, devil worshippers, or Protestants, like himself?

He also met with members of the Cofradia and the Hijos and found them apprehensive of Dimalanta. He sensed a tug-o-war between priest and icon. An elder gave Roger a pocket-sized laminated portrait of the Nazareno, an *estampita,* and told him it was antique and miraculous. He bought metal amulets with pig Latin inscriptions that were said to ward off evil as well as enemy bullets. He was all set for St. Christopher's in Baguio where he hoped to find out more about his uncle Gerard and perhaps retrace the man's route into the mountains. He would find the white Igorot.

That evening, he returned to Quiapo for a final walkabout. Something in its mix of religiosity and worldliness spoke to him: the jars of herbal concoctions right outside the church that he was told were abortive agents, the waxen bodily organs, the fortune tellers and prayer mongers.

He found himself drawn to a neon sign that read *Salaguinto*. He did not know what it meant but suspected that it offered erotic delights. If only it were so simple, he thought to himself, the distance between heaven and earth, or limbo perhaps, no more than a back alley.

Roger was quickly surrounded by petite brown girls in skimpy attire, but an older woman only shooed them away. She ushered the foreigner up a flight of stairs to the mezzanine, where he would enjoy more privacy and a better view of the stage. Some other customers eyed him curiously. He realized it was a girlie bar and that the petite girls would soon be shedding their clothes when the music turned mellow.

"What is your pleasure, sir?" the woman asked, trying out a phrase she had recently learned from another foreigner. After handing Roger a menu card, she quickly pointed him to a glass window. He went over and saw more brown women seated in two rows staring back at him. He knew at once that they could see him too and saw a few faces light up.

"Melanie," the woman beside him whispered, pointing to a girl in the corner, a shade darker than the others. "Exotic, huh?" She chirped. "She had just come from the south, virgin."

Melanie reminded him suddenly of Andrea Salas and he gagged.

"You okay?" the woman asked, alarmed.

"Yes," he said. "No problem."

"How about her? Cynthia, very good."

"Maybe later," he mumbled.

"Yes, of course. You relax first. Have a beer. We have great food. Try our bulalo."

The beer seemed to upset his stomach and Roger thought of leaving when the man joined his table. "You mind?"

Roger shook his head.

"Not very good stuff, huh?" the stranger asked. Roger shrugged. The man pointed to the glass window and to the stage where a striptease was ongoing.

"You want to check out other places?" the stranger asked. "I'm Eric, by the way. This is my neighborhood."

Roger shrugged again. They walked past other alleys with more neon signs and came to a place called *Maginoo*.

"Maybe you prefer this one?" Eric asked with a knowing smile. Roger wasn't sure why but he suspected that it was men, or boys, who sat behind the glass windows, here and performed on stage. He smiled and shook his head, although part of him wanted to look.

"Okay, maybe we eat something? You like Filipino food?"

"So far."

They moved on to a sidewalk eatery, where some guys were having drinks.

"This is my *barkada*," Eric said, "Roger from Sweden."

"Sweden?" the man named Felino lit up. "Stockholm, goulash… I've been there. I'm a *marino*… a seaman," he said.

The kaldereta was spicy. It reminded Roger of the goose his granny used to prepare.

"This is good stuff," Roger said. "It's goat, right?"

The guys chuckled. "What?"

"Goat, right?"

"Yes, goat," the guy called Pango said then howled: *Awoo….*

His mates barked after him: *Aw! Aw! Aw!*

The bile in Roger's gut rose to his throat. "No fooling, guys, it's goat. It must be."

"Yes, it's goat," Eric said finally and the bile settled inside Roger. "Hybrid."

"What?"

"Hybrid goat, half goat, half… you know?"

The gang burst into laughter.

"Goat," Pango said. "That's what I called him, *kambing*."

This time the laughter shook the wire and bamboo banisters.

Roger felt woozy. His head spun. It didn't matter what he ate anymore, he just wanted to chuck it out, all of it, all the way back to his grandmother's goose. Then his knees buckled. He had to sit, no to lie down. Then it was fuzzy. Then it was black.

He woke up with a severe headache in a room he did not know, wearing smocks way too big. Roger panicked. The woman saw him move and hurried away. Then a man came in, a white man.

"Calm down," he said.

"Who are you? Where am I?"

"You're in the Swedish Embassy. I am Consul Sven Bjorkman."

"Embassy? Why?"

"Some men dropped you off before sunrise. They said they found you sprawled by the Quiapo church, unconscious. They saw your passport and brought you here but refused to give their identities. They warned not to call the police to avoid trouble."

"Why?" Roger asked.

"I don't know. You tell me," Consul Bjorkman said. "What did you do?"

"Nothing. We were having drinks and … stew… then I felt woozy. It may have been dog meat."

"I doubt if any dog meat could knock you out like that. Your drink was likely spiked."

"Why? With what?"

"Ativan, perhaps. Heard of it?"

Roger shook his head.

"Never mind. Did you lose anything of value?"

Roger checked his wallet. "Maybe some cash but not much. I didn't have a lot on me.'

"Your flight is at six," Consul Bjorkman said, handing Roger his plane ticket. "Your stuff is outside. We got it from the pension house. Your bill's paid… just get out of here."

"Wait, I need to find out what happened. I have to go back…"

"We checked with the police. There were reports of a white man walking around the area disoriented and naked, late last night."

"What?"

"Care to find out more? Anyway, your father's quite ill. Go home. And… yes, they left this for you."

It was a small wooden statue of the black Nazarene.

In Stockholm, Roger found his father Stig at home drinking schnapps and smoking his pipe. The church group had told Roger's folks that their son stayed on in the Philippines and worried over his emotional state. Roger ranted, then slept for two days. When he awoke, he knew what he must do.

Roger entered the CICM seminary and left after two years. Then he went to New York to pursue a graduate degree in Anthropology. There he met Carmen Limhuatco, who was visiting, and they became fast friends. She stayed for a couple of semesters to audit social science courses, though close to a degree in Veterinary Medicine. He suspected that she was interested in him and didn't let on that he was gay for months. He wasn't sure himself until his counselor at the seminary suggested as much and urged him to spend time elsewhere in order to figure things out. Then he met Earl, a classmate, and they became a pair. Carmen left for home but they kept in touch.

Roger worked part time for the Swedish Institute for Development Assistance (SIDA) that allowed him to travel even as he pursued his research in "practical religion in transitional societies." He visited Manila occasionally and met up with Carmen. His interest in the Black Nazarene deepened.

He had written Jose Crenshaw back in 1998 after returning to Sweden and received no reply. His subsequent attempts to make contact were similarly unsuccessful until he received a letter in his office in 2009 from the Most Illustrious and Honorable Genuine Brotherhood of the Black Nazarene in Quiapo seeking assistance for training juvenile delinquents in IT and computer repair. It was signed by Crenshaw and had a separate note from him recalling the time he looked down from his cross and saw Roger. He further disclosed that there was a white man, a man of God who used to serve a false church, that Geisler may be interested in meeting. In his previous correspondence to Jose Crenshaw, Roger had written of his missing uncle. Then Crenshaw reminded him of another white man, who was seen walking in Quiapo naked and seemingly lost late one night many years ago. Roger felt an invisible hand, cold and clammy, grab his neck, causing him to choke.

Roger came to the Brotherhood of the Black Nazarene (BBN) Incorporated's one room office in Tondo in February 2010 but Crenshaw was unavailable. Roger couldn't wangle funding from SIDA for the BBN and none of the five people in the office seemed interested in him until he made a $1,000 donation to the non-profit organization. Manito Santos said Tata Peping would meet with him in a fortnight.

He was clad in a white gown and black skullcap that reminded Roger of West Asia. His beard was trimmed. He looked serene and the agony that Roger remembered from all those years ago seemed gone.

"So we meet again, Roger Geisler."

"Do you still do the crucifixion ritual?" Roger asked to break the ice.

"The time of the penitent is past, Roger Geisler. Now is the hour of the just. Perhaps that is why you have returned?"

"I'm a cultural anthropologist. I'm very interested in the veneration of the Black Nazarene among other things, of course. I see you have a social project going."

"They worship wood, Geisler. Matter. They have been doing so for centuries. Sleep walking... but the hour of reckoning approaches. And when they awaken, it will be as a tsunami to wash away all the lies that have ever shackled them."

Roger was taken aback by Crenshaw's words. "You agree with Fr. Dimalanta then?"

"That old fool," Crenshaw hissed. "He tells the flock to do good instead. Serve others" he says. "Love thy neighbor. God doesn't want your blood, only your love!" The black man roared, his laughter shaking the premises of the BBN, even as the others laughed with him. "He knows nothing. Penitents have nothing but their bodies, nothing but their pain. Whether or not they have money, the body is the only thing of real value. They must worship their body and they must treasure their pain: suffer from it and contend with it until it breaks them! Then perhaps, they can find a glimmer of truth."

"Is that what happened to you?" Roger asked.

The black man only grinned and walked away. Roger noticed that he touched everything he passed.

"Why are you really here, Roger Geisler?"

"You wrote about a white man…"

"Ah, the warrior?"

"Have you met him?"

"Who is he to you?

"He may be my uncle, Gerard De Bruyne. I think I'd written before…"

"I see. So this is all personal to you."

"Partly. My mother was close to him, they were cousins."

"She was in love with him," Tata Peping asked, smiling, almost elfin.

"No. I don't mean it that way. He was family."

"Family? Yes, it is always about family, isn't it?"

"You looked for your father too, once."

"Yes. In my time of darkness."

"I'm just curious."

"Why?"

"No one has ever done what he did… if the stories are true."

"No one?" Peping asked, and Roger was beginning to think this was all a mistake. What on earth was he doing here?

"Join the enemy, you mean?" Roger was speechless. "And Moses?"

"I'm not sure it's the same thing."

"No? You don't think your uncle might fancy himself as a liberator of an oppressed people?"

"I don't know. Perhaps I might understand more if I do meet him."

"He has taken heads, you know?"

"So I've heard."

"Mountain peoples revere heads just as lowlanders once did. There is no greater honor than to take a head in warfare or to lose one's own to a brave. There is no shame. Heads are treasured."

"I've read about it."

"Then the white folk came and told us to stop. It was barbaric, they said. Instead, believe in Him…." Peping turned to the cross hanging on the wall behind them, although he didn't seem to look.

"He, who was scourged and nailed to a cross, suffered a most undignified, ignoble death. Be rid of all those heads you've taken, they have no power. Valor will not save you, only this… the instrument of the Savior's death… be scourged, be nailed… suffer as he did, as he does, over and over."

"And *you* believed." Roger said, unable to still his tongue.

"Yes."

"What changed? I mean, do you think differently now? You seem to…."

"*You*." Peping said, nearly smiling.

Roger was dumbfounded.

"I saw you. I looked down from my cross and there you were below, staring… sneering."

"I wasn't."

"Who were you? The Apostle John? An angel? Are all angels white?"

"I'm sorry. I didn't mean to."

"Where was Mary? My mother… I remembered my mother. She was why I wanted to do this… once… I could not save her."

Roger was beginning to panic.

"What a fool I was: hurting, bleeding, screaming to the heavens, and there you were a white young man, a boy."

"I was nineteen."

"Mocking me."

"I wasn't, I swear."

"And I needed to be mocked. I could always hear them mocking, hissing from below, Itim na Nazareno: the Black

Nazarene. I couldn't care less. They were the fools! And then you showed up, at last. 'Today, you shall be with me... in Paradise,' you said."

"I don't know what you're saying. I said nothing. I was speechless, awestruck. It was the first time I'd witnessed anything like it."

"And all became clear. The clouds parted and the light shone through me."

"Glad to be of help," Roger whispered, not knowing what else to say.

"Here," Peping placed a polished stone on the table. "Take this with you. Go to Kiangan, Ifugao and find the police station. Look for the deputy chief, Abaya, and show this to him. He will know."

"Thank you."

"For what? What do you think this is about?"

"I'm not sure. But I've come far enough. What do you mean by the hour of the just?"

"That is for you to find out, Roger Geisler. That is why you have come."

An awkward silence ensued and Roger understood it was time for him to leave. He headed for the door then turned around. "So why do you keep it hanging on your wall then... if you no longer believe?"

The black man broke into a mild chuckle. "You of little faith," he whispered. "You still think its power comes from belief?" Peping then waved his hand to dismiss the younger man.

Roger remembered what it was he had really come to ask, "What happened that night?"

"Ah, the mystery, the not knowing is what really eats into the soul, isn't it?" Peping stared, but not at Roger.

"Who were they? Were they your men?"

Peping had to stifle a guffaw. "What do you think I am, some kind of mob boss?

"Did they do anything to me? I don't think I was harmed, or robbed."

"They were just having a bit of sport with you. Imagine, a strange white man roaming the back streets of Quiapo. Who did you think you were, Superman? Rambo? Elvis? The Beloved Apostle?" Peping couldn't hold back his laughter this time.

"Why did you come for me?" Geisler asked.

Peping turned, his eyes seemed uncertain. "*You* asked for me, did you not?"

Roger then trudged down the wooden stairs as an unseen insect nipping at the back of his nape. It struck him as he reached the bottom. As though clouds had parted and it became as clear as daylight that Jose Crenshaw—Tata Peping and the Black Christ—was nearly blind.

15
HAPPY BABY

CARMEN SAW HER mother now move about their home with the lightness and ease that seemed to have abandoned her for many years. She seemed younger, unburdened and this somehow disturbed and niggled the daughter.

"Don't you miss him?" Carmen asked.

Jackie eyed her daughter briefly then went back to marinating the duck. It was her turn to host their monthly book club meet. "He knows where *I* live," she said.

"So how is he?" the older woman asked after a while. "I know you're in touch."

"Okay, I guess." Carmen shrugged, playing with her hair.

Jackie frowned. "Has he involved you in some kind of trouble?"

"Of course not. Why'd you think that?"

Jackie eyed her daughter suspiciously. "You two are thick as thieves. I know there's stuff that's just between you and him."

"Not true!"

"He always wanted a son, didn't he?" Carmen asked.

It was Jackie's turn to shrug. "I guess every father wants one, deep down."

"Well, why didn't you... try?"

"Of course we did. But I've told you, my uterus' inverted, it was always difficult... then we sort of gave up."

"Maybe you didn't try hard enough?"

"What?" Jackie dropped her ladle and came at Carmen. "Listen, you, I don't know what lies your father's been saying behind my back but none of this is my fault. He left *us*!"

"I know. I'm sorry."

"I'm sorry too, I know it hasn't been easy for you as well, to be both daughter... and son."

"Oh, c'mon, Ma. You know I don't mind... I like sports, I loved Star Wars, I like the outdoors."

"Yes. You were always a bit of a tomboy..." Jackie smiled.

"Still am."

"So, are you?"

"Am I what? What are you asking Ma?"

"You know? I'm your mother. You can tell me things, *too*."

"So what do you want to know?"

"Are you a lesbian?"

"What? Women do sports! Women climb mountains!"

"And who was your last boyfriend? You're thirty-four. And what's with that white guy? What does he really want from you?"

"He's gay, Ma. And he's missing!"

"Is that what's bothering you? Have you and your father been looking for him?"

Carmen looked away. She was suddenly tearful.

"I'm not deaf. I hear you on the phone. So your father knows where this Roger is?'

"He knows someone who might."

"A woman?"

Carmen nodded and saw her mother turn away and walk back to her duck.

"But it's not what you think."

"Really? And what am I supposed to be thinking?"

"You know Dr. Duran... Anna Duran?"

"Ah... I might have guessed," Jackie whispered. "So what did he say? That she was the love of his life, and that I conspired against them, and so, now, I must pay?"

"No. It's nothing like that. She has a clinic in Quiapo. And I was brought there so father came..."

Jackie suddenly turned into a tigress, about to pounce. "Why were you in a clinic in Quiapo? What have you been up to?"

"I was looking for Roger and someone tried to mug me... I fainted."

Jackie exploded. "Maria Carmen! This has gone too far! Call your father! Now! I want to talk to him!"

Carmen knew it was impossible to deny her mother when she was in such mode. She went for her phone and waited for him to pick up. "I can't reach him."

Jackie poured herself a shot of brandy. "Carmen, dear. Listen, I don't care much what your father does with himself now. Maybe our time together is over, but you are mine, you are my life, you're all that matters, if should anything happen."

"Don't worry, Ma. It's all good."

"I don't want you going back there, promise."

She didn't like lying to her mother but the older woman's eyes begged her. She nodded.

"Did you love him?" Carmen asked.

"Well, how does that song go in Fiddler on the Roof? For twenty-five years I lived with him, fought with him, starved with him. Not *that* dreary, of course, we had money. And that's always at the back of a woman's mind... security. I didn't know about Anna and he never told me anything. I found out years

later, when he went back to climbing mountains. His mother…
your grandmother told me."

"Were you shocked? Bothered?"

"No. I was relieved."

"You didn't worry? That he might go back to her?"

"No. I knew, he wouldn't."

"Why?"

"You. He'd never abandon you. You were such a happy
baby.

"That's it." Carmen lit up. "Happy baby!"

"What now?" her mother asked.

"The message."

16
FUMIGATION

"YOU SURE YOU want to do this?" Jefferson asked Emily. The BBN had sent word that they would pick her up at the Horizons and that she was to come alone.

Emily nodded. She was beginning to remember the man speaking to her. Perhaps if she touched him the dam in her mind's screen would break and all her memories would come rushing back, but something told her it wasn't time.

"You don't have to do this," Carmen said. "It's too dangerous."

"I'm the only way in," Emily said. "You do want to find Roger, right?"

"Damn that Roger," Chester cut in. "He got himself into this hole. Let him find his own way out."

"Not exactly," Emily said, the others eyed her curiously. "I might have urged him on. *Him,* I remember."

"Him, you remember? You never even met! You communicated online, remember?" Jefferson said, exasperated.

Emily shrugged. "It had to do with my father, that's what I remember."

"That's what you *think,*" Jefferson said. As he pulled Emily aside, she pushed him off. "You're pregnant."

"What's it to you?"

"Well, is it mine, *ours*?"

Emily only stared at him, shrugging.

Jefferson was incredulous as Chester came between them. "This may not be the time to discuss."

"Stay out of this, chicken… Chester."

Chester glared at Jefferson and took Emily aside. They moved away from the hearing range of the others. "Look, Emily, I think you trust me by now. You have to tell Jefferson the truth. It's only fair. Is the child his?"

"I don't know," she whispered.

Chester balked. "Oh my. You may be blocking out a whole lot more. Listen, if you really want to do this, you have to trust Jefferson. He's your handler. He's the only one who can get you through this."

"Handler?"

"You're NBI. Both of you… at least you've been working with them for several months to find out what this Crenshaw is really up to. That's what Jefferson says, I believe him."

"He's a large, dark man, I remember." She scanned the place. "Lots of people were here, there was a party. Then someone came up to me, he seemed to know me and whispered that it might be best for us to clear the area. We should all leave now, he said, there would be fumigation."

"Fumigation?"

"Yes, that's what he said. Because of the crowd, I think…"

"Who was going to do it, the city government?"

"I don't know but I felt uneasy. I called to him, but he'd gone ahead and couldn't hear me. Then I started following, and running, and I saw this figure in orange, in a bio-hazard suit, with a contraption on his back. I sensed he was going to release something into the air. I saw the crowd. People were spread all over the streets, sitting, lying about. I raced towards the one in orange, then something, someone crashed into me. I was thrown to the ground then I saw him, the same one who warned me earlier. 'Get out of here! Go! It's happening!'"

"What? Were they going to poison the air?"

"I don't… then I …." She shook her head.

"You had your gun. Did you open fire? Did you shoot at the one in orange?"

"I …." Emily strained to recall what happened next but failed, hiding her face in her hands.

Jefferson approached, holding what looked like a pin. "Okay, if you want to do this, you know the SOP. You wear the transmitter. It's a tracking device," he said to Emily.

"What's that for? Drones?" Chester asked.

"What drones? This has a direct GPS link, Interpol. We'll be able to monitor her whereabouts constantly at the command center."

"Where's that?"

"Headquarters. I can set up a link, here, as well," Jefferson said and Chester tried not to seem too impressed. "We could send in the drones later, if need be."

"You think these guys won't suspect?" Chester asked.

"It must be placed where they wouldn't dare look."

Chester looked to Emily and Jefferson signaled for him to go away.

"No," Emily said.

"What do you mean "no"? This is protocol. You're an agent," Jefferson insisted.

"I don't remember any of that. All I know is that these guys are holding someone who may be my cousin, and in touch with someone who may be my father, and I want to know the truth. I'm not carrying any device or weapon that will endanger more lives."

"I can't allow that!" Jefferson said.

"It's not your choice. They're coming. If I don't show up, it's all over."

"This is madness!" Jefferson shouted and looked to Chester, pleading. "Chicken...."

"Shut up!" Chester retorted. "You might want to reconsider, Emily."

Emily only shook her head.

"We'll trail them! We've figured out... where their base is," Basilio said panting, carrying his biker's helmet.

"Who's *we*?"

"Him and me," Carmen said.

It was Chester's turn to balk. "No way! You've gotten yourself into enough danger, Nancy Drew!"

"Nancy Drew? What stone have you been sleeping under, Rip Van Wrinkle?"

"This is none of your business, have the cops trail them," Chester said, looking to Jefferson. "There's no actual case yet, and the bureau will want to know why our agent's not wearing a transmitter."

"It's near the Calinawan Caves in Tanay. That's the clue Roger left with Fr. Jaguar," Carmen said. "Lagos, he was referring to Laguna, then baby...bay... Laguna bay. Laguna de bai. Bai is "olden world for 'woman,'" mi lady...see? It's not too far from there; to the east are the Sierra Madre mountain ranges. That's the eastern mother, the caves are between the bay and the ranges, the fairy to the south is Mt. Makiling. Lastly, 'all that glister is not gold.' Once you enter the caves, you see fake glitter left behind by local and Hollywood productions."

"Why clues? Why not just say where he was or he was headed?" Chester asked.

"Perhaps he was having doubts about the group he was with," Carmen said.

Basilio chimed in, "I could smell pine and hear pigs last time. It reminded me of this place where we went to a few times as kids. One-eyed Gloria, Jose Crenshaw's adoptive *father*, occasionally organized these field trips for neighborhood kids to Tanay where she had a wooden *kamalig* for tomatoes and onions. We'd ride in her big jeepney. She'd tell us about farming and hard work then bring us to the nearby caves that she said the Katipunan once occupied. I remember how Jose always seemed embarrassed. He'd just sulk in some corner when we taunted him about his macho "papa." But then he would regale us later with tales about hidden Yamashita treasure that Gloria was supposedly digging for in other parts of the caves with his crew. Who knows, Peping maybe protecting a cache?"

"Not true, no treasure. These guys make money selling Wellington Lim's Vietnamese rubbers and Chinese sex toys and shaking down small time fiends. Tell them, Jefferson," Chester said.

"Well, in fact, there are people in the bureau looking into this hidden treasure business," he said.

"Oh, for Christ' sake, pokpok!"

Jefferson lit up like a hundred watts. "Hey, you remember?"

"Of course, you think you're the only one who recalls those blasted nicknames? Focus, man! You're the frigging NBI agent here!"

"Calinawan Caves? You know, there were reports of some dead crops and strange animal kills around the area, some months ago," Jefferson said. "I think some of our guys wanted to look into it."

"So?" Chester asked.

Jefferson shrugged. "I don't think they did. Cocaine showed up off the coasts of Isabela and Quezon and a lot of agents were sent there. "

"So what do we do now?"

"Well, if he wants to trail, let him trail. Those BBN guys will be here in a few minutes. What other move do we have? You'll need back up, though," Jefferson said to Basilio.

"No worries. He's here," Basilio said.

They saw another figure in a dark leather jacket come their way. When he removed his helmet, they saw it was Fr. Jaguar.

"This is Fr. Jaguar," Carmen said to Jefferson Po, "of Quiapo Church."

"So, you're the one. Are you allowed… to do this?"

"We serve where we are called," Jaguar said.

"We used to ride together, with some other guys, Quiapo's Angels," Basilio said, "before I went away, and he became a priest. It was only Hondas then, and Suzukis, two strokes, but we got as far as Pagudpud and Donsol."

"I knew you were a bad priest," Carmen said.

"The only kind there is," Fr. Jaguar replied.

"One of you should wear the transmitter," Jefferson said.

Basilio and Jaguar eyed each other.

"I want it on her." Chester pointed to Carmen, who brightened. "Well if you must, you must," Chester said.

"Don't worry, sir, I'll take care of her," Basilio said.

"I used to ride, too," Carmen said, turning to her dad.

"Those were the days," Chester sighed.

"Why did we stop?" Carmen asked.

"We got older, busier…."

"You feared I was becoming too much of a guy, right?"

"Your mom didn't like it and you were a bit of a daredevil."

"And you were a scaredy cat, who wouldn't go over 160. You were on the Harley and you'd lag."

"I'd worked on my fair share of accident victims."

"You had a Harley Davidson?" Fr. Jaguar's eyes lit up.

"Still there."

"Can I borrow it sometime? It will be for church purposes, of course, outreach programs."

"Why not? Poor thing needs some exercise, give it a blessing while you're at it."

"To stations," Basilio said and the bikers hurried off.

"Transmitter," Chester reminded Carmen and Jefferson handed it to her.

Chester saw both fear and gladness in his daughter and felt a swelling from inside him.

17

THE CHASE

BASILIO AND JAGUAR positioned their bikes at opposite ends of the road tangential to Horizons'. Manito entered the bar and patted down Emily in front of Jefferson and passed the metal detector across her body. He removed the cell phone from her purse, before leading her out to the monster truck. Jefferson was impressed with the vehicle and a tad intimidated.

Chester watched from the back room, the bar was still closed. "That's Crenshaw's right-hand guy, Manito," Jefferson said when the BBN left with Emily.

"I saw him," Chester said, "that morning, among the injured. He was trying to help."

"Maybe he was looking for Emily," Jefferson said.

Aboard the truck, Emily was ushered onto the back seat. She could see in the rear view mirror that the driver was eyeing her. She knew at once he was the one who came to warn her that night about the fumigation, the same one who rammed into her later.

"This is Brother Vergel," Manito said, "in case you forgot." He looked incredulous. "You really lost your memory?"

Emily kept her peace as she tried to recall the one named Manito. There was a tinge of acridness to the voice, she thought, or, perhaps, jealousy.

"You shot at Brother Mario. You caused a stampede. You know how many died?"

"He was about to poison the crowd," Emily blurted, unsure where the words came from, but her heart began to race. She could feel fear and anguish.

"Fumigating. They'd been pissing all over the place in case you hadn't noticed."

"Don't bullshit me," she retorted.

Manito hissed and shook his head.

"Nitrous oxide, know what that is?"

"Laughing gas?"

Manito smirked. "You're smart for a singer, aren't you? What are you, *really*?"

Emily shrugged. "I went to Philippine Science High."

"I see beauty and brains. And why did you have gun on you?"

"Protection, all sorts of people come to bars. Nitrous oxide.... You want to make people laugh? Don't they get enough of that from Wowie?"

"So you're a fan?"

"Yup."

"You think we want to kill innocent people? You think that's what Tata Peping wants? What *we* want?"

"What *do* you want, then?"

"To awaken them."

"From what?"

"From sleep. From over a century of slumber, of sleepwalking."

"What on earth are you talking about?"

"We were once a people with genuine spirit. Awakened. We threw off the foreign yoke, founded a republic and, when betrayed, continued to fight until they razed our villages, orphaned us, chained our spirit. Turned us against ourselves. We took to the mountains to protect our ancient spirit. Then they sold us more lies: Independence, New Society, People Power, EDSA Dos, EDSA Tres... they called us dirty, scum! Yet, we have not surrendered."

"And you think Crenshaw is about continuing the Revolution? You think he's political? You sure you're on the same page?"

"He plays the part, talks his talk. It's the only thing downtrodden people will buy—mystery, magic, miracle—that's how it's always been. Bagong Kristo, Bagong Herusalem, there will be poor pilgrims retreating to another Eden with another savior, another God."

"And isn't your Tata Peping another one of them?"

"No! He never claimed to be a Christ! *Itim na Nazareno*: that's what his enemies say, that's what the media, the Church uses to mock him!"

"Why?"

"Because they fear him, because he speaks the truth: Look into yourselves, he tells them, make of your lives your sword and shield, because people believe him."

"Because he's a big, black dude, with a beard and resembles the...."

"No! Stop! Don't malign him, not *you*! If anyone knows the real Tata, it's you. You've known him as no one else can."

"Oh no..." Emily felt nauseous as she placed a hand to her belly. She wracked her brains to remember what she should. She imagined throwing herself against the door in her mind's screen but merely bounced off. Then the serpent's head loomed large, bared its fangs, and she fell back.

"This time there will be no retreat, no mountain sanctuary. We make our stand where we were born, in the heart of our city, in the black heart of our city!" Manito said, but not to her.

"You have to be safe, no matter what. We'll protect you," Vergel said.

"Shut up!" Manilo growled at the driver.

Emily swallowed her tears. She would not show weakness but the dam was breaking, her memories were returning and she was beginning to see a life in ruins. "So were they supposed to laugh their way to enlightenment?"

"They would have been blissful, rested, all together, as one, slept as innocents, have their spirits renewed by Tata Peping and awoken at daybreak to a new truth. Imagine a hundred thousand people refreshed, revived, restored, walking away from the absurdity, from those lies, regaining their dignity and self-respect. Turning their backs on that insanity." Manito seemed entranced but she could hear doubt in him and knew he was as lost as her.

"Are you trying to get people hooked on laughing gas? Is that the grand plan?" She started to laugh.

"Shut up!" Manito pointed his .45 at Emily and she clammed up.

"It's not addictive! Tata doesn't hurt the innocent. It was you who got them killed bitch! You! I don't know what he sees in you but you don't fool me. I got my eyes on you! Now shut up and put this on!" He threw something at her.

She saw that it was a ski mask with no holes for eyes, but only for the nose. "No!"

"Put it on." He pointed the weapon at her once more, and she obeyed. Her world turned dark as an acridness shot up her nose into the back of her skull, and colors exploded in her mind's screen.

Basilio kept the monster truck in sight as he trailed three vehicles behind, while Jaguar was further back. They communicated by hand signals, but also kept their phones on speaker.

Manito looked at the side mirror and saw the motorbike with a black helmeted rider trailing. He looked to Vergel. "Basilio?" he asked the driver, who nodded. "Brother, your light is fading."

At the turnpike off Sta. Rosa, the truck took a sudden turn, veered off the expressway and headed into high grass. Basilio was surprised, swerving back, and turned into the grass as well and so did Jaguar. The truck crashed through high grass and shrub with the two motorbikes in pursuit.

"Hold on," Basilio said to Carmen, who clung to him for dear life. The thrill of riding rushed back to her as they sped past undergrowth and flew over tree stumps. The thought that they were being led into a trap hit Basilio a split second before they were airborne, caught inside the cargo net hanging between treetops. He grabbed onto the bike to keep it and himself from crashing down on Carmen. He pulled himself up by the hemp to let her settle safely. Jaguar looked up at his ensnared friends like a hunter marveling over a prize catch.

"Are you alright?" he shouted.

At Horizons, Jefferson and Chester were watching the monitor as the pulse speeding across the wilds of Laguna suddenly stopped moving.

Chester panicked, looking to Jefferson. "What happened? Do something! Send in your drones!"

"Calm down," Jefferson said as his phone rang. It was Jaguar.

It took nearly an hour for the chopper to find them. Two Special Action Team Police officers scrambled up the trees to cut down the cargo net.

Chester hugged Carmen for dear life as she scrambled out of the net. "This stops here! Enough of this!"

"Don't be a sissy, Dad. It's just getting fun."

"Fun? These wackos are seriously demented. It's police business from now on and we're out of it!"

"You can call in choppers?" Basilio asked Jefferson, impressed.

"I got some credit with the bureau," he said with some pride.

"You nearly got my daughter...." Chester started but stopped to demand: "Now fly us out of this mess!"

18
THE CAVE

SHE AWOKE TO a space that was both familiar and strange. A part of her had been here before, but it might be a part she had wanted to lop off like an unwanted, gangrened limb.

"It was a mistake," the thought flashed through her. She saw a charcoal portrait of herself and remembered the other one in Chester Limhuatco's place. Why were these men always drawing portraits of her? But there were other portraits: Women, men, children, animals and creatures she couldn't make out. Some were plain; others grotesque and unintelligible. They were of charcoal, ink, crayons and oil. There was a large oil painting of a woman with a transparent womb and a fetus that seemed reptilian. She balked. He was an artist, she remembered. The room was cool.

Then he knocked and entered with a cup of coffee he handed her. No longer robed or hooded, but a tall man in a blue sweatshirt and running pants. He might have been an athlete warming up, save that he now used a cane.

Glaucoma, she remembered. He was nearly blind in one eye and the other was also beginning to go. It happened after the last time he was crucified. He had thought it was temporary blindness caused by the trauma but the doctors said it was congenital. It was only a matter of time. There was little science could do.

But he started seeing with another eye—his third eye, his followers say, seeing things past and to come, and began healing with his touch. "The Lord blinded me so I may bask in his light," he said.

Other illnesses started appearing in his blood, his lungs, his liver and kidney. "What must be done must be done soon," he told Manito. "I do not have a lot of time left. And if I fall, you must continue."

His words had lifted the young man, filled the gaping hole inside him. Years ago, he had come to mock the black man in flowing robes, castigated him for being another charlatan out to fleece the poor. However, Tata Peping had held Manito's forehead and sent a heat down his spine that seemed to sear his every pore. Then he whispered into the younger one's ear: "Do not fear dragonfly, your wings grow strong."

Dragonfly. He was stunned. How could this guy know? It was what his mother often called him ever since he caught his first dragonfly at seven. She was a labor leader, and would be felled by bullets from unknown assailants six years later. Maybe this messiah was indeed different, Manito had thought, one truly inspired. He was willing to surrender his own logic to a different knowing, a higher knowing, perhaps. Through the years, Peping had seemed more and more a Nazareno who would inspire others to throw off the burden of their crosses rather than bear them for another millennia; one who would strike down the Pharisee and expel the moneylenders from the temple for good. He spoke of change, earthly and spiritual. "Nazareth was the seed," he once said to Manito who reveled in the man's presence, "we must bring to fruition."

Then she came into their lives, into their lair and the man seemed transformed, distracted and careless. Peping had asked Manito to check her out at the Horizons. He had recorded her singing "The First Time ever I saw His Face" on video.

When he saw Peping's eyes transfixed on the mobile screen, Manito felt the worm boring into his heart. "We are incomplete," Peping said. "She will be our other pillar. We need sisters as well. When the time comes, she will gather them."

Manito was stunned. "But we don't even know her. Let me check on her further."

"I will meet with her," Peping decided and Manito knew this was where everything went downhill.

"Emily," he said in his other voice, mellow and calm. "I hope you are well rested. I'm sorry for all that ruckus, but you were being trailed. And by Basilio, it turns out. I had hoped he could be won over, be a leader among us, but I fear he is set against us. He means to destroy all we've built."

Emily looked about, uncomprehending. "Where am I? What is this place?"

"You really don't remember?"

"I remember some."

"We're in the caves. This is our safe place, our place of power. You were here last month."

"Blindfolded."

"Precautions."

"Your headquarters?"

"This is the home of the Spirit, Emily. We have returned to the source of spirit and what the spirit can do is beyond imagining."

"What are you planning?"

"All will come to pass soon, but you are now with child, so you must stay with us and be safe."

"Did you drug me?"

"Emily? You really don't remember?"

She shook her head.

"We had some wine. I wouldn't have done anything against your will, Emily. You know that."

"I… I'm confused. I was tipsy."

"I swear."

"Was it here?"

"No, in your room, at the bar. That night, I came alone… in casual clothes. We sang a duet, that song. I sang in public after so many years. I couldn't help it. There weren't too many people around. I don't think anyone knew me. Then you invited me to your room upstairs. You said the manager wasn't around."

"It was a different you."

"Same, Emily."

"You said you wanted to drop all of it, that it was getting out of hand. You wanted a new life, you said we would have another life, together."

"I was tired and weak. It was a mistake, my Gethsemane."

Mistake. The word lashed across her mind's screen like a whip.

"But I will not abandon you, Emily, or our child. We must make things right. We must marry."

Emily gasped.

"I have made the arrangements. Don't worry, now I think there is someone you have been wanting to meet."

And with that, Peping left to give her privacy.

Someone then entered the room, who was shorter than she anticipated and thinner than on his social media photo. "Hi, Emily. I'm Roger Geisler."

Emily stared at the white man before her. "Are you really my cousin?"

"I'm afraid so," he answered and smiled.

"And you've met him… the White Igorot?"

"Twice, in 2010, then last week."

"Is he my father?"

"Yes. Your mother was Kalinga, she died shortly after giving birth to you. You were a weak child and her people feared you would not survive. So he asked the soldier to bring you to Maria Mahiwo."

"Does he have other children?"

"So I hear, with several women."

"How many?"

"You must ask him yourself."

"Is he here, in Manila?"

"No, but soon you will meet. He says it is time for the boulder to roll down to sea. When the thunder is heard, the sleepers will awake."

"Does he want to see me?"

"Yes, very much. He believes it's time."

"What's he up to? Is he working with Crenshaw?"

"They've met, in the north, that's all I know. They said he baptized Tata Peping on the Chico River."

"What a pair," Emily said sarcastically, gazing at Roger. "Are *you* working with them?"

"I'm in too deep. I have to see things through, but you don't have to get involved in any of this. Vergel, he can help."

"I have Peping's child," she said.

"Are you sure?"

She shook her head. "No, but I feel like time is running out. I want to meet Gerard De Bruyne. I must."

"You may not like him."

"He's still my father."

"We come through them, not *from* them, as the poet says."

"He's inside me too."

"Then steel yourself."

"Carmen Limhuatco's been looking for you."

"I shouldn't have gotten her involved. She should stay away from this…"

"Might be too late for that. I don't think she lets go easy. Is it really just laughing gas they're making down here?

"I hope so. I facilitated their imports from Europe. At least, I think my uncle got them to veer away from nastier stuff. Once I saw them inflate balloons with nitrous oxide from canisters, passed them around and inhaled from them."

"You didn't join?"

"I pretended to but I didn't inhale… not too much. Anyway they were all having a ball when Peping showed up. They perked up and gathered around him. He extolled the gas for all its benefits to body and mind. Still, it's just an instrument, he said. One must let go of the past in order to let the Spirit in. Blood must cleanse in the time of the just."

"What does he mean?"

"I don't know, though the others seem to because they nodded. Then he went into a trance and was soon channeling Jose Rizal, Bonifacio and some guy Bernardo Carpio…"

"A mythical hero. What'd he say?"

"That he had awakened and soon the mountains would rumble as he break free of his chains and the wrath of the just would be upon all. Then it turned all solemn and he was channeling the Holy Spirit, then the Nazarene, then God the Father."

"Like a lot of other mediums," Emily said.

"I know. I've seen my fair share in Banahaw and elsewhere, but he is different, Emily, He frightens me…"

"Why?"

"It's like there's this whole other side to him that doesn't want to do any of this. When he's not in robes, he's like some super hero without his cape who just wants to chill. Then wham! Something gives and he's the instrument of some higher power again."

"I think I know what you mean. What do you think the end game is, if any?"

Roger shrugged. "I suspect things took a turn when he met your father. From then on, he grew his ambition."

"He knows De Bruyne is my father?

"Yes."

"Who tipped off Peping that I was at Horizons? You or De Bruyne?"

The door opened and someone entered, buried it seemed beneath a big pile of clothing. It was Manito, who laid the dress wrought from jusi and nylon that had colors of the Philippine flag on the bed.

"Tata says for you to try it on."

"What's that?"

"Your bridal gown."

"What?"

"Yes. It seems your long lost father will not only be giving you away, but he's also agreed to officiate your wedding."

"Is this some sick joke?"

"You see me laughing?"

She looked to Roger as if for rescue.

"I've seen my fair share of those too," he said, looking at the dress.

Manito turned to leave.

"Manito," Emily called out. "You can't think this will all just end in some big laughing gas party that will turn people into patriots magically?"

"You think you got us all figured, don't you, Ms. Philippine Science? Well, you don't know shit, so just do as you're told. You're just another white priest's bastard." Manito said and marched off.

"They're holding the wedding here?" she asked.

Roger shrugged. "Some tourists did it last time I was here, in another part of the cave system. The Katipunan did so too, I hear, in their time. In the olden religion, caves were sacred sites."

"So my father's coming here?"

"Who knows? He's not left the Cordilleras in decades."

They both fell silent.

"What are you willing to do, Emily, when shit hits the fan?" Roger asked.

"What do you mean?"

"You shot at someone the last time."

"Did more harm than good."

"Still. Will you do it again, if you have to?

Emily nodded.

Roger looked down. "You were your father's trump card. The only way he could get Peping and his network and to work with him."

She felt a mix of anger and disappointment when they heard an explosion, causing the earth to shake.

"It's collapsing!" She heard someone shout.

19
CALINAWAN

"SO WHERE ARE your GPS and drones?" Chester insisted, trying Jefferson's patience.

"We don't have coordinates. We have to rely on ground Intel," the other man reiterated.

Despite Chester's protests, they all proceeded to the Calinawan Caves after Basilio and Carmen were freed from their trap, except for Fr. Jaguar, who rode back to Quiapo for evening mass.

"I thought you had it figured out?" Chester turned on Basilio. "So where's this *kamalig* you played in as a child? Where are your pines and pigs?"

They had entered the caves where some high school students were on a field trip, saw the glitters, scoured the nooks and crannies but could find no sign of Tata Peping or any of his followers, who took part in the dark ritual Basilio described.

"We were inside a cave," Basilio said. "I know it's here somewhere or maybe another branch of this system, away from the tourist area."

"Maybe we should go home," Chester said.

"There." Jefferson pointed to a structure around twenty meters away, as they emerged from the cave.

"Looks like a *kamalig* to you?" Chester asked.

"Maybe more concrete now than bamboo and wood, let's check it out," Basilio said.

"Really?" Chester whined.

As they approached the structure they could see a fence, then men in blue overalls unloading blue plastic barrels from two trucks.

"Wait," Basilio whispered. "Keep out of sight, I know those guys. They're with the Kapatiran."

"You sure?" Jefferson asked.

"I don't forget faces."

"Well, there you go. Call in the drones and the Special Action Team," Chester said.

Jefferson glared at him.

"They may be stockpiling chemicals for nerve gas or God knows what?" Chester insisted.

"Or manure for their organic farm," Jefferson said.

"They have organic farms?" Carmen asked.

"According to Intel."

"Or Tata Peping's bath water," Basilio said.

They all stared at him.

"Some of his diehards think it has healing properties," he went on. "They plan to bottle the water and sell them in Quiapo for twenty pesos each."

"Serious?" Carmen asked.

"Well, surely you can arrest them for *that*," Chester argued. "No way any of it is FDA approved!"

"Shut up, chicken. Look over there," Jefferson said, taking out a pair of binoculars from his bag as he hid behind a clump of rocks. "I saw pictures of that at the bureau."

"Give it here." Chester grabbed the binoculars from

Jefferson and peered into them. "It's just a field of rotten tomatoes. So what?"

"They seemed sucked dry and two meters from that… warehouse. Who knows what goes on in there?" Jefferson wondered.

"And that's what they teach you at the NBI? Beware of rotten tomatoes, two meters from a warehouse with blue barrels?" Chester sneered.

He scanned further with the binoculars and saw a backhoe and what appeared to be a huge water pump and drill.

"And what's that?" Chester asked.

Jefferson retrieved the binoculars and looked. "Seems someone's digging."

"Mining?" Carmen asked.

"Treasure hunting," Basilio said. "They've long been rumors of Japanese war booty buried hereabout. Peping used to tell us about one-eyed Gloria hunting for treasure in these parts."

"Child's talk," Chester dismissed.

"I'm checking it out," Basilio said and hurried over, followed by the others.

They found what seemed to be an abandoned mineshaft.

"There's no one around," Carmen said.

"Probably private property," Chester added.

"Seems like they've given up finding anything," Jefferson surmised.

"Doesn't look safe, could be caved-in," Chester noted.

"I'm going in," Basilio said.

"You nuts?" Chester asked. "We need a warrant, right, Jefferson?"

"This could be it, the passage to the Kapatiran's lair," Basilio said and moved down towards the opening. "I can feel it."

"So now you're psychic, too? What's with you people?" Chester mocked.

"I'll come," Carmen said, following Basilio.

"NO!" Chester shouted but failed to grab Carmen as he slipped on the loose earth.

"Alright, I'll lead the way," Jefferson said, taking out his torch as Chester hung back, exasperated.

"Are you coming or not?" Carmen asked.

Chester trailed the group reluctantly as they wound their way through the tunnel. In the darkness, the walls glittered.

"Fool's gold," Jefferson said, to keep the others focused on moving forward until they reached an ornate wooden door.

"This is it," Basilio said. "I was here, but on the other side. Emily's there, too."

"And how do we get to her?" Chester asked. "Should we ask nicely?"

"Maybe we can trade you for her," Jefferson suggested.

Suddenly, a phone rang.

"Whose is that?" Carmen asked, peeved.

"We're too deep for any cell signal to reach," Chester said.

"It's mine. It receives ground penetrating signals," Jefferson said.

"You and your…" Chester was beginning to say when an alarm went on.

"Oh, no…" Jefferson groaned. "Might have triggered a booby trap. Run!"

They scrambled out of the tunnel chased by sporadic explosions. The earth began to shake and rubble fell on them. Chester felt a rock hit his face but charged ahead as he led the rush towards the entrance. Then he saw daylight and leapt. He crawled out of what was now a man-sized hole then pulled Jefferson to safety. Jefferson in turn pulled out Basilio, who then pulled on Carmen but a wooden beam fell on her. It did not hit her directly, though, as rocks were in the way. Still, Carmen was trapped as more explosions sounded from inside the tunnel. The men each gained enough grip on the beam, and at the count of three, managed to lift it high enough for Carmen to slip through. They scampered to safety before a final explosion caused a landslide that closed down the shaft completely.

Chester hugged Carmen for dear life. She was hyperventilating. He had to calm her, massaging her back.

"Dear Lord, no more of this," Chester lamented. "No more."

20
AT THE BBN

"DID YOU KILL someone in Japan, Brother Basilio?" Peping asked. He had requested Basilio to meet him at the Kapatiran office in Quiapo over urgent matters. Basilio suspected that Peping distrusted him but pretended nonchalance.

"What? Of course not."

"Yet you fled, with another man's passport?"

"To be safe. I was an illegal, I knew the victim, lived in his place. I was an easy suspect. How come you know this?"

"We have our means. This victim was your friend?" Peping asked.

"Yes. He took me in."

"He was one of peculiar ways, they say."

"He was gay; a homosexual, if that's what you mean."

"And this bothered you?"

"Of course not. Why would I stay with him otherwise? I have many gay friends."

"You share their ways?"

"No!"

"I've disrespected you. I'm sorry."

"No. I'm not gay, but I don't mind them."

"Still, you might have had a few to drink? He might have said something, touched you in a wrong or strange way."

"No! What are you trying to do? I told you, I didn't hurt him. I left!"

Basilio stood up and paced. "I left his place. I went to bunk with another Pinoy."

"Brother Hiroshi."

"You know him too. Did he tell you?"

"It doesn't matter, Brother Basilio."

"I never said anything to him."

"Memories are fragile, brother, as in the case of our sister, Emily. We know you've been in touch with her. It's okay, this is all part of Gód's plan. We remember what we will. It serves our purpose, His purpose."

"She was looking for Roger Geisler."

"Yes. And she's found him. He was your herald?'

"Who?"

"The Swede. The spirit employed him to summon you home."

Then it struck him. "Ponce," he whispered inwardly. He was Peping's source. Ponce had been a penitent himself and was "crucified" once. He works on vessels that sail to Rotterdam regularly, hangs out in a place frequented by Filipino seamen. That's where he must have met Roger. It was Ponce, who sent Roger to him, Basilio figured. He balked. He seemed trapped in an elaborate web spawned by Jose Crenshaw that spanned the globe.

"I did not kill Akiko—James Rosales," Basilio insisted.

"So it is, as you say. Still, the Tokyo police have not solved the case and they continue to look."

"It's been twelve years."

"I've told you, the brotherhood is near and far, Basilio, and we protect our own. Do not be distracted, in any case, as your moment approaches."

"How so?"

"We would like you to be among the Hijos who will protect the Nazareno during this year's traslación. I'm sure your father's former colleagues will gladly welcome you and your friend, the deputy Parish priest will not object."

Basilio felt his gut stiffen. "I've done it only once, so long ago. I wouldn't know the first thing to do."

"You will be guided by the Spirit, Brother Basilio. Do not worry."

Basilio could do nothing but nod.

"I sensed a heavy burden on you, brother. "Cast your burden upon me all you who are tired and heavily laden," our Lord says."

"It's nothing. I'm still acclimating."

"If you will allow me, brother," Peping began and stood up. He moved behind Basilio and held the other man's shoulder before he could react.

Peping squeezed Basilio's shoulders and he felt like a ball suddenly deflated, with oxygen rushing out of him. He felt light as air and wanted to sleep. Then Peping held Basilio's head. He massaged the man's scalp and nape. Basilio relaxed and lost track of time. Then he felt warmth in his crown that spread and flowed down his spine like hot liquid. Basilio imagined a snake reaching for the pit of his spine then there was only the air-conditioned breeze and birds chirping and an ocean. He was afloat, drifting to the far horizon.

Akiko was in his blue kimono with embroidered white sakura. He was massaging Basilio's scalp, nape and back. Basilio was drowsy. Then he felt spines tingling his neck. When he came to, branches from the sakura crept all over him, intent on strangling him, it seemed. He stood up and pulled off the vines. Then he grabbed Akiko's throat as Akiko backed off.

"No!" he begged.

Basilio squeezed harder than he intended, his hand doing its own bidding as she started to choke.

Basilio awoke in a fit. He turned and saw Tata Peping staring at him.

"You had a good sleep, brother?" Peping asked. "You needed it. What's the matter, bad dream?"

Basilio shook his head.

"You had a vision perhaps?"

Basilio shook his head again.

"Don't worry, it will come when the time is ripe," Peping said.

"It's not true," Basilio whispered and Tata Peping peered at him.

"Not true." he whispered again and hurried off.

21
NATIVITY

"BE HOME FOR Christmas, dad, that's all I ask," Carmen had said to Chester after that incident in Laguna.

And so he had arrived on the eve of the nativity at their house in Polk Street in Greenhills, after nearly a year. It was the home he had shared with Jackie for thirty years, where Carmen grew up. It was the house his parents Raul and Emma had built for their firstborn as a wedding gift. Chester had fulfilled his father's wish that he become a cardiovascular surgeon. Raul always feared that heart trouble ran in the family, as his own father died from an attack. The brokerage business was left to the care of his younger brother, Denis to the relief of Chester, who did not have a business bone in him.

Denis died of pancreatic cancer at thirty-five and he had never married. His parents fell into a deep depression, sold off the business and stayed cooped up in their home in Dasmarinas Village, Makati. Chester visited regularly and almost moved back into his old home to care for his parents, but they refused. Carmen had turned sixteen then. Within eight months, Emma died in her sleep. Raul suffered a fatal stroke a year later.

There was nothing Chester could do. He wanted to quit medicine but Jackie threatened to leave with their daughter, so he came out of his funk. His trust in his abilities and in his science was deeply shaken though.

Jackie herself had grown up in Greenhills. Not long after her marriage, her parents and two siblings migrated to Canada when their real estate business went bust, followed by death threats.

Since then, family had always been just the three of them.

Chester brought roses for Jackie. It was the first time he had done so since the first years of marriage. He wasn't sure what he wanted it to say, whether it was a peace offering or preamble to coming home.

Did he wish to come home?

No, he quickly realized when he saw Jackie. She was beaming and he knew it was all due to his absence. Couples either became closer or they grew apart, but what he feared most was pulling her down with him once he could no longer tread water. He felt affection for her still, but wondered now if he had ever loved her and vice versa? He knew he was doing this to appease Carmen. Her growing recklessness, he felt, was her way of reaching out and pulling him back.

"I'm not coming home," he wanted to say to both women but thought better. It was Christmas, a time for good cheer and lies.

I will die alone, the thought struck him suddenly, profoundly and he sipped his wine. "What a year," he whispered a toast.

"I have a friend who's looking for a place, dad, near your condo, I was thinking...," his daughter started.

"I'm buying it, Carmen. I've told my landlord."

Silence descended upon the dinner table. "An angel passing," Chester thought.

"Property is property," Jackie said, "not a bad buy."

Carmen left the table.

"I'm not coming home," Chester whispered.

"I know," Jackie said. "You have to tell her sometime."

"She won't listen."

"Why was she in Anna Duran's clinic? What's going on?'

"She's been looking for her friend, Roger Geisler, the one who researches the Nazareno."

"Are you with Anna?'

"What? No. No, it's not like that. Someone injected her with a mild sedative and bystanders took her to the clinic. She had my card in her purse."

"She's all I have left, Chester."

He wanted to cry suddenly, but he knew he would never leave if he did. He would have to return to this place, to his old life. "Not yet," he thought to himself, "not yet."

"I know," he said to his wife and held her hand.

"Did you ever want me?"

He touched her face. "It's been over thirty years," he whispered.

"That's not what I asked you," she said, so he nodded slowly. It was Christmas, after all.

22
NAVEL

THE CAVERN WAS well lit. There were AV/TV monitors and WIFI connection though the signal was sporadic. An air vent funneled fresh air in. Emily realized that this was the true headquarters of the brotherhood. She had been here before.

The men were in *camisa*. Some were snorting gas from small balloons. She knew they were doing laughing gas. She felt relaxed herself. People seemed to be enjoying themselves with none of the eerie tension she remembered from before. Someone was playing the guitar, a Spanish sounding tune while another danced. Emily suddenly realized she was the only woman in the place but felt no unease. It struck her that this was the true lair of the Brotherhood, its "navel."

Then Tata Peping appeared and the crowd hushed. The music stopped. All eyes turned to the half-naked man with a python wrapped about his torso. Emily was stunned. She saw the serpent's head and a light seemed to burst inside her. Peping seemed aglow. The coconut oil on him, that he used to heal others, made his body glisten. She realized how well built he was. He could have stepped out of a gladiator movie and she felt her heart racing like a wild stallion.

"The time of the just is near, our power grows," he intoned. "The gas is good. It helps open our minds, to hear the silence, see into the deep, but the steel in your character, you must draw from within. Our task will not be easy. It has only begun. We may be mocked and vilified, persecuted, hunted. Be strong, be brave, be true."

His words send a chill up her spine. This was the side of him she feared and it was growing stronger.

"Master, is this right? Is this the instrument we need?" It was Manito, imploring. He had refused to partake of the gas. It was an aberration, a dangerous distraction, weakening: an opiate. He was agitated. Things were taking a destructive turn. He feared the worst, feared that he might have to take things into his own hands.

When he first joined the brotherhood, a light seemed to have shone through Manito's mind like a laser vanishing all doubt, but now there was only confusion. His Chemical Engineering degree had impressed Tata Peping, who kept him close, and Manito felt he had found a mentor worthy of utmost loyalty. Jose Crenshaw kept faith in science and technology as much as in the Spirit. They were the twin pillars of the brotherhood, he averred—its sword and shield.

Two doctors and four nurses eventually joined Peping for the BBN's healing sessions weekly at the Quiapo office, part of which was turned into a medical clinic. Peping asked Manito to hook up the Brotherhood's operations to the Web and organize IT training for street kids; many of whom were brought in as staffers to help spread the BBN's work online.

He spoke to Manito about developing organic fertilizers for use in pilot farms in Laguna and Nueva Ecija that would be funded by Swedish monies and linked to European markets. Manito wondered where all the resources were coming from but was not privy to the group's finances. He only knew that

Tata Peping had access to Wellington Lim and there were the hawker fees and dues from members. Peping gave Manito a monthly stipend to manage the group's open projects. It was enough but money was the least of his cares.

Then Tatang Peping sought audience with Fr. Dimalanta to clear the air but was rebuffed. He was beginning to see himself as an important leader after a TV interview. He hoped to meet with the archbishop but the call never came. Then Tata Peping asked Manito to register the BBN with the Comelec so they could run under the Party List system in midterm elections but was again denied. Manito saw Peping turn morose.

"They will never listen," he said to Manito.

When Fr. Dimalanta started to denounce him from the pulpit, Peping went to church one Sunday and marched right up to the Parish priest during Holy Communion, parting the crowd effortlessly. It was the assistant Parish priest Fr. Jaguar who came between them. Dimalanta had to be taken to the hospital shortly after. By then, critics were becoming scurrilous. He was being dubbed the "black mamba."

"The rot is too deep," Peping said to Manito, hearing the pain and steel in his voice. "We have to uproot weeds, vermin, plow and let fallow before we can grow."

"Nitrate is used for fertilizers," Peping went on. "It is used for explosives as well, yes?"

Manito felt his heart pound against his ribcage. He stared into Peping's eyes and saw why, alas, he had been kept close.

"We may have to defend ourselves," the older man had said. "We wont be like the Lapian in '67".

Manito knew Tata was referring to the Lapiang Malaya, a 40,000-strong movement founded by another spiritual leader, Valentin de los Santos, in the 1940's. He too communed with spirits and revolutionary heroes. In October 1966, one thousand members armed with bolos tried to disrupt a summit among seven nations allied with the U.S. during the Vietnam War that was being hosted by Pres. Marcos in Manila and were dispersed by the police without incident. The following May, De los Santos called for the resignation of Marcos and declared the formation of the Lapiang Malaya government. The Philippine Constabulary (PC) and the local police cordoned off the Lapian's headquarters in Pasay. On Saturday, May 20, newspaper publisher Chino Roces and Pasay Mayor Pablo Cuneta visited the group's headquarters to urge De los Santos to stand down, but his "generals" refused, claiming they were "sons of Andres Bonifacio," and feared no one.

At dawn on May 21, as members of the movement tried to break through the security cordon and march on Malacañang, the PC and police opened fire, killing scores of De los Santos' followers along Taft Avenue. Valentin and his lieutenants would be arrested and thrown into a mental asylum, where he died years later. Manito had heard of it from his father, Ricardo, a bystander then, as was Manito and his uncle in May of '86, when police opened fire on peasants in Mendiola, just outside the Presidential palace, killing many.

But, in February 2001, he was no bystander. He had marched on Malacañang with his mates, who called for the restoration of Erap who had been ousted and jailed. Erap was no Bonifacio, for sure, but he was the people's choice and had every right to finish his term. Wasn't this the promise of democracy? Wasn't this why people flocked to EDSA in '86? But they were sneered at and mocked by priests and matrons, deemed unwashed and misguided. It was a night of rage and mayhem. The politicians, who had fired pistols and called for the palace assault, would later disappear. Manito had rushed headlong into a phalanx of riot police in Mendiola to protect his girlfriend Karen, whose parents would fly her off to Cebu after the incident, and suffer a beating that would scar him deeply. He would remember every blow to the head, the back, the groin; someone pulling his hair, dragging him along the street, his back burning, a boot on his face, his neck, his gut! Spitting blood!

And now, Manito saw the woman entranced by the man and his python. She was the worm inside the fruit—the mole. He was never more certain now that she was the enemy. Then he saw her being summoned to the stone altar by Tata Peping.

Peping held out his hand to Emily and they knelt by a manger beside a bull's head hanging on a pole beside a live goat. He took off the coiled python and gently laid it on the manger, the BBN's nativity set. Then he touched her forehead and prayed over her. The crowd knelt as well and he laid his hand now on her navel.

Manito touched the handle of the knife that had been entrusted to him for safe keeping, Basilio's knife. He was certain now of its purpose.

23
TRASLACION

THE LAST TIME he was atop the *carroza* of the Nazarene Basilio, he was twenty. It was fifteen years past, a lifetime ago. He had never imagined doing it again. He had already fled from this, crossed two oceans to be away, now he was back to replace his father, to avenge his death.

When Basilio asked to be an Hijo in the year's traslación, he was welcomed with open arms by the group. He was an Ambahan, after all, and it was his rightful place. Alderman Nico Bragais, Conrado's old friend, embraced Basilio, tearful. "Thank God you have returned, Basilio," he said, "but you must swear to have nothing to do with that madman Peping."

"I will never have anything to do with him," Basilio said, his windpipe tightening. The Hijos were the last people he wanted to deceive, but this was the only way for him to gain Peping's trust, to find out what the BBN's end game was.

This much he had told Jefferson Po, who still was wary that the BBN was planning something horrendous. "They may wreak havoc and you'll be in the midst of it. What happened in Pasig may have been a dry run," Jefferson said.

"I have to take that risk. I can stop it, whatever it is," Basilio replied. Peping had asked him to serve with the Hijos at the traslación and to get Vergel on board the carriage as well. They would be given instructions at dawn before the procession left Luneta.

"He must have hinted at something?" Jefferson insisted.

"This is my confession. It clears you just in case," Basilio said, handing Jefferson a flash drive. "Put a chopper in the air with a sniper on. If there is something planted on me or if I'm supposed to do anything terrible, I will tell you, so keep your mobile line open. Shoot me down, one shot, in the head. I will wear a bonnet so the blood won't spurt. Make it clean so no one panics, make sure."

"This is too crazy. Find out beforehand what they're up to," Jefferson insisted.

"He won't say. This is the only way, I swear!"

"Put this on," Jefferson handed Basilio a transmitter. "This has a GPS link. There will be no cell phone signals along the procession route and throughout much of the city for 36 hours as a precaution. The police will have two drones over the procession route. They will be the only ones allowed to fly over the area aside from our chopper. We'll have a tranquilizer gun ready."

"No, that won't do," Basilio disagreed. "You'll have to take me out… and anyone else who makes a bad move."

"We won't be able to tell. We can't be sure."

"It'll be your call when I'm out. Swear."

Jefferson nodded. He shook Basilio's hand.

On the eve of the procession, a multitude had flocked to the Luneta Grandstand from where the traslación was to commence. The faithful made a beeline for the backstage to wipe the protruding feet of the Black Nazarene. Handkerchiefs, face towels, shirts, rags were thrown at the Hijos, who wiped them on the Nazarene feet, then threw them back. Sometimes, one got a shirt in lieu of a kerchief, or towel instead of a shirt. It didn't matter. They had all been blessed. Devotees also strove to touch the icon's right shoulder that bore the crucifix.

At around 9 p.m., the Master of Ceremonies introduced the evening's main speaker, a popular Bishop that Basilio had not heard of. The Bishop's voice boomed across Luneta from giant speakers. He spoke of God's creation and man's co-creation but the crowd seemed mostly to ignore him. They prayed their rosaries and novenas even as the vendors went on hawking their wares. To whip up the crowd, he would sometimes raise his voice and punctuate his sentence with a loud "AMEN." But all he could evoke was a tired and obligatory echo from the crowd. Talking was a distraction to the devotees' own religious experience; a nuisance.

By 10 p.m., the Bishop was done and a multitude of young people in maroon and yellow swept in, rejoicing. They would rather be with Jesus and walk with him to Golgotha.

At dawn, Basilio climbed up the *andas*, the icon's carriage, after a high mass officiated by Fr. Dimalanta with four other priests. The Cardinal delivered the Homily. He called upon the patrons to have a faith that transcended miracles.

Basilio was given the main post right beneath the Nazarene. Vergel was at the opposite end. But beforehand, Vergel had shown him two large plastic sacks filled with pint sized yellow balloons. Basilio was astounded.

"Just give them away gradually along the route," Vergel whispered. Then he gave Basilio another bagful of canisters. "Spray the stuff on towels and hankies they throw at you after wiping them on the Nazareno before tossing them back to the crowd."

"What are they?"

"Perfumed disinfectant."

Basilio glared at Vergel, who only shrugged. "You know how finicky Tata is about hygiene. Spread joy, not viruses!"

Basilio took a can and sprayed its contents on his wrist.

"No!" Vergel nearly shouted, attracting the attention of the other Hijos.

There was a strange whiff in the air. Basilio eyed him, and then sniffed his wrist. A sharp, pleasant scent shot up his nostrils. He thought he smelled some cannabis. It settled him after a while. "Balloons," he whispered into his phone. "We're giving away yellow balloons."

"What?" Jefferson asked, as he arrived at the heliport. "Are you sober?"

As the carriage pushed off, the crowd broke through cordons and surrounded it like a storm surge of humanity rushing in from all sides. Basilio, at the helm, felt like the captain of a boat pounded by giant waves. They rocked. Men immediately started climbing up the carriage and had to be fended off. Basilio grappled with a hefty guy, allowed him to wipe his towel on the Nazareno, then tossed him back down to the crowd. Another one was right behind him but Basilio pushed this one off. He threw a kerchief at him, though.

"What the fuck is going on, Basilio? Talk to me!" Jefferson said over his transmitter. He could imagine how Basilio now had his hands full, with devotees climbing every which way on to the carriage. The chopper took off from the air base in Cavite and headed for Luneta.

Along Roxas Boulevard, Jefferson could see yellow balloons handed from the carriage, slowly spreading to the crowd. Others were handing them out as well to the crowd. People were snorting from the balloons and stopping on their tracks or wandering off. Some sat down on their haunches. They disrupted the surge of people towards the carriage and caused tension in places but no big scuffles were breaking out. Some people in the crowd were laughing and in good cheer, rather than grimly fanatical as in the past.

"Damn it! What's in those balloons, Basilio?" Jefferson demanded.

The sniper cocked his weapon. "Sir, I have a clear sight right now, sir!"

"No, wait… people might stampede if they see blood." Jefferson switched on the TV monitor and saw Carla Villa, the reporter, with a devotee holding a yellow balloon with a portrait of the Nazarene. The young devotee was laughing and telling Carla that he saw someone snorting from a balloon and followed suit. He said that it was nice smelling gas that made him feel great.

Then some others came by and shared, "It's a wonderful innovation."

"What do you think it is?"

"Don't know, but it's enhanced my experience."

"How?"

"I know why I'm here. I feel this oneness, with all of them… all of them…," he said, spreading his arm towards the crowd.

"Are you high?"

"High on Jesus."

"So, whatever's in those balloons, appears to be making them happy. But we'll keep you updated on what's really inside," Carla Villa relayed on live broadcast, staring at the camera.

"It's looking more like a Sto. Niño, or an *ati-atihan* fiesta than a traditional traslación," the studio anchor, Myra La Vina said.

"Reminds me of Woodstock," another commented.

By 3 p.m., the carriage had crossed the Ayala Bridge and social media was abuzz with news that laughing gas had been spread among devotees.

The procession made a stop at Plaza del Carmen along the southwest flank of the neo-gothic San Sebastian Church, the only one in the world made of pre-fabricated steel.

After praying the rosary inside the church, the resident Recollect priests removed the image of Our Lady of Mt. Carmel from its principal niche on the *retablo mayor*. It was placed on a scaffold at the southern end of the church. There, it was lifted by priests to "see" and "meet" the Black Nazarene, as devotees prayed the Our Father. Then the image was turned as it watched the Nazarene go on its way to Bilibid Viejo Street towards Quiapo. The scene strangely reminded Basilio of his mother, and he felt a slight aching inside him.

Towards nightfall, Basilio could feel fatigue set in. He struggled to fend off zealous devotees but was nearly tearful when a paraplegic was borne on the shoulders of the ocean of men towards the icon. He pulled the man up so the man lay prostrate on the Nazarene's feet. "Get up! Get up! What are you doing?" He wanted to shout but kept his peace.

The man wept. It was a while before Basilio could convince the paraplegic to remove himself from the icon's feet. He decided it was too dangerous to send the man back down the ocean of bodies and found a niche for him atop the carriage.

It was close to two in the morning when the carriage approached the Quiapo Church plaza and Basilio pulled Vergel to his position and decided to get off. He knew he was now a marked man, with his face all over the news and social media, giving away yellow balloons, and spraying stuff on towels, as per Jefferson.

He leapt onto the crowd and surfed across heads and limbs until he managed to plant his feet on the ground. He walked away quickly from the crowd, but heard someone shout from behind. "Stop, you! Saboteur! Stop him!"

More men in maroon shirts looked towards him menacingly. Basilio started to run. The men gave chase and Basilio raced through Echague when a Harley was suddenly appeared.

"Get on!" the rider barked. Basilio knew at once it was Jaguar. They cut across a maze of side streets and landed on Quezon Avenue. Jaguar gunned the bike and Basilio held on to his old pal for dear life.

"It's a tidy mess you've made!" Jaguar shouted above the din.

"Laughing gas, man. It didn't hurt anyone, did it?"

"Made a travesty of the event. They're going to want your hide!"

"It wasn't my idea. I just wanted to make sure it wasn't anything fatal."

"Still a dangerous stunt to pull. It could've caused big trouble."

"Anyone died?"

"Hope not."

"Where are we going? What's the plan?"

"Shut up!"

"Will you hear my last confession?"

"NO!"

Finally, they arrived at Chester's condo, as Carmen and her father monitored social media and the news on TV. Carmen rushed to Basilio and hugged him tight, her head on his chest. Chester was taken aback but kept his peace.

"They're pinning it all on you," Chester said.

"I know."

"The police raided the BBN headquarters and the Laguna warehouse. They claimed to have found firearms and stuff that may be toxic. They suspect the use of laughing gas may be a prelude to something else."

"They have nothing," Basilio sneered.

"They have a book, in English, by Shoko Asahara, the cult leader who masterminded the Tokyo sarin gas attack in '94. It's signed by him and dedicated to you," Chester said, staring at Basilio.

"Oh my God," Basilio gasped. "James gave it to me, back then. I lent it to Manito."

Jaguar and Chester look to Basilio questioningly.

"James... Rosales. I stayed with him in Yokohama... he... it's a long story. I didn't even read most of it."

On TV, BBN lawyers have issued a statement denying any wrongdoing by the group but indicating that "rogue members" could have acted on their own. A taped message from Crenshaw was broadcast saying that an applicant on probation, Basilio Ambahan, who was an illegal in Japan in the '90s and recently returned to the country, might have been among the Nazarene's protectors this year. Ambahan, whose family was a line of Cofradia, had been suspended for spreading "dangerous ideas" among the BBN. Crenshaw urged the Hijos to apprehend Basilio and for him to surrender to the authorities. This was followed by reports of Ambahan's involvement in the unsolved case of James Rosales' death.

"I had nothing to do with that!" Basilio insisted.

"You have to ask Jefferson for help," Jaguar said.

"He'll be looking to cover his own ass now," Basilio said. "He should've just put me down."

"Don't say that," Carmen said. "You're not a dog."

And Chester realized his daughter was already fond of the man. "Leave town," he suggested. "This will blow over. No one died."

"He can stay here," Carmen offered.

"Call Jefferson," Jaguar said.

Chester retrieved his phone.

"Tell him I know where they're taking Emily," Basilio said.

24
DAUGHTER

CARMEN WAS ADAMANT on joining the trip to Kiangan, despite her father's protests. She was convinced that Roger would be there as well should Tata Peping indeed show up with Emily.

Jefferson and Chester drove the van alternately with Basilio, Carmen and Maria in the back seat. Chester thought Jefferson should've brought along another agent for security, but Jefferson said things were messed up enough as they were. Basilio had been implicated publicly, and who knew what Emily had been up to?

"My ass is on the line too, Chester," Jefferson intimated. "There are people in the bureau who want to see me stew. I can't afford any more loose ends."

They reached the mountain village close to 4 p.m. after an eight-hour drive with a lunch stop. The elder greeted them and a group of women mobbed Maria. These were her childhood mates, Carmen surmised, whom she hadn't seen in forty years.

They sat around the *dap-ay* drinking coffee with the elder who spoke in a mix of Ifugao, Tagalog and English. Maria translated some of what he said.

"Our daughter Bagiw has returned to us after many seasons," the elder said. "She has heard Kabunian. Here, none can harm her or her daughter. Her daughter is our daughter; her friends, ours as well."

When the skies began to bleed, the white man arrived, still in loincloth but wearing a pair of Nike's and a dark blue jogging suit. His hair tied back in a bun. He greeted the elder.

De Bruyne bowed to Maria and there was a moment of silence between them. Then they repaired to the *dap-ay* with the rest of the group from Manila. De Bruyne had wanted to speak to Maria privately, but she insisted the others hear what he had to say.

"I owe you a huge debt of gratitude for raising my daughter, Maria," he began.

"Bagiw," she averred. "I am home."

"Bagiw," he resumed. "Now you must let her fulfill her destiny."

"What destiny?" Bagiw asked. "What have you done? She is with child." Bagiw looked to Jefferson across her. "His."

"The child is not yours," De Bruyne said to Jefferson, who lit up.

"How do you know? What kind of deal have you made with that mad man? How can you pimp your own daughter?"

"No deal. You were the ones who used her as bait. And now she has chosen your prey."

"No way! He's tricked her, played with her mind with that crazy gas or some other junk."

"How can such a thing happen?" Bagiw asked, distraught.

"Who knows? How was it between us?" De Bruyne asked.

"There was nothing between us!"

"Really?"

"One day you left. That is all. You abandoned your office, abandoned...."

"I found my calling."

"You found a wife, that's all you ever wanted. You fraud!"

"Maybe, that too, but now things have fallen into place. The light has shone through the haze. I know why I came to this land. The black one must perish for this time of darkness to finally end."

"What darkness? You're the mad one! Always was! You intend to kill Crenshaw?"

"Crenshaw's a fool, but a useful one right now. He is the means to an end."

"You baptized him in the Chico," Bagiw said.

"Stokes his ego. He would not have listened to me, otherwise."

"So you're his John the Baptist?"

"He read stuff I wrote back in the day about head hunting…"

"And power," Bagiw cut in, "I remember. You were wrong. I always wanted to tell you."

"I know."

"He thinks you're powerful, doesn't he?"

De Bruyne looked at her tenderly.

"Just because you took heads…you never understood."

The white man nodded.

"That's the big lie, isn't it?" the woman went on.

He smiled.

"You had to go away to be a man," she said, staring hard at him and he looked away.

"My nephew Roger came to him," De Bruyne said, "to find me."

"Where is he?" Carmen asked, alarmed.

"He's safe, don't worry."

"You used him too?"

"It was meant to be. Peping's people made contact with me and we met at Tabuk. He was fascinating at first, I admit, and a bit scary. A force of nature, I felt, for good or evil."

"What's he planning?" Jefferson asked.

"To marry... tomorrow."

"Then?"

He sighed and shook his head. "When they banned the BBN from running for Congress, things changed. He started talking about the Lapiang Malaya next time we met. I reminded him how those guys were massacred. He said he was no illiterate peasant. The BBN had cops, military, media people, even people in government. He talked about that Japanese guy, Asahara who used sarin in Tokyo in '94."

"It's Manito, his aide, the guy who framed me," Basilio said.

"Manito had this grand scheme to spread nerve gas during the Nazarene procession, not enough to kill anyone he said, just to create panic. Muslims would be blamed and mobs could attack the Quiapo mosque, causing mayhem in Manila. The BBN moles would take over three vital police stations while the core group with Peping would capture Quiapo Church and use it as their base to launch the genuine people's revolt, to declare a spiritual revolutionary government. Then Mayor Erap would be offered the choice to complete his presidency, governing alongside Tata Peping."

De Bruyne's revelation left his listeners dumbfounded.

"Manito's more fucked up than I thought," Basilio said.

"Are you shitting us?" Chester asked the white man.

"Wish I were," he replied.

"Actually, it's not as crazy as it sounds," Jefferson said.

Chester stared at him, incredulous.

"And Peping? He supports this?" Jefferson asked.

"Maybe not entirely but he humors the guy like one would an acolyte, keeps him guessing. He treats Manito like some weapon kept holstered. Manito started experimenting with nerve gas, causing a leak somewhere in Laguna," De Bruyne said.

"Calinawan," Jefferson concluded.

"Yes. It killed crops and a few livestock but it bothered Crenshaw.

So I intimated to Peping a different plan, a larger one, one that would truly shake the world, rouse people from slumber, change things. It came to me in a dream. And I suggested using laughing gas instead for a dry run. I tried it in Europe once, and I know how it can be made in large quantities."

"Why?" Carmen asked.

"Why not? Didn't you see how people enjoyed themselves? Recognized themselves? Why should they agonize all the time over fate and faith? We have made a fetish of agony in worship, abandoning ecstasy. That's why these frauds in checkered suits attract crowds and make fortunes from people who just want to enjoy God."

"There's the Sto. Niño festival, the Sinulog," Carmen said.

"Kids' parties, clown shows." De Bruyne sneered. "I've lived with shamans and seen things that no lowlander can imagine."

"And you have become one?" Bagiw asked.

He shook his head. "No, it is not in me, but I have found my purpose. In any case, I believe I did enough to save lives, or stop a disaster, at least, and buy time for the real work."

"Which is?" Jefferson asked.

"You will know... soon."

"What can we do?" Basilio asked.

"Nothing. Stay away. Let things take their rightful course."

"How do we know it won't be a worse disaster you intend?" Chester chimed in.

"Trust me."

"Trust *you*?" Bagiw echoed skeptically.

"You have taken lives," Chester interjected.

"The only deaths will be deserved, necessary," De Bruyne said, looking deeply pained now. "The militia killed my family… my wife and son. They killed the village chief. I saw how the people were lost, dying inside, the village wasting away even before any dam would be built. They looked to me. I was a priest, after all they said, a man of God. I had to do something. We had to restore the old ways, be warriors once more."

"How many have you killed?" Carmen asked.

"That doesn't matter now. There is just one more thing to be done." A thick silence fell as the fog moved in.

"So you've found your devil," Bagiw said. De Bruyne looked at her curiously.

"You once said the devil existed only for those who have not suffered any real tragedy or pain. So you went looking for him, didn't you?"

"I was as much a fool then as Crenshaw is now, maybe more so. Strange, you should remember."

"You used to fidget a lot back then, so uneasy, your fingers were always drumming on the desk, the cupboard… like that hamster of yours, running endlessly on that wheel, inside his cage, going nowhere. I see you are more settled now."

De Bruyne raised a hand. "I couldn't keep it steady… you remember."

"You are healed?"

"I don't know if there can be any true healing.'"

"You have killed… that is all."

"I claim no more."

"Did you try to kill yourself that night? Before you left?" De Bruyne scowled, seemingly alarmed.

"I picked up the crumpled paper from the trash basket," she went on. "I read what you wrote: "We must undo ourselves." I saw the knife. It was stained with blood. I always cleaned the knives before leaving. Your wrist was wrapped the following day."

"Enough, Maria! This isn't about me or us."

"We touched nothing more."

"It wasn't about that."

"What happened to Luke, my hamster?"

"I drowned him."

"What?"

"I let him go."

"He wouldn't have survived the wild."

"You did," Bagiw reminded him.

"I need a puff," Basilio said suddenly, getting up. He couldn't stand the former "lovers" bickering.

"Me, too," Carmen piped in, following suit.

"You smoke, too?" Basilio asked, surprised.

"No," Carmen quipped, causing Basilio to smirk.

"There's a pack in the van," Jefferson told them as the two went out of the *dap-ay*, with Chester glaring after them.

But then, there were more serious issues at hand. "Why are you marrying them? What good will it do? Does Emily want to do this?" Chester asked De Bruyne.

"*We* will marry them, Bagiw... Maria... in the ways of your people ...and mine, you and I. Tomorrow, here. The mountains and the lowland will become one. You shall all bear witness. Then we will part ways and wait for our new dawn. We must undo ourselves." De Bruyne looked sadly at the woman. "And now Bagiw and I need to be by ourselves."

"The elder says we can use the *ulog*," Maria said.

De Bruyne nodded.

"They have prepared another dwelling for the rest of you," she said to the two other men.

"Can we all fit?" Chester asked.

"I suggest you let the couple have it," Maria said.

"Couple?"

"I think she means them," Jefferson said, indicating Carmen and Basilio, who were now by the van, Basilio lighting up a cigarette.

"No way!" Chester protested.

"Oh, don't be a wet blanket, Limhuatco."

"She's my daughter!"

"Who's what? Thirty something? She'd be a grandmother back in the day, in these parts, right, Maria?"

"He's a felon! The cops are after him!"

"It'll pass," Jefferson said and called out to the two younger people. "Hey guys, there's a room for you. Go with these two!"

"You!" Chester growled at Jefferson.

"Relax, I brought sleeping bags or we can sleep in the van. I bet that's more comfy than hardwood, or rock."

Carmen came over, tugging a reluctant Basilio, making Chester's blood boil.

"We'll do a few hours, then you guys can take over if you need to," Carmen said as she marched away with Basilio, trailing after Bagiw and De Bruyne.

"We're fine," Jefferson said.

Chester wanted to chase after them, but Jefferson held him back. "Oh let them be, old man. Let the kids have some fun, you've had yours."

"I'm not going to let that…."

"Hey, we have to plan for tomorrow. I need your help, man, come." Jefferson urged Chester to come with him to the van, only the latter was seething.

Jefferson opened the trunk of the van, unzipped a bag and pulled out bulletproof vests and four automatic rifles. Chester was stunned.

"I have four: for you, me, Basilio and Carmen. Maria's safe here," Jefferson said. "You did your ROTC, right? Anyway, it's like a child's toy, point and shoot."

"Are you insane?"

"They won't come unarmed. You know that."

"Well, then I'm taking my daughter with me. You and that rake can shoot it out with those psychos all you want!"

"And where are you off to? See any taxis around?"

Chester kicked at the van in exasperation.

"Hey, that's government property. Simmer down. Weren't you the one so calm and composed earlier? Listen, we need to keep our heads cool; this is just for protection. Don't sweat the small stuff, man. You always do that, even when we were kids."

"How would you know about sweating, you bully? How would you know how guys like me felt?"

"Whoa, I never bullied you chick—Chester. I always thought you were one of those guys who didn't care much about nothing, or didn't take sides."

"Sure…"

"In fact, I sort of envied you."

"What?"

"You were aloof mostly. It's like you didn't give a shit; nothing, no one could bother you. You had nothing to prove to no one, you were just above it all."

"No shit! I took no sides to save my hide. What I always wanted to do was kick your ugly mug in! That would've been the highlight of my high school, you prick!"

"Really? Well, why don't you do it now?"

"What?"

"Okay, do it. Get it out of your system. Wallop me one if it will clear your head for tomorrow," Jefferson said, spreading his arms wide.

"Christ… what are we? Fourteen-year-olds?" Chester spat out his betel nut.

"You have to be with me, Chester. I'm not letting go of Emily tomorrow. No matter what happens, she stays with me," Jefferson vowed.

Chester was suddenly relieved he brought along a surgical kit, then swallowed down his vomit.

"What do you think he means by real work? Was yesterday just a ruse, to take our eyes off the ball? What's the end game?" Jefferson asked.

"Beats me, you're supposed to be the spook," Chester said. "You think it's yours? Emily's child?"

"I truly hope so. We did shag a few times. And she doesn't remember, man, that's what hurts."

You know what hurts? That full back's broken jaw way back when. Chester was tempted to retort but kept his tongue. He had never sensed more sincerity in Jefferson.

"Perhaps, it's an act, to get to Crenshaw?" Chester guessed.

"I don't know, man. I don't know anything anymore."

"What if it's *his*?" Chester asked, feeling sudden sympathy for the other man. Jefferson's eyes lit up. "What if the baby turns out a curly-topped black kid?"

Jefferson stared at Chester, almost imploringly. "Won't matter," he said. "If she'll have me, nothing else would matter."

"Wow! And you used to taunt that brown kid in school, Enrique Bello, and wrestled with him by the river."

"I love her, Chester. I love her like I've never loved anyone before."

Chester could do nothing but believe him as they saw the lights go out inside both huts.

25
ENTOURAGE

JEFFERSON AWOKE TO the sound of gongs that snapped him out of his dream of shagging Emily. He had slept inside a sleeping bag for the first time and felt pleasantly invigorated. It was almost like emerging from a cocoon. He sauntered towards the *dap-ay*, where Maria, the elder, Chester, Basilio and Carmen and De Bruyne were having coffee brewing over the hearth and boiled taro.

"They'll be here soon," De Bruyne said, looking at his mobile.

"I don't like this," Jefferson said.

"No guns," Chester said.

They all look at him curiously, then to Jefferson with some alarm.

"Dad? Did someone come here with guns?" Carmen asked.

Jefferson stared at her. "You all know what we're dealing with. If you think they're handing over your friend Roger without any fuss, think again."

"There will be no violence. We do what must be done and move on," De Bruyne said.

"This is my home. I am in charge," Maria said.

The BBN drove up in a single SUV, which strangely disappointed Jefferson. He was expecting an entourage. "Amateurs," he whispered.

Manito emerged first with an escort decked in black and an uzi submachine gun and approached the welcoming group. Jefferson looked to Carmen, who smirked.

"Lakay De Bruyne, Nanay Maria and… friends. Tata Peping is most honored to join you on this auspicious day," he announced.

"Where is he?" De Bruyne asked, peering at the SUV.

"Oh, he and his bride are eager for your ministering, Lakay. We just want to agree on protocol."

Jefferson felt a nip in his groin and instinctively felt for the pistol inside his leather jacket.

"You come upon us with guns, and ask for rules," Maria said.

"Oh, excuse Brother Andres, force of habit," Manito said and made a gesture to the armed one to hurry back to the SUV. "We have come a long way, we had to be prepared for any trouble."

"What do you require?" Maria asked.

"Tata only wishes that the ceremony be private. You and Lakay are to minister. I shall witness."

"You came to us. This is our village, we all bear witness to our daughter's fate," Maria said.

"The others must stay ten meters away. We will form a security cordon," Manito stressed.

Emily was in a white gown. She refused to wear the outfit previously laid out for her, and Tata Peping did not insist. He himself was in a *barong* that reached to his knees and white slacks. His hair was tied up in a bun and he seemed like a south Asian or African dignitary.

"Where's Roger?" Carmen insisted to Manito.

"He refused to come. He's a friend, so we could not force him," Manito said.

"The deal is, the Swede is released," Chester chimed in.

"He is not a prisoner," Manito replied and brought out his tablet. He showed Carmen and Chester the screen and played a video of Roger Geisler. He was holding the day's newspaper and told Carmen that he was safe and chose to stay at the BNN headquarters to help. He asked her to contact his parents. Carmen eyed Manito suspiciously after the video was over, but left it at that.

A group of highland women and men began a mating dance that mimicked birds, as the beating of gongs grew louder.

"How long is this going to take?" Crenshaw whispered to De Bruyne trying not to seem peeved.

"You asked for this," De Bruyne replied.

Carmen tried to reach Emily but was kept away by two armed guards. Only Maria was allowed to be with her daughter by the *dap-ay*. After nearly an hour, a pig tied to a pole was brought near the *dap-ay* for slaughter. A young man stuck a sharpened bamboo into the pig's carotid artery and it squealed horribly. Emily cowered and Maria hugged her tight. The animal would not be allowed an easy death. Its squealing was to exorcise the unappeased presences all about. The ruckus seemed endless as well for Jefferson, who tried to keep tabs on Emily. He sensed she was distraught and primed himself for the worst.

When the pig finally died, it was disemboweled and the liver presented to the shaman and other elders, including Maria in the *dap-ay*. Crenshaw saw the shaman frown as he peered at the liver and made the sign of the cross something nipped Peping in the gut. Soon, what he suspected was confirmed.

"The signs do not bode well," De Bruyne whispered.

"I don't care, you said this was no more than a formality," Peping said.

"It's what it is. We must wait if we must."

"I'm not leaving without a wedding."

"Old man says we have to wait two more days at least," Manito whispered as he approached Peping.

"No way. I don't have the time, we don't have the time," Peping said and entered the *dap-ay*. "I beg your indulgence, esteemed friends, Aling Maria, honored mother of my bride, but there is some urgency to the matter at hand. My bride and I...."

"My daughter can speak for herself," Maria cut in.

Peping caught himself and breathed deep. "Emily, please tell your folks that we need to... we wish to marry now."

"The signs are not good. You must wait for a more auspicious time," Maria said.

"There is no time."

The others looked to Peping curiously.

"Listen, Maria," Peping resumed haltingly. "You are a convert, a Christian, you can't believe in this."

"Do not presume to know my heart, Mr. Crenshaw."

"I meant no disrespect. But if two people... Emily, please, tell them."

"Is it your wish to marry this man at this time, daughter?" Maria asked.

Emily looked up. "No," she answered bravely. "Not at the hour, not ever."

"You're confused, Emily. All of this has weighed on you. Go back to the car, and we'll talk."

"No."

"Go to the car, I say!"

"My daughter goes nowhere with you, Crenshaw!"

Crenshaw looked to his guards, who held up their weapons.

"No, not like this," De Bruyne pleaded.

"You used me, white man. You never intended for this marriage to take place. You betrayed me as you betrayed your white Christ, but this time you pay."

"This can wait."

"No, it can't."

"Once things are in motion."

"Quit your bullshit!"

"He's right, Tata," Manito said and Peping eyed him and the white man suspiciously. "It can wait."

The gongs resounded echoing across mountains. Warriors, some armed with automatic rifles, lined the surrounding hills, pounding the earth with sticks and rifle butts.

"Patience, Crenshaw," De Bruyne said.

"I'm not saving your white ass," Peping whispered.

De Bruyne turned to Peping, astounded. "I don't know how blind you really are, Crenshaw, but you should at least sense that I'm your only ticket out of here."

"We will do this some other day, if God allows," De Bruyne announced to the gathering as he approached the shaman and the elder and hugged them. Then he came to Maria and Emily. "Thank you again for everything," he told Maria. "You raised her well, so take care, both of you."

"Where would we be now, if we had ran away instead, you and I?" Maria was tempted to ask her once parish priest but only said as she smiled wistfully, "You too, Fr. Gerry."

Emily hugged her father. "We must meet again, Dad. This has been too brief, and I want to know you."

"God willing, child. I'm sorry for my shortcomings, but soon all will be made right."

"I'm afraid."

"Be brave, child. A new world beckons, and we make way."

De Bruyne moved briskly towards the SUV. "Let's go," he called out to Crenshaw, who was torn.

Peping's eyes pleaded with Emily but she looked away. "I shall return."

"And you," Peping shouted to Basilio before boarding the SUV. "You cast no more shadow!"

As the SUV drove away, a gun shot was heard and a body thrown out. Basilio rushed down the road followed by Jefferson and Emily. He knew he had only one shadow they could slay.

"It's Vergel," Basilio realized, "an Hijo, and my confidante."

"My God," Emily turned away and found Jefferson's shoulder.

He felt sudden gladness despite the corpse before them. "There's a body now, we can charge them," he whispered, putting an arm around Emily.

"They might hurt Roger," Carmen said, as she joined them with Chester.

Basilio shook his head. "It's De Bruyne's show now."

26
BLACK POPE

"WE HAVE TO bring the corpse to a morgue under NBI jurisdiction," Jefferson said. The Ifugao elder had allowed Vergel's remains inside the *dap-ay*, after wrapping it in a ritual blanket.

"And what do we say happened?" Chester asked.

"Exactly as happened."

"And they'll take our word for it, I suppose?"

"I work for them, Chester!"

"Really? I'm beginning to doubt that."

"I called in choppers, didn't I?"

"Well, why don't you call in one now?"

"And where is it supposed to land?" Chester smirked.

"This isn't official business, remember?" Jefferson reminded him. "We're on our own."

"And you want to drive this corpse all the way to Manila, that's eight hours."

"The BBN can pin this all on me again," Basilio said. "My photo's all over social media."

"What's the alternative?" Jefferson asked.

"Mummify?" Carmen asked.

"They don't do that anymore," Emily said, "but my mother says there is a Christian graveyard not too far from here."

"He has a family," Jefferson said.

"We bring him to Lagawe, look for a funeral parlor, keep him there for a while, then have him transported to Manila when its safe," Chester suggested.

"I'm not authorized," Jefferson insisted.

"And you're authorized to transport him all the way home?" Chester sneered.

"Look, we bring him back to a morgue I know, in Quiapo where we can keep things hush in the meanwhile. We have to go back to Manila, anyway, to figure out and stop whatever the BBN are up to," Jefferson said.

"You know he's going to… decompose in a few hours," Chester had to mention.

"Well, let's get moving then. Help me put him in the van instead of yapping."

Jefferson, Chester, Basilio and three locals helped carry Vergel's remains to the SUV.

"Put him inside the sleeping bag," Chester said as Jefferson glared at him.

"This was your idea, not mine," Chester reminded his former schoolmate.

"Basilio, you can stay here until this blows over. They will protect you," Maria said.

"You too, Emily." Jefferson added.

"No," Basilio replied. "I'm not afraid of them."

"I have to see this through," Emily insisted. "He's my father."

"So we all pile into this thing with… *him*?" Chester asked, indicating Vergel.

"Get in!" Jefferson ordered, taking the driving seat.

They had reached the lowlands by noon with four hours left at least of travel time to Manila.

"Vergel killed my father," Basilio said, rousing the other passengers from stupor. "He was sent to collect gambling debt my father owed the BBN. My father was drunk, there was a scuffle and it was an accident, or so he said. They wanted me to kill him in turn, during the initiation. I refused and they made him kill some pedophile instead. He became my shadow."

"Your darker self," Carmen said.

"Spy shadow come forth," Jefferson quipped. "Remember that, Chester, when we were kids, the cartoon show on TV, where this detective would summon his shadow to do stuff for him? We used to taunt the darkie Enrique."

"That's it!" Chester suddenly said.

"What? He has a spy shadow?" Jefferson asked.

"*The black one must perish!* That's what he said."

"Who?" Jefferson asked again, confused.

"De Bruyne."

"He's not going to kill Crenshaw," Jefferson said. "They've got some crazy deal."

"The Pope," Chester said.

"What pope? Me?"

"No, idiot! The Pope *Pope*! He's coming to Manila tomorrow, visiting for three days, staying at the Papal nunciature..."

"Where did that come from, genius?" Jefferson sneered.

"He's Jesuit."

"So?"

"Remember when we were kids, the head of the Jesuits, Fr. Arruppe came to say Mass at school and I was chosen to be sacristan? I heard some adults call him the Black Pope so I thought he was African but he turned out to be a white man."

"That's what some church people call the head of the Jesuits, the Black Pope," Carmen said.

"Why?"

"There's always been rivalry among the orders. They vie for influence in the Vatican, a lot of backbiting. Their rivals say the Jesuits have their own agenda, that they're the anti-Christ."

"*Solve fasciculos possumus nosmetipsos*," that's what he whispered to me," Emily said. "More or less."

"It's Latin for: We must undo ourselves," Carmen said after a while, "I think."

Chester was impressed. "You know Latin?"

"Learned some, for my research."

"De Bruyne was a missionary who came to proselytize, lost his purpose, then went native… Now, he sees it his final mission to undo what the Catholic Church has done in the colonies. What better way to achieve that than to slay the head of the Church right here, in the only Christian majority country in Asia."

"And Crenshaw's part of it? Why? What does he get out of a dead pope? They'll never elect him as the next one?" Jefferson asked.

"Who knows? De Bruyne might have sold him a whole different scenario," Carmen said.

"So how are they going to even get close with all the security?" Chester asked.

"Earl." Carmen said.

27
EARL GRAYSON

HE AWAITED THE SMS message from the roof deck, the only place in the building where electromagnetic signals could be received. It came at 8.30 p.m., which was "five minutes away."

He rushed downstairs and informed his chief security aide, Jurgens, that a black Revo with plate no. ZGB 1225 would be by the premises in three minutes escorted by three motorcycle cops. It would deliver a "package" that must be led through the back gate with his only one companion, who would also be donning a maroon-colored friar's frock. They must both be checked for weapons or cell phones and the back door to the pantry locked after they have entered. He showed Jurgens photos of both men on his mobile.

"No one else enters," Earl repeated.

The message first came through his Facebook account. It was a certain Gerard De Bruyne, a former priest who first made contact. He was a strange-looking dude with long white hair and wearing an old priestly garb. He explained how he needed to have a personal audience with the Pope, with whom he'd had previous correspondence. It was a matter of millennial importance. "I am Fr. Gerard De Bruyne. Tell the Pontiff, he will know who I am," the man said.

Then Earl saw the gaunt white man beside De Bruyne and knew at once it was Roger Geisler. It was at least eight years since they were last together and he was unsure how and why they parted. Was it in Boracay or Patpong? Was there a third party involved? He had left all that behind, buried it in the pit of his brain, gone to his mother's country, Switzerland, where he held citizenship, and applied to be a Swiss guard to the Pope.

Was it to atone for his ways? No. It wasn't about atonement or forgiveness. Then he remembered that there was someone else. Another time Roger had picked up a Thai boy, a she-boy, and Earl had lost it. He had charged at Roger and the teen with a knife he had bought at the antique shop, close to stabbing them both. Earl fled into the Bangkok night, confused but grateful that something or someone had stayed his hand. He understood finally, what his mother had told him once—that he had murder in him, like his father, that he was inclined to kill. So he must do so for the right reason, for a sacred duty if possible.

"You have to arrange for the Pope to meet with Fr. De Bruyne. It's awfully important, Earl. I would not ask you if it weren't so," Roger pleaded, before a hooded being in a maroon frock came up behind Roger and placed a knife across his throat.

Earl felt his body turn to stone and his heart racing like a runaway horse. He turned off his electronic tablet and fell to his knees wanting to pray, but not knowing why. Should he plead for mercy? Should he ask for a reprieve? For what? From whom? He had always warned Roger about becoming too intimate with his research subjects, but the man was reckless, naïve, impressionistic, and easily taken by every nut case with a fanciful scripture. He scoured caves and lived among derelicts and druggies, slept in jungles and whipped himself along with penitents, trudged the darkest alleyways of the earth as if his whiteness was an amulet that protected him from all sort of savagery.

But when he spoke of being crucified in the Philippines, Earl knew it was time to cut loose and save himself from Roger's death wish. Now, the worst had come true. He had been drawn into Roger's web of madness. He was sworn to protect the Pope. He would die first before exposing the Pontiff to any danger. The job of Chief Security had fallen on him after Capt. Schumann became ill before the trip. Earl knew he should ignore Roger and De Bruyne and turn away from the darkness. However, Roger's visage weighed on him.

After an hour, he sought an audience with the Pope. Francis' personal secretary, Fr. Auguste, said the Pontiff was meditating and could not be disturbed. Earl insisted that he needed to confess a personal matter. Fr. Auguste conferred with the Pope, who agreed to see Earl. The Pontiff listened carefully to all Earl had to say, blessed him and sent him away and asked for Fr. Auguste.

Later, Francis would tell Earl to set up the meeting with De Bruyne inside the Nunciature. He gave specific instructions on how things should proceed. Earl felt a dam break inside him tears and gushed forth. He shook violently until he felt the Pontiff's hands on his shoulders. He looked up and saw Francis' calm mien while Fr. Auguste sent dagger looks his way.

28

TUNNEL

THEY HURRIED TO Anna Duran's clinic in Quiapo after dropping off Vergel's remains at a nondescript funeral parlor where Jefferson made Chester sign the death certificate. Jaguar had called Basilio to say that Roger Geisler was now in Quiapo after escaping from the BBN lair in the Calinawan caves.

Roger wore a week-old beard and looked so gaunt that Carmen hugged him. "What have you gotten yourself into now?"

"They plan to capture the Pope," Roger said.

"Capture?"

"De Bruyne's made contact through Earl."

"I knew it," Carmen said.

"They threatened to harm me if the Pope didn't meet with De Bruyne, who's offered to surrender personally to the Pontiff."

"And how did you get here?" Jefferson asked.

"Vergel helped me escape. It took me a while to figure out where I was. Is he with you?"

The group fell silent.

"Let's stop here. We should tell the authorities," Chester said.

"It's happening tonight. Earl's head of security, and all contact goes through him. The Pope has agreed to meet with

De Bruyne. Police members of the BBN are escorting my uncle to the Nunciature. It's all been arranged."

"What do you mean, capture? What exactly are they planning?" Jefferson asked.

"I'm not sure. I suspect they want to take him hostage, create an international incident then have Tata Peping negotiate for the Pope's release. He'll become world-famous then."

"I don't trust De Bruyne," Basilio said. "He's playing Crenshaw."

"*The black one must perish.* That's what he said, right?" Carmen recalled.

"Could be metaphorical," Chester mused

"He's killed before. He's a warrior," Carmen said.

"Only blood can cleanse, that's what Tata Peping has been saying since meeting my uncle. I think he's echoing De Bruyne."

"We can go online, alert the media, broadcast the plan beforehand," Chester said.

"And create an incident ourselves? This is all speculation right now. No one will broadcast anything without proof," Jefferson replied.

"Proof? We have a body in the morgue," Basilio pointed out.

Roger Geisler gasped as the others fell silent once more. "Sorry, Vergel's dead," Carmen whispered to Roger. "They killed him."

"Then we have to go crash the gates if we must," Roger insisted, fighting back tears.

"I know a better way in," Jaguar said, "I served briefly at the Nunciature as a seminarian. I know someone inside. The meeting will occur at nine in the evening. There is a tunnel that leads from the Paco Church to the Nunciature."

"This," Fr. Jaguar spread a moth-eaten map across Anna Duran's table. "Got this from the archive. Here." He pointed to a spot. "It was used until the 19th century, a lava tunnel that the

Dominicans remade into an escape route in case of popular uprisings or government reprisal."

"It's maintained?"

"Partly, that's what the overseer says, he can guide us maybe halfway, beyond that we're on our own."

"There are snakes and rats down there," Chester said.

"It's worth a try," Jefferson added.

"Why don't you send in your drones instead?"

"Drones won't see anything. We have to get in."

"We?"

"Fr. Jaguar and I."

"Me too," Basilio replied. "It's personal now."

"And me," Roger said. "It's my fault too, all of this…"

"I'll come," Carmen said.

"No!" Chester shouted.

"Your dad may be right this time. There's no point for you to risk…" Basilio started saying but Carmen cut in: "If Roger goes, I go."

"And I," Emily said.

"No!" Jefferson shouted this time.

"He's my father."

"Well, why not?" Chester chimed in sarcastically. "Send in the marines."

"So we're all coming, except for dad," Carmen said looking to Chester, who fretted.

"Alright, I'm in, but if anything goes wrong, I'll have your head, you moronic police stooge! NBI my ass!" Chester railed at Jefferson.

"Relax, Chester. This is what you've always wanted to do, right? Save the world? You were with those "junior crusaders" back then, weren't you? In Grade Four, you were ratting out classmates even before we grew any pubes. So don't get high and mighty on me, snitch."

"Shut up! That's kids' stuff."

"But I bet you just wanted to glimpse that pretty novice nun Ms. Roco's panties, didn't you? Had the hots for her, yes? So what color were they, immaculate white or magenta?"

"Nothing! She wasn't wearing any! Satisfied?"

"Dad!"

"Just kidding. Okay, Fr. J., let's go to church," Chester deflected, turning away.

They were met by Mang Mario behind the Paco Church, in a centuries-old cemetery for priests. Mang Mario led them to a crypt with a stone Madonna and unlocked the rusty gates.

Jefferson passed out torches, gas masks, and two small oxygen tanks.

"No firearms," Jaguar reminded everyone though he was almost certain Jefferson was packing at least a taser, and felt some relief in the thought.

Mang Mario told them that nearly six kilometers of the tunnel had been cleaned up, strengthened and refurbished a few years ago by the parish priest, who was convinced that the end days were at hand as revealed in the final message of our Lady of Fatima and that the tunnel could be a sanctuary for the elect once the Apocalypse began.

After the priest died from a sudden heart attack, Mang Mario took it upon himself to maintain the tunnel but had to sell off some of the original supplies for finances. Still, there were rice stocks, dry goods and water down there, he explained.

As the team descended the stone steps they felt the underground chill. Solar lamps lit up the environs and they marveled at the rows of canned food and sacks of rice, water bottles neatly stacked on the sides of the tarred walkway. There were bunk beds, wicker chairs, even a coffee maker in dug out caverns.

"It must have taken an army to do these," Jefferson said.

"Twenty workmen, all from out of town, some from Mindanao, Muslims. They were never told what it was all about. It took them four months," Mario said. "I replace some of the rice stock and the water every six months, sell the old stuff to buy new ones."

"He did all this through Church funds?" Basilio asked.

"There were two rich donors, a man and a woman, both have since passed on, too."

"How long you intend to keep this up?" Carmen asked.

Mario shrugged. "As long as I can, I feel Fr. Aurelio wants me to. He gives me strength. When I'm gone, maybe you can maintain it. You're the only ones besides me who know about it."

"Oh, I'm sure Mr. Po will be interested. He's quite into secret caverns and hideouts," Chester said.

"Put a lid on it, chicken."

There was a painting of the Last Supper a la Da Vinci on a wall.

"Perhaps we should just stay here and await the end days," Jefferson said.

"You're the end of days," Chester quipped as they reached an iron curtain.

"This is as far as I go," Mario said. "I don't know what lies ahead. I was told that four or five kilometers more and you would find the stone stairway that lead to the Nunciature."

"Okay, this is it, people. No turning back once we proceed." Jefferson moved to pull back the curtain. There was a deafening silence.

"Let's do it," Chester said.

Jefferson led the way with Basilio at the rear. Pavement turned to cobbled stone and dirt, then some mud.

"We're at the water table," Jefferson said.

"Manila's below sea level," Emily reminded everyone.

"Sinking even as we speak," Chester added.

Carmen was reminded of a movie version of the Divine Comedy she once saw and half expected an angelic or underworld guide to show up and lead them into the bowels of purgatory or hell, where they would witness some notorious souls burning in cauldrons.

Basilio thought he saw gold dust on the wall. As he flashed his torch, the earth shook wildly and debris fell. There was nowhere to hide as the team scampered forward like rats.

"Don't panic!" Jefferson shouted. "It's just huge trucks passing." The shaking died down after a while and the group rushed onwards until they reached stone steps.

"We're here!" Jaguar shouted and directed his light on a steel door eight steps above.

"Closer than expected," Chester said.

Jaguar went up the steps and knocked on the door three times, before stopping for three seconds, and knocking another five times. Jefferson suspected it was a Masonic code and became ever more doubtful of the priest's true loyalties.

The lower part of the door opened and light shone through. Jaguar signaled to his mates to follow him, as he crawled into the light. They crawled inside one after the other and crawled further on the hardwood plank.

Damp air turned into air-conditioned cool. They emerged behind a dark screen with slats through which they could see a dining table. The two hooded men were led in and Pope Francis was three meters across seated on a hardwood chair, hands clasped to his chest, calmly waiting. The one in a white cassock, who let them in, gestured for them to be silent and whispered to Jaguar.

"We're here to witness, that is all," Jaguar reminded the others.

"God help us," Chester whispered.

29
THE PRODIGAL

A CONSUMING SADNESS spread through Manito as he led a hooded De Bruyne past the sentries. As agreed upon, De Bruyne was brought in a BBN SUV escorted by a four motorcycle cops. There was only the driver and another cop inside the van aside from De Bruyne and Manito. The back door was locked behind them.

It felt like the time after being released from prison following the EDSA 3 fiasco when he seemed cloaked in the immutable, rock-solid, rusted-iron certainty for the likes of him. Manito was certain now they had been deceived yet again. This white man had no intention of doing what he said he would do. He came here to do one thing—to kill the other white man across the table. It was all too late now.

He saw De Bruyne walk over to Francis, who stood and opened his arms to welcome the prodigal. De Bruyne took off his hood as they embraced, then the Pope sat back on his chair and the other man bent a knee and kissed the Pontiff's ring. Then they huddled and whispered to each other for what seemed an eternity to Manito with the Pope nodding and touching the other man's face tenderly.

When De Bruyne finally stood up, Manito knew what was coming. De Bruyne reached inside his robe and drew out what seemed a wooden cross, pulled off a wooden cap and revealed a sharpened edge. He raised the crucifix over his head.

"No!" Manito shouted, but Earl had burst in with two other guards.

"Drop it!" Earl shouted. "Stand back!" His .45 was now aimed at De Bruyne.

"Don't move!" Another security personnel drew his weapon on Manito.

"No, father!" Emily shouted as she had rushed into the kitchen, followed by the rest from the tunnel.

"Back off, all of you!" Earl barked.

"Bless me, Father, for we have sinned. Undo the crime!" De Bruyne shouted. "We must undo ourselves! *Solve fasciculos possumus nosmetipsos!*"

"No, Earl!" Roger yelled but shots were fired. De Bruyne was thrown back and his blood splattered on the Pope. De Bruyne stood and staggered but another shot felled him. Blood gushed from his head as he hit the floor.

Earl and three other security aides and the priest from the kitchen rushed over to surround the Pope and bore him away, locking the door behind them.

Everyone who came in from the tunnel and the dead De Bruyne were now trapped inside the kitchen.

Manito rushed over to pick up a stray fork from the table then grabbed a stunned Emily from behind. He poked the fork against her jugular. "Stand back or she's next!" He shouted.

"Let her go, Manito, it's over. De Bruyne came here to die. He used you. We used each other. We could still all walk away from this. The Pope's safe, the authorities won't want any of this to get out, because of too many questions to answer," Basilio told him.

"That's what you've always been good at: walking away, but not this time. We take our stand here, or we all die. End the abomination here."

"Tata Peping wouldn't want you to do this. She's pregnant with their child," Carmen added desperately.

"That fraud! I was blinded. Didn't trust my own instincts. I let that suicidal priest feed Crenshaw's megalomania. They've turned the movement into another clown show, but this joke's not going to be on us!"

"What do you want?" Jefferson asked.

"I want you all to take out your cell phones and show this to the world. I want everyone to know what's going on here, right now!"

"There's no wifi or cell signal in this part of the building. All communications were shut off," Jaguar said.

"Turn it back on!"

"Take it easy. We'll have to inform security, or whoever's in charge," Jefferson told him.

"Do it!" Manito ordered, and they all gasped as a pinch of blood dribbled from Emily's neck. Manito had a lock on her arm and neck, making his own arm shake.

Basilio suddenly remembered that Manito used to be a top varsity wrestler. Emily was breathing hard, her eyes wild.

Jaguar went to the kitchen door, signaled to security through the small glass window. The door was opened a little, as someone pulled Jaguar inside with the door locking behind him.

After some minutes, Jaguar was pushed back in, stumbling as he did, and the kitchen door was locked once more.

"They won't turn on signals, but if you put down your weapon and let her go, the Pope will grant you an audience," Fr. Jimenez said to Manito.

"That's great, Manito. It's what you want, a global audience," Jefferson said.

"No. We talk on my terms," Manito insisted.

"But if anyone gets hurt…," Jaguar was beginning to say

"Someone's dead!" Manito cut in.

"Take me instead," Carmen volunteered. "She's pregnant. I started this. I urged Roger to get in touch with his uncle, despite the danger. I wanted the research." She started to move towards Emily.

"Stay back," Manito shouted.

"No!" Chester protested. "It's my fault. I found her. I didn't do the right thing, I wanted to keep her for myself, and it led to all this, so take me."

"I'm a priest. I shouldn't have kept secrets with Basilio. I thought it was a game like when we were kids," Jaguar said. "It's me who you should take."

"I just wanted revenge, Manito. You're right," Basilio acquiesced.

"I was blinded by my fascination for my uncle. I could've stopped him, somehow, but I enabled him instead," Roger said.

"You're all crazy, crazier than those two. You think I care about any of that now?" Manito yelled at them.

"It's on me, Manito. I'm with the NBI. We've been monitoring you," Jefferson confessed.

"We know! You think we're fools? We had a road map, a program. She changed Peping. He was willing to give it all up for her! And this is the price we pay! I want media access now!"

An electronic bell chimed. Jaguar knew it as a call to late prayers, making Manito distracted and Basilio lunged at him. Emily wrestled free but blood was already gushing from her neck. Jefferson, Chester and Carmen quickly came to her aide, even as Basilio and Manito wrestled. Jaguar rushed to the door to signal for help.

Basilio and Manito went to ground grappling. They saw the sharpened crucifix near the fallen De Bruyne and both men scrambled to reach it ahead of the other. They tussled for it and Manito had the upper hand. Manito suddenly grabbed Basilio's hand, his grip like steel.

Before Basilio could react, the stake was thrust into Manito's chest. Basilio was shocked but powerless to pull his hand from Manito's grip and the crucifix from Manito's chest. Basilio's tongue retreated as Manito glared at him.

"You are now my shadow, Basilio," Manito told him, his hand shaking. Blood oozed from chest until it gushed from his mouth and his head dropped.

Basilio gasped and pushed Manito away, wiping the blood on the dead man's cassock and standing up.

Meanwhile, Earl and other security men had finally entered the kitchen.

"She's bleeding bad and needs to go to the hospital." Jaguar pointed to Emily, who was being attended to by Jefferson and Chester. "The two others are dead."

"It wasn't me. He did it to himself," Basilio stammered.

"Put pressure on this," Chester commanded Jefferson, as he held a bloodied cloth to Emily's neck.

"There is an ambulance on standby, for the Pope," Earl said. "But only authorized personnel are allowed."

"I'm a doctor," Chester said, flashing his I.D.

"The pontiff has his own doctor."

"You want him involved in this?"

"Okay, just you," Earl said.

"I'm coming," Jefferson said. "NBI," he added, showing *his* badge.

"Me too," Carmen said as Earl eyed her.

"I know you," he whispered.

"She's a vet... my... nurse, an E.R. nurse," Chester stammered.

"All right, you guys get going. There's a paramedic on board. Don't tell him anything he doesn't need to know," Earl said. Security personnel carried Emily to the ambulance in the driveway.

"I'm a priest," Jaguar said to Earl, as the ambulance left.

"Cross my heart," he said, making the Sign of the Cross over his chest.

Earl turned to Basilio.

"He's with me," Fr. Jimenez said, "an acolyte."

They turned their attention to the corpses.

"It was a suicide, Earl," Roger said. "I saw the whole thing... two suicides. One stabbed himself and the other shot himself."

"Oh, yes... yes," Jaguar confirmed, as he quickly blessed both remains.

Earl looked at them wide-eyed, and shook his head. "Then you better vanish as well now," he said.

The two nodded and hurried off.

"Back door," Earl instructed. "You were never here."

Roger was about to leave when Earl asked him to stay.

As Jaguar and Basilio slipped past the Nunciature gate, they could see media amassing outside. They hurried towards a group of big bikers. Quiapo's Angels fortunately bore away their mates into the safety of Manila's night.

30

ST. BENEDICT'S

AS THEY ROLLED Emily into the emergency room, Dr. Limhuatco shouted out instructions. "Pregnant woman with injury to carotid, she's lost a lot of blood. We need a transfusion. Check her type."

"AB," Loretta said as she rushed towards the patient. "A Dr. Duran informed us. She's here, on your call, she said."

"Yes," Chester said, lighting up. His mood lifted a bit. "She'll monitor the fetus, clear the O.R."

Dr. Anna Duran was waiting when they reached the Operating Room. Dr. Limhuatco scrubbed in. As he prepared to suture Emily's wound, she went into cardiac arrest. As they placed the defibrillator pads to Emily's chest, Chester recalled the first time he saw her and his knees slightly buckled. He bit his lips to be in the moment.

"Sixty," he barked, ordering an increased voltage for the defibrillator. Emily flat-lined and the room went into a tizzy.

"All right, I'm going in!" he said.

"You sure?" Loretta asked.

He looked at her, then at Anna, who nodded.

"Fetus is stable," she said her stethoscope to Emily's belly.

"Yes," he said.

Loretta cut open Emily's clothes and stripped her. Chester saw her naked for the first time and felt a jolt of electricity surge through him. He settled himself.

"Scalpel," he instructed Loretta.

Her ribs gave way rather easily, Chester thought. As he put in the spreader to open up her chest cavity, he could feel power in his hands that had seemingly abandoned years ago.

As he stared at Emily's heart—darker and smaller than he imagined. Chester thought that all he had done, all the life he had lived was meant to prepare him for this moment, to hold this one heart in his hands and urge it back to life. As he held Emily's heart, he imagined passing his life force into her. Loretta tapped him and Chester started massaging the organ, kneading it like dough.

"Please," he pleaded silently. "There is so much life in you yet. You're too young."

He remembered the time with Dr. Ortiz and something kicked from inside him. This was a life-and-death struggle! *This was war!* He pressed harder. *The heart is a muscle! Only a muscle!*

Then it happened. He felt a niggle, like a finger brushing his gloved hand, then a prick, a throb; a beat! The muscle came alive, squirming, undulating; pumping! An animal awoken! Wounded and fierce! Unbeaten! Triumphant!

A cheer went up, the team applauded. Chester felt his head inflating and his own heart leaping out of his chest. He imagined himself as a prehistoric hunter, who had just ripped the heart out of a terrible beast. He raised his hand to remind the team that there was more work to do.

They closed up Emily's chest and her heart rate returned to normal, her vitals stabled. She remained comatose, and there was minimal brain activity that was monitored. The neurologist, Dr. Isaac Sy, did not offer any prognosis but Chester could sense his pessimism. Meanwhile, Anna continued to keep tabs on the other heart inside Emily and felt good about the fetus' chances.

"That was brave," she said to Chester as they repaired to the cafeteria for a break.

"I guess I grew a pair coming here," he whispered, sighing.

She smiled and buzzed him on the cheek.

Just as he was about to kiss her back, his mobile rang. It was his wife Jackie going on about the news on TV, the Pope, and ambulances going to St. Benedict's. He could hear Carmen beside her mother, trying to explain stuff and calm her.

"I want your father to tell me! What's going on, Chester?" was the last thing he heard before his phone went dead and he was overcome by fatigue.

31
QUIAPO REDUX

ROGER REMEMBERED THE time he was here, when it had turned dark and his head spun from something he imbibed. He heard Mass inside the old church, visited a few nightspots, drank with guys on a side street and ate what might have been goat or dog meat. Then he had awoken inside the Embassy, cleaned up and sent home, never to know what exactly happened that night.

He always thought that night changed everything, that he would have to come back again and again, that his life was now tied up to this place. He thought he had seen in parts what his uncle had seen in whole; had stared into an abyss that would never close, never leave.

And now he was back to ground zero, with that other enigma in his life: Earl. A man who might have loved him, might have killed another because of him but turned away, gave him up for a life of dispassion and duty.

When he told De Bruyne about Earl, Roger was little convinced that it would matter. Earl had found a calling nobler than anything they had shared. Why would he even consider risking the Pope's well-being for the sake of a lover who had authored his own undoing? But things were already spinning out of hand. Manito wouldn't stop talking about sarin and De Bruyne was clutching at straws.

His uncle knew better. He held Roger's face in his hands. "You are his instrument, Roger, you."

The SUV was geared with a military grade GPS. Earl stopped the vehicle a block off Quiapo Church. "This is the spot, right?" Earl asked him but Roger couldn't be sure. "This is where the priest said we should leave the bodies?"

"One body," Roger answered. "He said to keep them separate."

"No time, too dangerous," Earl insisted. "We leave them here."

"But...."

"We let the priest figure it out," Earl said. "He'll know what to do. They always do."

The body bags were heavier than Roger imagined. They heaved with all their might and ended up dragging the bags towards the broken lamppost just outside the church, making sure they were not sighted. But even if they were, it was all too late now, Roger thought. They were both in hoodies.

"This is where we part ways," Earl said, on the way back to their vehicle.

"I'm sorry," Roger replied. "I didn't know what else to do. I was afraid something worse might happen."

"He was my first," Earl said.

"What?"

"The white priest, De Bruyne, your uncle. I've never killed anyone before."

"You had to."

"You always imagine the moment, and fear it. Pray it doesn't come and yet a part of you yearns for it. Did he intend to stab Francis or himself?"

"I… don't know."

"What did he mean? We must undo the crime, undo ourselves?"

"I don't know, Earl, I swear to God."

"What did you make me do?"

Roger dropped his head as vomit crept up his throat like the time he roamed these streets. "Forgive me."

"Here," Earl said, handing Roger De Bruyne's crucifix/stake.

Roger remembered it from the time in the Cordilleras when he saw De Bruyne sharpening it over a fire. "It took four hundred years for the symbol of Roman terror to become the Christian standard," De Bruyne had said. "In the end, this served the same purpose."

Roger saw the lines in his uncle's face, some of them were scars he now realized in the flickering light.

"You know the early Christians' symbol for Christ?" De Bruyne asked the younger man.

"Fish," Roger said.

"Fish… food, sustainer of life, everywhere. An instrument of death is finally valued over a provider of life."

"The fish is still used."

De Bruyne shrugged. "You see people risking life and limb to reach for a likeness of fish? Did armies plant fish totem over conquered lands?"

"It's the burden of Christ, his passion and suffering people want to share."

"Why?"

"Makes everyone else's suffering and mortality worthwhile, doesn't it?" Roger asked, suddenly fearful of his uncle.

"The pretender saw a flaming cross in the sky and found his destiny and the Christians sold out their heavenly kingdom for an earthly empire," De Bruyne had said, and Roger had left it at that.

Now, he saw the crucifix being thrust at him suddenly.

"Take it," Earl told him. "*You're* family."

"No," Roger repeated and started walking away. Suddenly, he ran, embracing the dawn.

32

THE PRIESTS

THE PARISH PRIEST found Fr. Jimenez praying at the altar. It was nine in the evening.

"Do you wish to confess? Father Jimenez?" Fr. Dimalanta asked.

Jaguar seemed jolted: "I won't deem to bother you at this hour, Father."

"You may think I'm senile." Jaguar wanted to reply but the elder priest stopped him with a stiff finger.

"So you found those remains by chance?"

"Yes, Father. I rose before dawn for a jog and…."

"A ranking member of that madman's cult, of whom you seem to know many, and a long-lost Belgian priest, what are the chances?"

"I don't know what to say," Fr. Jimenez whispered.

"A bird told me that it wasn't a kitchen staffer who was rushed to the hospital from the nunciate the other night," Fr. Dimalanta said and Jaguar felt rocks in his throat.

"You're not the only one with friends in certain places," the parish priest went on.

"I'm sure you have many, Father," Jimenez said and the older one glared at him.

"I hear it was actually a female devotee who managed to worm her way inside the nunciate, another fanatic who wanted to get close enough to the Pope and was stabbed with a fork by an overzealous Jesuit. What do you think?"

"I think it's quite improbable. Perhaps we should not indulge these wild stories."

"Really? Well, what do you expect from these Jesuits? The end is near, Jimenez, the enemy is inside the gate. It's those masons."

Jaguar gazed at the parish priest, dumbstruck.

"You think they'll stand for a communist Pope? They'll do him in sooner or later, just like they poisoned that other one."

"Perhaps we should not...."

"And I supposed you weren't anywhere near the nunciate the other night?"

Fr. Jimenez shook his head. "I was in Paco."

"Nor any of your rogue friends?"

"I'm not sure I know who you mean?"

"That lowlife Ambahan, that abortionist Duran… and God knows who else? Just the sort that Francis loves to hobnob with. I know you want to be a parish priest, Jimenez…" The elder raised another stiff finger to stifle any protest from Jaguar. "I admire ambition. It wouldn't be the worst thing for a local boy to finally run the show hereabout. But are you sure you're doing the right thing? Do you have a real vocation?"

"As I've always said Father, I would prefer a small rustic parish."

"Save that for the media, Jimenez, or is it Fr. Jaguar you prefer these days? You don't fool me. I know your kind. The priesthood is a playground for you, isn't it? You think you can play hide and seek with your little demons safely while here under the mantle of the church. Sooner or later, those demons are going to grow up, Jimenez. You won't last."

"Pray for me, Father. May the Lord grant me more strength," Fr. Jimenez said, and Dimalanta smirked. "I only wish to do as much as I can for the parish."

"You're going to the Vatican."

"What?"

"For six months. Go do your research on mystical theology or whatever you've been bugging the Cardinal about. You might prefer it to your small rustic parish."

"But I haven't applied for leave lately?"

"It seems someone close to the Pope asked about you from the Cardinal. So you do know people in high places, after all?"

"I've no idea…"

"The parish can do without cultists and reporters sniffing around for the time being. You attract the sort, Jimenez."

"Me?"

"You might end up an exorcist yet, Father Jaguar."

"I serve where I'm called."

Dimalanta sighed. "Of course. You leave in a week."

As the elder turned to leave, Fr. Jimenez called out: "By the way, Brother Gerry, our I.T. technician has installed a second system. He says you can use the old one for research…in case you need to access certain websites."

Fr. Dimalanta looked askance at Jaguar. "Don't make me angry, Jimenez. You won't like me when I'm angry," he said and walked on.

Jaguar was stunned. "The Incredible Hulk," he mumbled. It was the iconic line of Bruce Banner in the old TV series whenever he was about to transform into the monster-hero. So was the older priest mocking or toying with the younger one by mimicking the Hulk, or was he going senile, confusing fantasy with reality? Had he fancied himself a comic book hero once?

Yet Jaguar felt a sudden affinity with the other man. He had an urge to run after Dimalanta and ask him if he was indeed quoting from past TV but thought the better of it. Then he recalled the one time the parish priest had asked his opinion on whether or not it was appropriate to refer to Batman in a sermon.

"What about the Batman?" Jaguar recalled asking. "Are you talking about a recent movie version?"

"Is he more good than evil?"

"He's... complicated," Jaguar had said, hoping for a lengthier talk on the subject but Dimalanta had frowned and walked away as well back then.

"But weren't you and I supposed to be caped crusaders as well, once we took our vows and donned our vests?" Jaguar had wanted to ask the older one back then, but knew it was all too late now.

As he passed the Nazareno's glass niche, Fr. Jimenez noticed a yellow balloon. He picked it up and saw the printed image of the Nazarene. Before he knew it, the priest had ingested the contents of the balloon. A therapist friend had told Jaguar how he tried out different stuff just to better understand his patients.

"It's okay," the therapist explained, "as long as you don't have an addictive personality."

Jaguar always thought of himself as even-keeled, able to be the master and not the slave of any pleasure, even that of worship. In a while, he felt suffused with a lightness that seemed to fill every pore of his body. He relaxed thoroughly. Blocks of ice that he imagined inhabited parts of him melted away. There was no fear in him or rancor, only peace and yes, joy! Was this it? The joy coveted by all? Sought for in years of study, service, dedication, self-abnegation, and worship? Delivered almost instantly in a balloon of gas?

He tried to snap out of it. It was all biochemistry, he reminded himself. The gas had released dopamine or endorphins in his brain. This wasn't the real thing. But what *was* the real thing? Why *did* one serve, and pray, and worship? Did flagellants and those nailed ritually to crosses also experience hormonal rushes that altered their brains?

Then he saw her at the corner of his eye, staring at him just by the church gate.

"Kitty!" He called out.

He raced outside but she was gone. There was only the night and some vendors packing up.

She will always be in my shadow, he thought, *always*.

33
SHADOWS

"HE WAS A dear friend of your father," Vergel's widow, Esmeralda, said to Basilio, clasping his hand. "Ever since Conrado died, Vergel had become distraught. Perhaps now, he too would be at peace."

It was a white hardwood coffin with ornate gildings that Basilio had chosen. He had bought it at a discount rate of five thousand pesos. Basilio had returned to St. James Funeral Homes, where they had dropped off Vergel's remains to make the arrangements for the wake. Jefferson had produced two witnesses, who swore they found the body at a nearby side street and somehow a police report was written up wherein five strangers delivered the corpse to the funeral parlor and a cardiac surgeon signed a death certificate. The proximate cause of death was heart failure. The bullet wound through the skull was sutured and never mentioned. Basilio then went to Vergel's home to inform his family. Only Esmeralda was around.

"Are you filing charges?" Basilio asked Emeralda.

"Against whom?" she asked, dazed.

"He made enemies of late, working for that Tata Peping."

"Was he a member of the Kapatiran?"

The woman shrugged. "To be honest, he hadn't been home most of last year. I barely saw him. I could hardly talk to him. I think he was a sort of body guard of that Peping, collected debts for the guy, and carried a firearm."

"He used to be a cop."

"Yes. Retired early after that scandal, a protection racket. He tried to raise poultry but it all came to naught. He was so down until he met Tata Peping, and gave him a new purpose."

"Did he talk much about Jose Crenshaw?"

She shook her head. "Only that he was a special person, destined for something big."

"Are you requesting an autopsy?"

"What for? I don't want to know about his death. I just want to remember him when we were a happy family?"

"Where are your children?"

"Rima died in a car accident in Taiwan. Ben's an engineer in Dubai. He remembers you. He'd like to meet with you when he returns home day after tomorrow."

Basilio felt an urge to tell Esmeralda all he knew about Vergel, his once "shadow" but managed to keep his peace.

She lit up, as if realizing suddenly whom she had been talking with. "Is it true what they say on TV?" she asked, peering. "Did you pass out those poison balloons at the Traslación?"

"No," he disagreed vehemently. "It's all a mistake. Not me. And there was no poison, just some funny gas."

She frowned. "Did you kill someone abroad?"

His forehead stiffened. "No, no, it's all fake news. The Kapatiran's been spreading lies about me because I wouldn't join them."

"So you're with them too?"

"No. Look, I should be in jail now if I did all those things, right?"

She nodded slowly. "All sorts of criminals are out in the streets. Be careful and thank you for all this."

"It's the least I can do. He was my ninong. Do you have a family crypt, we can arrange for the funeral?"

"At the north cemetery. He would like to be beside his parents."

"Okay, we'll do that. I'll go over to Manito's a while," Basilio said.

She lit up again. "Oh yes, that young man, he's a local boy, I remember. And he was a follower of that Tata Peping?"

"I'm afraid so."

"And they found his remains near the Church, right?"

Basilio nodded.

"Poor thing, they say he's been disowned. No one's shown up at his wake. What's happening to us, son? Why all these killings? Do you think it's true what they say? The dark days are here?"

"People have been killing each other for ages, Auntie. It might be scarier if they suddenly stopped," he said, trying some levity then realized that Esmeralda had just assumed both deaths were violent, though there had been no such reports or autopsies.

"See you later, Auntie," he said and hurried over to the adjoining chapel where Manito laid in state.

After Fr. Jimenez found the two bodies near the church, he blessed them and informed the funeral parlor that quickly picked up the remains. Jefferson Po did the rest. Manito's body was soon identified. It took three days before the CICM and the Swedish Embassy issued statements about Fr. Gerard De Bruyne, basically confirming his identity. The embassy took charge of his remains. They were interred in Kalinga as per his wishes, according to his nephew, Roger Geisler.

Esmeralda was right. Manito's wake was more lifeless than him. No one was around. Basilio scanned the place and wondered if he had done the right thing? Perhaps he should have informed Manito's family first or the BBN. He sat on a plastic chair and gazed at the coffin.

"Are you a colleague associated with that black guy, the cultist?"

Basilio looked up and was shocked to see Manito, but in female form. He knew at once it was Manito's younger sister, Amanda. He remembered her from back when they were teenagers. She had grown into an attractive, if sad-looking, woman. He recalled briefly that his friendship with Manito had to do as well with his desire to be closer to her.

"No… no," he stammered. "I know those guys too, but I'm not a member. Manito was a classmate in high school, a close friend." He swallowed hard.

"Basilio," she said.

"You remember? Amanda?"

She nodded and a wave of warmth passed through him.

"Where's the rest of your family?"

"No one else wants to come. When our father passed away two years ago, Manito didn't even show up."

"Maybe he couldn't."

"He gave us up for them, those cultists. *They* should be here."

"I don't think it's convenient, right now."

"They used him."

Basilio shrugged.

"So who's paying for this? Are they?"

"I am," Basilio said

"Why?"

"He was my friend. I help out in the Church, with Fr. Jimenez. Sometimes we do simple wakes and burials for long unclaimed remains the parlor wants to dispose of. I've had some good years abroad, though it might be a way of giving back. And then I saw it was Manito."

"Who did this? Those crazies?"

"What do you mean?"

"We know he was killed. Everyone does. They covered it up."

"Here," he said, handing the woman a blue note book. "This was found on him, might tell you something."

She waved it away. "No, keep it. I don't need to know anything more. He was never the same after our mother was killed. We were just kids but he waged war in his heart. He wouldn't let go of his anger. Was that wrong?"

"I don't know. I know he stood his ground while others fled or looked away."

"I hope all that's done now. That he can be happy, at last."

"Are you married?" he asked.

She nodded. "Two girls, five and two."

"I married Delfin Pantoja, Remember him? Tondo High?"

Basilio did not know him, but nodded.

"He's an accountant. How about you?" she asked and he shook his head. "You were abroad?"

"Long time," he whispered.

She looked down at her feet.

"How about the funeral?" he asked.

"My brother, Elmer, and our other relatives don't want him buried with our parents," she said.

"What about cremation? The church doesn't prohibit it anymore. What with the price of plots? We can do that, if you like?"

"He always said that wakes and burials were so much waste. I think he'd prefer to have his remains donated to science, but do what you think is best," she said and handed him a white envelope that he knew had cash.

Basilio refused but Amanda insisted. "He was my brother," she reminded him and he had to accept. "Thanks for everything, you're a good man, take care." She squeezed his arm and left abruptly.

Basilio thought he would cry, mourn all these deaths finally since coming home.

Suddenly, a cold, clammy hand was on his nape. He shot up.

"Family? Was that the sister?"

It was Jefferson Po.

"What's it to you? What are you doing here?" Basilio asked.

"I'm not the crime suspect here," Jefferson retorted.

"You have nothing on me. Leave me alone."

"Did you tell her anything?" Jefferson seemed truly concerned.

"No, but I wanted to. I think I should."

Jefferson shook his head. "No, no… not yet. Be patient. The key to any successful investigation is patience."

"Stop it."

"What we say and to whom is of vital importance now," Jefferson said.

"Go away!"

"We shouldn't scare away Crenshaw for now. I'm sure he'll make contact with you Basilio, keep in touch with him. Give him some rope…

"I'm done with him! And you!"

"And you think he's done with you? How safe do you think you are with him and his zealots at large?

"I don't give a fuck what he wants."

"Tolstoy once wrote that you may not be interested in war but war sure is interested in you, same thing, man. You know Tolstoy? Russian writer, ask Chester, the nerd knows that stuff."

"It's not me he wants," Basilio shot back. "I'm no use to him now. I'm not the one who screwed up his wedding and got his bride in coma with his child still growing inside her."

"Could be mine, Basilio," Jefferson persisted. "We're still not sure…"

"He wants your hide, Po, and he wants his child… and bride. Who knows? Maybe he wants to stash her somewhere like Snow White until he can wake her up with a kiss? He's a healer, remember?"

"All I know is that I received this strange email about evidence implicating a Basilio Ambahan in the murder of one Nemesio Dayrit, who escaped from police custody months ago and went missing."

Something nipped Basilio.

"The dagger they used to kill him," he mumbled. "I may have prints on it."

Jefferson shrugged. "So what? They likely dumped the guy's remains anyway."

Basilio sneered.

"Still… this could be messy. You seem to be around a lot of stabbings," Jefferson said.

"What do you want?"

"I know you want him," Jefferson said, "I know you can never let go of what he did to your father… We can work together. I have a nose for talent, Basilio, and you're a natural born spook."

"I'm not going to be your bait. Your last one is comatose. How stupid do you think I am?"

"She didn't listen to me!" Jefferson yelled, then caught himself as he carefully looked about.

"You're right," he went on calmly, whispering. "No one is really safe while Crenshaw's out there plotting and getting madder—not me, or you, or Emily. Think of your family."

"I will deal with him myself!" Basilio retorted. "I'm not going to be your stooge!"

"Just hear me out."

Basilio knew Jefferson was right, but then, he would never be rid of the guy once he agreed to any deal.

"I need some air," Basilio said and slipped out of the funeral home. He looked to the night and saw a shooting star race across the quarter moon. He felt he knew now how it was to be the shadow of a shadow.

34
C-SECTION

"WE'RE INTO THE 28th week, the chances of the fetus surviving outside the womb are very high. It's our best shot. I don't like to wait any longer," Anna said to Chester, Jefferson, and Maria Mahiwo.

Chester sighed and nodded. "I agree. Her heart's been erratic. We should save the baby now."

"Will removing the fetus improve her chance of waking up?" Jefferson asked.

"We don't know that," Anna said but there could be less stress on her system.

Chester looked to Maria.

"Do what you think is best. Save first the one with the better chance of survival," she said.

"But once the baby is secured, I recommend we move her to a hospice. Dr. Anna knows a good one," Chester said.

Jefferson scowled. "What are you saying?"

"It's been seven months, Jefferson. Time to let things take their natural course," Chester said.

"What natural course? You're a doctor!"

"The hospice will provide basic, palliative care, she will

be comfortable. No more tubes or artificial respiration, or extreme measures."

"You want to kill her? You murderer!" Jefferson shouted.

"You see the EEG monitor, Jefferson? She's gone, already brain dead!" Chester argued.

"You don't know that, you're not God! There's still some activity!"

"So you're a believer now?"

"Better Him than you! You think you're infallible? Always loved to play genius, didn't you? Well, not this time! You're throwing her out of this hospital over my dead body!" Jefferson railed.

"I don't own the damn hospital. Management has bent over backwards but I don't have bottomless credit!"

"So, it's all about money? You money grubbing, greedy pig doctor!"

Anna had to get between the two men as Chester attempted to throw a punch at Jefferson.

"I'll pay! I'll pay, you greedy bastards!" Jefferson yelled.

"Really? You paid her back wages yet? Government rat!"

"I will decide what happens to my daughter, once my grandchild is safe," Maria Mahiwo declared.

At the O.R., Dr. Isaac Dy monitored Emily's heart, even as Chester remained on standby in case emergency heart surgery was needed. Meanwhile, Anna performed the Cesarean section to deliver Emily's baby.

Chester was first to approach Jefferson after the procedure. His anger for the man had passed, now replaced by a tinge of sympathy. "The baby's fine. You sure you want to see?" he asked.

"She's my daughter," Jefferson said.

He and Maria proceeded to the nursery and glimpsed Emily's baby at the incubator. They saw a reddish brown baby with a lock of curly hair and thick lips. Maria smiled. "My granddaughter,"

Jefferson nodded, tears in his eyes.

Upon returning to Emily's room, they found a medallion lying on her bed. Jefferson immediately recognized it as BBN, as there was a serpent coiled around a tiger's head, and grabbed it. Beside it lay a note that read: "The Brotherhood is near and far. Keep this with her at all times if you want her safe. I will awaken her when the time is right and restore my family."

It was signed: *Itim na Nazareno.*

"They're here!" Jefferson raced to the station and blew up on the stunned nurses. "Who entered Emily Mahiwo's room? Who placed this on her bed? Get security! Lockdown the hospital!"

A guard approached and Jefferson was all over him. "How did these crazies get in? What security is this? Lockdown the place!"

"I'm sorry, sir, what is this about?" the guard asked.

"I'm NBI. I order a lockdown!" Jefferson yelled and was about to manhandle the guard when a voice boomed from behind.

"Jefferson! Stop it!" Chester ordered.

Jefferson turned and saw Chester glaring at him. But he paid no heed as he rushed to the front door, suddenly noticing a figure in black helmet and leather jacket aboard a motorbike eyeing him by the hospital gate.

"Stop!" Jefferson pointed at the figure riding away.

Jefferson rushed back inside. "It's someone in black, on a motorcycle," he told Chester, gasping for breath. "I can catch him."

"No, you can't. He's gone. This isn't a prison, Po. People come and go. Emily's safe. So is your daughter." Chester put a comforting hand on Jefferson's shoulder.

Jefferson calmed down and nodded, putting a hand over Chester's. "Thanks, man," he whispered.

Back in Emily's room, she had just been wheeled in. Anna came with the incubator. She took the baby out. Chester looked at her and shook his head. She nodded. "We have to try," she said.

Anna brought the baby to Emily's breast and placed her lips by the nipple. The infant sucked instinctively, cautiously at first and then hungrily. Milk dribbled from Emily's breast.

"She's going to make it," Jefferson said, biting back tears. "Both of them, I know it."

Chester held Jefferson by the shoulder again and shook it.

After some minutes, Anna took the baby back to the incubator and her team wheeled the infant back to the nursery.

Meanwhile, Jefferson took out the metal medallion and examined it. He showed it to Chester, who shrugged.

"What do you think?" he asked.

"I don't know. What's to lose if we put it on her."

"What are you saying?" Jefferson insisted.

"You think there's something on it?" Chester asked. "A computer chip maybe?"

"That's it, big brain science guy? That's your logic? What's there to lose?"

"You're the detective! You tell me!"

"And what do you suppose will happen if we don't put it on her?"

"I don't know? You want to take the chance?"

"You hear yourself?"

"*You* asked *me!*"

Maria grabbed the medallion from Jefferson. "Nothing from that man touches my daughter again," she said and put the medallion inside her bag. She then pulled out a silver cross, the one De Bruyne had left on her daughter all those years back, and placed it inside Emily's gown pocket.

Maria laid her hand on Emily's forehead. She closed her eyes and seemed to go into a trance. She started chanting in a language neither man knew. Chester guessed it was her tribal tongue.

"My daughter will return when Kabunian deems it wise. She will ride the wind with two eagles and cross the fire clouds," Maria said before turning to walk away.

The two men looked at each other.

"Emily will have to leave, Jefferson," Chester told him sadly, and the other man looked away.

35
BAPTISM

ANNA CLEARED SPACE for Emily at her clinic. Her vitals improved after delivery and she breathed normally. And though she continued to be fed intravenously, some color returned to her face. Chester visited her regularly to check on her heart, and sometimes it seemed she responded to stimuli.

Once the baby was strong enough, Anna brought her as well to her clinic.

Maria came four times a week to help care for her.

Jefferson said he had posted agents around the clinic for security, and Chester chose to believe his classmate.

At first, Jefferson had wanted to bring her home but Anna reminded him that Emily needed to be monitored. Safest place would be the home turf, Quiapo.

"Do you, Magiting Bagiw, accept Jesus Christ as your Lord and Savior?" Fr. Jimenez intoned as Maria Mahiwo held baby Bagiw over the baptistery.

"I do," her godparents replied.

"Do you renounce Satan and all his works?"

"I do."

"I baptize you in the name of the Father, the Son and the Holy Spirit."

Maria turned the three-month-old Bagiw to Carmen, who kissed her and then gave her to Chester, who did the same, followed by Basilio and then Jefferson, who held her tight.

Maria had decided to have Bagiw baptized to celebrate Emily's seeming improvement. A part of her felt this might hasten her daughter's full recovery. "Your mother's waiting at home," she told the baby. Home had been Anna Duran's clinic.

It was 11 a.m. one Monday and the crowd was sparse at church. Jaguar thought there was a huge figure in a dark maroon cassock walking towards them. He gasped and blinked to see, but then the figure was gone.

"What is it?" Carmen asked as she noticed Fr. Jimenez.

"Nothing. I just… thought…."

"He's in our heads," Carmen said.

"I've got eyes on him and his gang 24/7. He's not getting anywhere near our daughter," Jefferson said.

He had called Bagiw daughter ever since, although Maria only had Emily declared as mother on the birth certificate while she and Jefferson were appointed as guardians.

"He won't win," Basilio said. "We won't let him, right?"

"So you're staying?" Carmen asked and Chester noticed the glint in her eyes.

"Yes," Basilio replied.

Chester felt a niggling in his throat.

"Good, *kumpare*," Jefferson said, squeezing Basilio's shoulder heartily.

"I'm moving back into our ancestral place to work things out with the bank. It was mortgaged by father and we're in arrears on the payment," Basilio said.

"I'll go with him to see Vivian Lee. She's bank VP now, my high school classmate," Carmen said.

"What do you plan to do with it? The property won't pay for itself," Chester asked.

"Pawn shop," Jefferson chimed in. "Best prospect for this area."

"Always the blood sucker," Chester quipped.

"Food. People will always want good food. You were a cook right?" Carmen suggested.

"I'll figure it out later, maybe some kind of school…" Basilio started to say but Jefferson cut in, "For beauty pageants! Everyone wants to be a beauty queen these days. You have foreign contacts, right? Put up a modeling agency, or a talent outfit."

"Music, that's more your line," Chester said.

"You can still play bass at Horizon's on Saturday nights, right?" Jefferson asked.

"He said we'll… *he'll* figure it out later," Carmen replied, and saw her dad stare at her.

"I have to clean it up first, as my cousins left a mess. Can you come give it a blessing, Father?"

"Of course, just say when," Jaguar said. "By the way, I won't be going to the Vatican yet. The trip's been deferred again. Fr. Dimalanta's retiring. I've been asked to take over his functions in the meantime."

A cheer went up, and the others applauded.

"Great!" Basilio enthused. "Finally my *kababata*, parish priest! I'm proud of you, *'tol*!"

"Acting Parish priest," Jaguar stressed.

"So no more bullshit over the women's health center?" Anna asked.

"We'll see… if you behave," he said with a wink.

"This calls for a celebration. Lunch at Ramon Lee's, on me," Chester announced.

"Okay, but let me run some errands first," Fr. Jaguar said.

"And let's bring this girl home first. She needs feeding," Maria said. She, Anna, Jefferson and Chester repaired with Bagiw to Duran's clinic as Jaguar sped off in the Harley that Chester had donated to the Church.

"So are you with the Cofradia now?" Carmen asked Basilio when they were alone.

"I'm taking over my father's place with the Hijos as well," Basilio said.

"Have you become a believer?"

"I am home now."

"You made some deal with Jefferson Po?

"Nothing I can't handle."

"Roger asks about you." Carmen said with a playful glint.

"Well, tell him I say 'hi.'"

"Tell him yourself. I'll give you his email address. I think he likes you," Carmen teased.

"Think so?"

"He might be able to help fund your plans, you know?"

"And what are you suggesting, Ms. Limhuatco?

"I'm suggesting that we go to your place and figure things out," she said.

Back at the clinic, Chester approached Anna when they found some privacy.

"Listen," Chester began, but couldn't find the words. He reached for her face, but she grabbed his hand and placed it on his chest instead.

"It's okay," Anna whispered. "Everything's fine."

36
HOME

HE WAS ALWAYS fascinated by the possibility of alien abduction. Once, Chester had a nagging sense that he was abducted and was divested of some vital essence that he could no longer recall.

And now watching the TV series on how the earth was possibly seeded by extraterrestrials who created a hybrid race that became *homo sapiens,* he felt a strange consolation.

"Anyone can be sold anything, Dad," Carmen told him.

"The universe is unimaginably vast. It's just arrogance to assume we're the only sentient beings around," he retorted.

"Whatever, take care," she said.

The area where his condo sat was rumored to be a UFO landing site but Chester was now back in Greenhills "house sitting" their home while Jackie was off to China to take pictures with her photography club and to "consider her options."

He understood now a bit of what Jackie had gone through the past year. It was a big house to be alone in, even as the help had taken the weekend off. Chester had bought the Pasig condo he rented. He, too, had options to consider.

But if not for himself, he planned to gift the place to Carmen and hope she would settle down, even with a guy like Basilio whom Chester found too reckless and compromised for his daughter. Still, grandkids would be nice.

When Fr. Brix came to the hospital for his post-op check-up earlier, Chester had unloaded on his old mentor. He didn't mean to confess.

The priest stopped him. "Oh, I'm retired, so no more of that." So they just shared stories that he might have told Jackie otherwise. Chester had to unburden himself, lest he explode like a death star. So he told Fr. Brix about an Igorot woman who raised the child of a foreign priest, a doctor who found a beautiful, unconscious woman in a crowd of injured folk and longed to keep her like a prized doll, a black man who declared himself a black Christ, nerve gas experiments, laughing gas at the Traslación, a botched attempt to assassinate the Pope in Manila and a comatose woman who suckled her infant child.

Fr. Brix listened with good humor. His hearing aid needed repair.

"You were always blessed with a wild imagination, Chester," Fr. Brix said afterwards. "You were one of those boys who made up crazy stuff for confession just to get out of class. I knew you wanted to shock or perhaps try out your stories on an adult. I did enjoy some of them, I must confess. Even looked forward to hearing them at times. So I just gave you the usual penance. What was it? Can't even recall."

"Three Our Fathers, Three Hail Marys."

"That was it? None of you did penance, anyway. I expected you'd become a writer or perhaps a politician, or even, who knew? A priest. But the Lord knows best. The storyteller always trumps the truth teller, right, Chester? I was your first audience, wasn't I?"

"What did I confess?"

"You don't recall? Let's see. We're you the one who saw a UFO or was abducted by aliens? I think there was more than one."

"I had schoolmates who were abducted by ET?"

"Did you see your father having sex with the house help?"

"Of course not! I bet it was Jefferson Po!"

"Yes, probably. But he did a number on that Don Bosco hotshot, didn't he? Won us the game."

"You remember?"

"Think I'm senile?"

"But what if they were true? What if someone was, in fact, abducted or traumatized?"

Fr. Brix shrugged. "We didn't dig too deep into those things back then, because they're too messy. Anyway, the crazy ones always survived, didn't they?"

So what's the difference between the stories you told us in religion class and what we told back then? He wanted to ask, but remembered Fr. Brix was a heart patient. "Will you give me my penance?" He requested instead.

"What for? You don't pray. Just keep an eye on that Jefferson Po before he goes to hell. You still in touch?"

"Unfortunately. By the way, Jackie says hello."

"Who?"

"My wife, Jackie Dy. You married us."

"I did? Married a whole lot of you, didn't I? Are you still together?"

"We're trying."

"So you're not sure? There's a time to be a boy and time to be a man, Chester," the priest blessed him. "Can I smoke again?" He asked the younger man afterwards.

"Go ahead. The Lord giveth and the Lord taketh away," Chester said.

"Amen."

Now as he scanned the night sky from the patio eyeing the little dipper, trying to make out the shape of the "ox herd" and the "weaver girl," Chester wondered how many of those points of light were still alive or exploding stars? How many long dead? How many event horizons of black holes? Where was Jose Crenshaw? Was he another charlatan who had ruined so many lives; a false sun that had imploded? Or was he in fact a man of power? Could he indeed awaken Emily? Could he launch a revolution?

He felt a throbbing in his veins. His heart raced and sweat poured. He had held her heart in his hands and urged it back to life. Could he also restore the rest of her?

In his dream, it was a dark hooded man, or perhaps a shadow, that reached into his chest, through his ribs, held his heart and squeezed to the point of near shattering. Then, suddenly, he saw Emily on top of him, holding his heart. He struggled for breath and awoke in a pool of sweat only to realize that his phone was ringing.

It was Anna. "She's back!"

That was the last thing he heard before a thousand points of light exploded from inside him and filled him to the brim.

photo by Javier P. Flores

CHARLSON ONG is a writer, film producer, and director. He has won the Philippine National Book Award for both short fiction and the novel. He has four short story collections: *Men of the East and other stories* (1999); *Woman of Am-Kaw and Other Stories* (1992); *Conversion and Other Fictions* (1996); *Of that Other Country We Now Speak and Other Stories* (2016). He has three novels: *An Embarrassment of Riches* (2000), *Banyaga, A Song of War* (2006); *Blue Angel/White Shadow* (2010). He is writer, co-producer, and co-director of the acclaimed film *Tanabata's Wife*, which won Best Picture in the Tofarm Film Festival for 2018, and Best Adapted Screenplay for 2019 at the Filipino Academy of Movie Arts and Sciences Awards (FAMAS).

White Lady, Black Christ is set in Paperback, a font family designed by John Dewer for House Industries, harkening to the time when typefaces were designed and used for specific sizes: readability for small specimens, and sophistication for display-sized ones—a craft now lost in modern desktop technology with multitudes of font options.

Ivan Reverente's cover art is reminiscent of the period when book art was made under strict production limitations. Here, the cover art is produced only in three colors, similar to the silk-screened t-shirt and handkerchief designs sold during the Traslacion.

This book comes in two print editions: a limited edition hardcover, and paperback.

www.ingramcontent.com/pod-product-compliance
Lightning Source LLC
Chambersburg PA
CBHW020116180726
47992CB00018B/92